LIAM WILSON

The Malignancy

First edition

This book was professionally typeset on Reedsy.
Find out more at reedsy.com

Contents

1

Chapter 1

A crash. Footsteps. Someone was in my house. Multiple people. I could hear the crunching of feet on glass. Someone had broken something, maybe a window. Neither of my parents were home. Thankfully, I didn't have to worry about that. My mind raced. I froze on my bed. Even with the hunting knife my uncle gave me, they could overpower me. I could try to jump out the window, but if this was a robbery, they probably didn't realize that I was home alone. Besides, it was wintertime, and I already knew that the window had frozen shut. To be honest, I didn't really want to jump, anyway. From such a height, it was likely that I would break an ankle. I decided the best course of action was—

A man burst into my room and aimed a pistol at me. He missed. Something hit my pillow three inches to the left of my head. I impulsively rolled off my bed and grabbed the bedside lamp. He fired and somehow missed again. I felt something whizz past my ribcage.

The man scowled and tried to fire again, but I swung wildly with all my strength and swatted the gun out of his hand. He cried out in pain. I swung again and smashed the lamp against his face. The light bulb shattered, and the man stumbled backwards and collapsed in the hallway. A crimson puddle formed around his head. How did I do that much damage? I didn't even swing that hard. Where were the other guys? There had definitely been more. I slowly approached the man, who might not have been fully unconscious. The person who entered with him likely heard the disturbance. Where were they? This guy sure didn't look professional. He wore jeans and a stained sky blue winter coat, seemingly fresh from goodwill. His greasy hair may be because of the blood. Jesus, did I kill him?

I felt something sharp prick my neck. I frantically glanced around; there was no one to be seen. It must have been some sort of dart. I started gasping for air. What if they messed up the dosage of whatever drug they just injected me with? Who were they? I tried walking back to my bedroom but only made it two steps before I sunk to my knees in overwhelming fatigue. Dots covered my vision and I could see darkness creeping in all around me. My body simply no longer obeyed my commands. Nothing was working. I felt my face plant into the carpet. I think I fell hard, but it was difficult to tell because my face was so numb. Before passing out, I only recalled the vague voices of my captors.

Darkness. I was in a dark room. It was pitch black. I sensed being in a small room despite nothing. So tiny. I could feel the four corners. The ceiling keeps my head down. Both sides are compressing me. The bottom was too shallow. Far too shallow.

Cold. It was cold, and it was getting colder. I was naked. Nothing at all. No underwear, no blanket. I could feel my nakedness, but I couldn't see it. I couldn't see myself.

Silence. There was silence. The silence that devours you and spits you out like you are nothing. The silence that buries itself deep inside you and hollows you out. The silence that makes you lie in bed for hours and stare at the ceiling. My kind of silence, I suppose.

Wet. I was wet. Why was I wet? I could feel the water. Moving. Rising. It took me a few seconds to realize I was going to drown. I tried to scream, but no sound came out. Just that silence. That god damned silence. It wouldn't go away. I screamed and screamed, but the walls seemed to grow tighter.

The freezing water rose higher. Gooseflesh. Eventually my throat hurt, so I gave up screaming. The water rose above my hips. And then my stomach. Finally, I noticed that the water had reached my chest, and I realized I was done for. My fate was to perish in this tiny enclosure. This little, dark, cold, wet, silent box.

The water rose above my head, and I was...

"Hello, there," a young, attractive blonde woman shook me awake. Her steely blue eyes penetrated me in a way that made me feel uncomfortable. I shifted in my seat, blinking desperately to try and remove the dryness in my eyes.. Where was I? It looked like some kind of private jet. I was sitting in a big white leather seat. It was the type of plane only seen in the movies, not in real life. I glanced out the window and realized with horror that we were already in the air. I felt weak, sick.

"Where.. where am I?" I asked. The woman smiled. I noticed her dress for the first time. It was white and expensive, just like the rest of the airplane.

"Don't worry. You are perfectly safe." The woman kept her PR smile painted on her smug, beautiful face.

"Jesus..." I muttered, rubbing my eyes. My head was pounding. Worse, I was nauseous, and not solely because of nerves.

3

The woman approached me with a garbage bin, and I snatched it out of her hands just in time. I've always hated throwing up. You can't breathe. It burns, it stinks, and the water tastes sweet after. I guess it's sort of a silly thing to say. I doubt anyone enjoys it.

"Sorry about that," I groaned after a few minutes. Why was I apologizing to my kidnapper? I apologize too often. Was that a bad thing? I wasn't sure.

"Don't worry about it. Would you like some ginger ale?" The woman asked.

"A napkin first. But yes, I would actually," I burped. It was grotesque.

"You must be wondering what's going on," Her smile faded a bit.

"Yes," I said. My heart was still pounding.

"You've been taken,"

"I can see that."

"There was an excellent reason,"

"Which is?

"We selected you for your unique genetic traits."

"What are you talking about?"

"Only a few people like you exist, and only you are fit for what lies ahead," the woman declared. I realized that they had changed my clothes. I was wearing a comfortable white sweater and white dress pants. They had even had the audacity to put on a belt. At least the belt and shoes were black. How bizarre.

"Sounds like a lot of bullshit to me," I blurted out. I immediately regretted it. To my surprise, she burst out laughing. It was an annoying laugh.

"You...you just don't hold back. Do you?" She could barely

catch her breath as she stood up, taking her hand off my shoulder. The jet smelled like vanilla. Fresh vanilla.

"I guess I get like that when people shoot me and haul me onto a jet against my will," I grumbled.

"Don't worry, this is all safe," the woman assured me.

"You've already mentioned that."

"Within a few days, you'll be home,"

"You still haven't explained what the hell I'm doing here. What do you want with me?" I demanded.

"You are actually very lucky,"

"Lucky?!"

"Mr. Mattheson has chosen you to take part in a study,"

"What kind of study?"

"It has to do with—"

"Wait, did you just say Mr. Mattheson? As in Matthias Mattheson?" I asked. Her smile broadened once again. Where were the other passengers? I suddenly realized that it was just me and her on this plane.

"Yes, the same. Now, the study,"

"Yeah, yeah. Continue,"

"Well, Mr. Mattheson has invented a time travel device,"

"You're shitting me,"

"No,"

"That's not possible. I read somewhere that Einstein's theory of—-"

"Mattheson found a way,"

"How?"

"I don't know. None of us do. It was just him and his team. It's a closely guarded secret. I'm sure you understand."

"Yeah, I guess,"

"Good,"

"Has he used it yet? How do they know it works?"

"Oh, they've used it dozens of times,"

"Why do you need me, then? What's the connection between my genetics and this?"

"One of Mr Mattheson's team members hypothesized that someone with your traits could be immune to the travel sickness,"

"Travel sickness?"

"There is a cost for device usage. A violent illness that causes one to lose one's mind. We know it's not permanent or fatal, but it is unpleasant and we would like to avoid it at all costs,"

"Oh,"

"Yes, an appropriate response, I think. I apologize on behalf of Mattheson Enterprises for the unpleasant experience you had.

"Why like this? I'm sure I would have agreed."

"No, you wouldn't. Besides, this isn't strictly legal. The entire operation is in danger of discovery by the Canadian government. They are aware of our project but are unsure of its nature. We couldn't risk exposure,"

"Fair enough,"

"I hope you understand,"

"Do I have a choice?"

"Not really," she chuckled.

"What's your name?" I asked.

"Margarethe,"

"I'm Ashton, but I guess you already knew that."

"Indeed. Well, I hope I have answered some of your questions. We actually just got in the air about twenty-five minutes after you woke up. So we still have about six hours left on our flight,"

"Where are we going?"

"Turkey. If you need anything, let me know. Food, drinks. I know you are feeling a little sick. That's just from the tranquilizer that we used. A side effect is nausea. It should pass soon,"

"Thank you." I sighed and rested my head on the soft head-rest. I felt a bit more relaxed, but many questions remained. I had no control over this situation whatsoever. There was nothing I could do. Perhaps that thought allowed me to drift back to sleep somehow.

I woke up drenched in sweat, so I drank the water Margarethe must have left beside me. We were already descending.

2

Chapter 2

Margarethe said nothing until we landed. The nausea was gone by then. I looked out the window and saw nothing. Only a runway, hangar, and small building. Where was this big facility that they were taking me to? We must have to drive somewhere.

"Ashton?" Margarethe tapped my shoulder. We had been parked for some time and I didn't hear her approaching.

"Yes?" I cleared my throat. I hadn't spoken in a while, so my throat was a little sore. Must have been from the stomach acid. The back of my throat still held a nasty taste.

Margarethe smiled again, signaling that it was time to leave, but her grin couldn't hide its obvious falseness despite years of practice. The circles under her eyes began to seep through the thin layer of meticulous makeup. I assumed she hadn't slept on the flight, although the source of her haggard appearance could have been much more complex than that.

"Okay," I muttered. I didn't have much choice. We exited the plane and walked out onto the tarmac. The weather was quite nice out, but I realized I was overdressed. It was way too warm for me. I could smell salt in the air. We were in a hilly area, probably close to the coast. If she didn't lie about Turkey, then it must have been the Mediterranean I smelled.

We entered a small building that resembled a construction office in the city. Cheap wood paneling, yellowed lighting, and a messy desk with a styrofoam cup of coffee on it. At the desk sat a fat, sweaty man. A small fan buzzed in the corner.

"Early?" the guard grumbled.

"Yes," Margarethe replied.

"Ain't that a blast? The guard activated a hidden lever under the desk, causing the room to descend. The office was an elevator. The whole thing seemed rather familiar.

"I don't suppose you've watched the dark knight, have you?" I asked Margarethe.

"No, definitely not," Margarethe said, her grin appearing to be genuine. We descended slowly, and for what felt like forever. It was probably like five minutes, but it was impossible to tell. No words from the obese man during the descent.

Upon the elevator's halt, a blond man in an expensive suit greeted us. It was Matthias Mattheson, billionaire extraordinaire. I guess it was comforting to know that was true, at least. I wasn't really sure why, but I always liked Matthias Mattheson. He seemed like one of those billionaires that might actually have a net positive on society. He solved the language barrier with his brain chip and had revolutionized healthcare with his nanotechnology. Of course, neither was widely available to the broader public. That didn't mean they weren't important, though. A home computer cost untold amounts of money when it first came out in the 1980s. Now, they were still somewhat pricey, but vastly more affordable. I always figured that Mattheson's inventions would face a similar fate in the future. It's regrettable that geniuses frequently prove to be child-rapists.

"Mr Beachum! Pleasure to meet your acquaintance," Mattheson said in a strange British accent.

"Are you British? I thought you were Canadian," I blurted out. Mattheson laughed.

"Just pulling your todger! Let me show you around, eh?" Matheson chuckled. Pulling your todger? He waved away Margarethe, and she walked left down one of the many concrete hallways. I was amazed at the cleanliness of it all. How fresh the air happened to be, given the obvious depth of the facility. It was also very bright, and I had seen no one aside from Mattheson so far. I supposed that was about to change. The fear from before remained, and my palms were quite clammy, but curiosity began to take precedence. This was amazing. Where the hell was I? It was like something out of a movie.

"Where are we going?" I asked as we started walking down the ostensibly endless hallways. Like the plane, everything smelled like fresh vanilla. It wasn't intoxicating, though. It was refreshing and authentic. Nothing like those car scent things that can give you a headache after a while. This was the real deal. Mattheson's shoes clacked against the floor, echoing down the halls.

"I'm going to show you my machine,"

"Your time machine, right?"

"Ah, you'll believe it when you see it work. Still, I want to show you until then. You're the first person, apart from my employees, who will witness it in action."

"Right,"

"Now, tell me, Mr. Beachum,"

"Yes?"

"Are you afraid of me?"

"Well, you did kidnap me,"

"You must be terrified,

"Uh—"

"That's good. Because you should be."

"What?"

"Just messing with you. A tug on the todger! God, your generation has got to lighten up. Stressed about this, stressed about that. Gimme a break. Just relax, and trust in humanity. We aren't all bad, are we?"

"I don't know? Are we?"

"Now, that's funny. Mr. Beauchum, people are complicated creatures. However, bad people do not exist.

"I disagree,"

"Of course you do. You'll see, even in the distant past, people had morality. It is the foundation of consciousness. Self-understanding. Without some sort of morality or beliefs, self-understanding can scarcely be achieved,"

"Morals can be twisted, though. Evil, even. The Nazis had morals, didn't they?"

"You got me,"

"What?"

"There are bad people out there. Just wanted to ensure you were aware.

"It's pretty obvious,"

"Not as obvious as one would hope. Too many optimistic people are out there. Sunny worldviews are dangerous on a trip like the one you're going on. You won't be able to trust anyone."

"Sounds fantastic,"

"It will be. Just be careful," Mattheson grinned. What a

weird fucking exchange. This whole thing was just making me uncomfortable. The hallway widened into a massive room. There was a big metal ball with a hatch sitting in the middle of the room. Wires and cords attached to it. A yellow step ladder was positioned to give access to the hatch. There were dozens of people scurrying about. Some in white lab coats, others in orange safety vests. It was strange that we saw no one in the hallways on the way there. I supposed it must have been a coincidence.

"Here we are," Mattheson beamed, his fluffy blond hair gleaming in the bright industrial led lights.

"Is that—"

"My machine, yes,"

"Have you actually,"

"We've used it dozens of times. Did Margarethe not—"

"Yes, she told me. I'm still in disbelief." To be honest, I didn't believe it all. Mattheson's dedication, both in terms of time and money, was clear in this thrilling undertaking. Traveling through time was impossible. Despite not being into science, I still knew it defied physics. It simply wasn't possible, no matter how advanced technology might be. Time travel, if possible, only works for traveling to the future. It was impossible to travel to the past. The entire room still smells faintly like vanilla.

"Oh, you must be just exhausted! Let me show you to your room," Mattheson exclaimed. We exited the large space and returned down the hallways. It was about a five-minute walk before he showed me my room. I tried looking for exits, in case I wanted to escape later on. But everything looked the same to me. It was challenging to discern my whereabouts. It was like a fever dream. Besides, I did not know where the hell we were, anyway. Somewhere in Turkey? I didn't see any buildings before the plane landed, but then again, I was asleep for most of the approach.

Mattheson gave me a key card and showed me the room. It was modern and quite large. A flat screen tv with Netflix and amazon prime, a large shower and separate tub, a king sized bed, and a painting of some sort of rocky coast. The painting looked like it must have been somewhere in Scotland. Maybe Shetland? The Isle of Skye? I had no idea, though. It was beautiful.

"You'll have an hour to wind down. Then you'll come and meet your crew at suppertime. Training begins tomorrow." Mattheson inspected his fingernails.

"Training?" I asked.

"Oh, yes. You'll need to complete some quick courses before going back in time. It would be absurd to send you to Ancient Antioch with no knowledge of the local customs, history, and such. You'll get to talk about it some more over supper. Fair enough?"

"I suppose I don't have a choice. I'm your prisoner, right?" My heart rate rose a bit.

"Guest! Please, you are lucky to be given this opportunity. Show some grace," Mattheson kept a straight face. I couldn't tell if he was angry or didn't care. He was very careful with all of his movements and expressions. Just like Margarethe.

"Of course. Sorry," I mumbled.

"Now, I will leave you be. You must be just overwhelmed," Mattheson exhaled and left.

"I guess," I sighed and examined the room. It was largely empty. Nothing I could use as a weapon. Mind you, did I really want to escape? This could be the real deal. This rich weirdo might have actually built a time machine. It was just all too hard to believe. I didn't know what to think anymore.

I face planted on the bed. The sheets were nice and cold. I moved my arm around to feel the soft, chilled sheets. Goose-bumps spread all over my skin. I yawned. Why was I tired? I had slept on the plane, it made little sense to me. The sleep must have been no good because of nightmares. Did I read somewhere that when someone dreams, their sleep is shallow and therefore counts for less? Or was I just imagining this? I wasn't sure. All I knew was that some billionaire had locked me up in his Turkish basement, and my parents had no idea where I was. For what? Why? Because of my genetic traits? What bullshit. Nothing was adding up.

I wondered what my mother was doing right about now. Was she feeling the same way? Trapped? Trapped in her grief, her hatred, her regret. She hated me. I could see it on her face. It wasn't what she said, though that was hurtful on its own. It was the look in her eyes. I've never seen her look at me like that before. I've never seen anyone look at me like that before. There was no other way to describe it other than pure contempt. Resentment. That my mother could look at me that way was beyond unsettling.

I watched a few episodes of Seinfeld on Netflix, and I was just finishing up the third episode when someone knocked on my door. I got up and slowly approached the door. No peephole, unlike hotels. I decided I had no choice but to open up. An attractive Indian woman, appearing to be in her early thirties, stood on the other side of the doorway. She was wearing a comfortable looking white sweater and loose jeans. It was mostly her face that was attractive, I decided.

"Hello," I said.

"So you're the kid," the woman stated, expressionless.

"Yeah," I said.

"Follow me," her face softened a bit, and I followed her. We started walking through
the labyrinthine tunnel network.

"Did I do something?" I asked. She hesitated for a couple of seconds before answering.

"No. I'm Priya." Priya glanced over at me and offered a weak smile. Okay, then.

I see some people weren't onboard with this whole thing. Good to know.

"Do you know how I got here in the first place?" I asked.

"Yes," she sighed.

"And you're okay with that?"'

"No, that's why I scowled when I saw you,"

"I see,"

"The fact of the matter is, you're just a kid. You shouldn't be here."

"Then can you help me get out of here?'

"No,"

"Why not?"

"It's not possible. But this should still be fun for you,"

"Is the time travel thing—-"

"Yes, it's real. I'm the chief engineer. I've worked here for seven years. Before that I was at MIT. Mattheson hired me straight out of school. I should have never accepted,"

"Why? If it works, then—"

"Just try to enjoy yourself and you'll be home soon enough," Priya said simply. Before I could ask anymore questions, we reached the dining room. A hall, large and filled with numerous tables. There were thousands of people here!

The hall smelled like buttery seafood, and the heat of the food warmed up the whole room. The sudden manifestation of the crowd's chatter took me away. There was definitely some sort of serious soundproofing going on here. We had entered through some double doors and it was like turning up the volume on your headphones from mute to an eight. It was absolutely insane.

Priya guided me to a table with an old man in a tweed suit and a muscular guy in sweats and an undershirt. I expected a buffet, but they served the food. Everyone was getting the same thing, though, no menu. I supposed that was fine. I was lucky that I had no allergies.

"This is Professor Charles Knotts," Priya said. The professor gave a polite smile and nod. I did an awkward little wave.

"And I am David," the buff man stood up to shake my hand. He had a firm shake. His hand was surprisingly dry and calloused. I smiled and sat down. A server brought me my food almost immediately. It was a crab rice pilaf with garlic butter broccoli. After scarfing down my meal, I properly examined the surrounding people. The professor looked like he was in his early seventies, but he was extremely fit for his age. No belly or anything. David was probably ex-military or police based on his haircut and how he was scanning the room. Maybe I watch tv too much. I don't have any idea what I'm talking about half the time. Priya was sitting next to me.

"In three days, we'll travel to Antioch in 115AD," Priya announced. Antioch? Where was that?

"Where exactly is Antioch?"

"Well, it's in modern day Turkey. In 115AD it was one of the largest cities in the Roman Empire," professor Knotts explained.

"I see," I muttered.

"So, Ashton, do you have an interest in history?" He wheezed.

"I don't think about it a lot, but I enjoy learning about certain things," I say.

"I see. How familiar are you with the time period we're visiting?" He rasped.

"Not much. Nothing, really. I know some basic things about the Roman empire, but nothing specific to ancient Antioch. That's for sure," I say.

"Ha! Of course you wouldn't. That's perfectly understandable," He chuckled warmly.

"Yeah,"

"Would you like to know some more?" The professor asked.

"Sure?"

"Antioch, 115AD. Some like to use CE and BCE because they are supposed to be less christian oriented but I guess I'm just traditional. It was the height of the Pax Romana, the Roman peace. The Roman Empire enjoyed peace from Octavian's triumph over Mark Antony in 30BC until Commodus took the throne in 180 AD. By this I am speaking in relative terms. The Emperors still went on plenty of wars of conquest, and there will be one picking up pace when we are there. We have chosen this time period and location to pop study because—-"

"I don't think he needs a full history lesson. He'll learn enough over the next few days," Priya interjected. I was actually finding it all very interesting, not least because of the knowledge that I would actually be visiting. I was still, despite everything, a little in disbelief.

"What about you?" I looked over at David. David sighed.

"I'm David. Former Israeli special forces. I'll be protecting you three," David had a deep voice.

I was at a loss for words. It was all very awkward to me. A stranger whisked me away to my room without further conversation. He failed to introduce himself and was much less friendly than anyone I had encountered here. Someone had laid out some expensive-looking pajamas for me on the bed. I didn't usually wear pajamas, but I was still tired and I decided to put them on. They were very comfortable. It didn't take long for me to fall asleep.

Trees.

I was back in the forest. I know where I am. It is the campsite where Caleb died. Birds scatter from the trees, and I hear the familiar croaking of the crickets.

Running.

I'm running. Running away from something. Whenever I attempt to glance behind, I fear stumbling or colliding. So I keep my head forward and pick up the pace. My heart is pounding in my chest, my stomach cramping. The dry gravel crunches under my feet. Salty sweat pours down my face as I run and run.

Rain.

As I run, I feel rain start to pour down my face. It's surprisingly warm. I expected it to be cold, like the air. It's very warm. It's too warm. I look and see that the rain is blood. I'm drenched in it. The gravel isn't so dry anymore. It's soaked. With every movement, my feet sink further into the bloody mud.

Falling.

I trip and fall into the ditch. Fall and fall. Tumbling into a black abyss. Slamming into rocks and branches and bushes. I try to grab a hold of a branch but it breaks. I start to grow dizzy and a fear starts to emerge. Fear creeps in, then overwhelms. I am afraid that this fall will never end. That I am in hell. That this is my punishment. That–

Eating.

In a ditch, eating something. Something raw. It tastes warm and bloody. Chewy as well. Very chewy. I look down and am shocked to discover I am consuming a human intestine. The stomach is just completely chewed right open. I scream and choke on the meat. Gagging, I stand up and try to vomit. Nothing will come out. Reluctantly, I look at the face. I see myself looking back with glazed eyes.

3

Chapter 3

I woke up soaked in sweat, so I took a shower right away. It was impossible to tell what time it was given the lack of windows, but the alarm clock claimed it was six AM. I looked in the drawers and found a fresh change of clothes. Putting them on, I laid back down and watched some more Seinfeld. Someone knocked on the door at 7am. He led me back to the dining hall, and I sat back down with the same group of people as the night before. I couldn't help but feel like I was being herded around like cattle. We said nothing to each other apart from the usual morning pleasantries. Towards the end of the meal, which was pancakes with fresh fruit and sausages, Priya said that I was to begin my training immediately.

"What exactly is this training again?" I had to speak up over the clamor of the dining hall.

"We just need to be sure you understand basic etiquette and safety procedures to ensure that everything runs smoothly," Priya explained.

"I think I have you this morning," Professor Knotts coughed. I followed him to a small classroom, complete with a smart board and about twenty desks. Knotts informed me I would be his sole student, so I could sit where I wanted to. I sat at the front.

"So what exactly am I supposed to learn?" I asked.

"Etiquette and behavior. You are going to stick out enough as it is, so it's my job to reduce that as much as possible in these next few days. You will undergo a procedure this afternoon that will enable you to speak Latin fluently, just as if you are speaking English."

"I'm getting a language chip?"

"Yes,"

"Aren't those worth like half a million dollars?"

"The current price for a Latin Translator is only three hundred and twenty thousand dollars. That's because it's a rare language only really used in the modern day in formal Catholic ceremonies,"

"Wow, it's cheap enough that regular people could sell their house and have just enough money to buy one," I exclaimed.

"You remind me of my nephew."

"Did you kidnap all your nephews?"

"I didn't kidnap you,"

"So you're held hostage here too? They aren't paying you?"

"No, I work here,"

"Voluntarily?"

"It's not so simple,"

"Whatever. Just start this lesson of yours already," Knotts droned on about how to walk, how to stand, how to socialize, etc. Supposedly, slavery was normal back then, so he talked about that for a bit. Also, he said there were some cultural things that I would have to get used to, such as the Romans' tolerance for violence. Public nudity was ok in certain situations, such as baths and certain parties. However, there were some conservative Romans who were against such things. Also, in Antioch, there was a hodge-podge of various religions. Roman paganism, Early Christianity, and Judaism were all coexisting within Antioch. So I would have to keep all of that in mind. To be honest, though, I wasn't paying attention. Most of it went completely over my head, and the old man's delivery was boring and unenthusiastic. Besides, I had other things on my mind.

The nightmares weren't going away. I supposed that my mother must have triggered something deep inside me. Caleb was dead and my mother hated me. She resented me. Now, there was a fresh problem; I did not know what these people had in mind for me. Whatever was going to happen, I realized that for now I had little choice but to cooperate.

After the etiquette lessons, we had lunch all together again. Just like breakfast, it was silent. As soon as I finished eating, Priya guided me to a medical room to undergo the brain chip implant procedure.

"How do I know that this is safe?" I demanded.

"You have no choice," Priya replied, and that was the end of it. A team of about five people in full surgical gowns and masks surrounded me on all sides. I was forced to lie down on what reminded me of a dentist's chair. They put a gas mask on my face and told me to count backwards from 100. I drifted off halfway through 97.

Running through the redwoods. The red blinding my vision. Burning my corneas. Scorching my skin. Boiling my organs. Radiating my brain. So much red. Why was there so much red? It

22

made little sense. All I could see was RED, RED, RED, RED, RED.

I tripped and fell. There was no way I was getting up. Lying there in the red sunlight. Letting my skin bubble and burst. Steaming, rotten flesh. The grass is cold, though. Was it gray? I couldn't tell. It wasn't green, though. There was no life in this hellscape.

A wail. Such a bloodcurdling, desperate wail. I recognized it instantly. Something from my memories. I knew what it was. It echoed through the woods like a wolf's howl. A wolf searching for its pack, or perhaps just alerting the others to the next victim.

I cried, but it just burned my skin even more. I could feel my eyes drying up, shriveling. Darkness crept in like the uninvited guest it had always been. I tried screaming, but there was no noise coming from my throat. Just burning, blinding pain. So much pain.

Just as my vision was on the verge of fading away from the heat of the toxic sun, I saw a deer eating its child.

"How are you feeling?" Mattheson was standing over me. He was wearing a different, but impeccable, suit. I realized this was the first time I had seen him since the previous day. I was lying on the reclining surgery chair, but all the surgeons were gone. I felt groggy but otherwise fine. I ran my hand over my head and found a minor cut at the base of my skull.

"Good," I muttered.

"I'm afraid that little scar is permanent. However, it will be scarcely noticeable. I believe the benefits outweigh the costs."

"That's not for you to decide. You, and all these surgeons here, are criminals. Not only did you kidnap me, you've now forcibly performed surgery on me. That's some shady shit," I growled. The fatigue was already wearing off a bit, and the more I thought about it, the angrier I got. This whole thing was both absurd and terrifying.

"Well, now you can speak Latin."

"So? The time machine won't work. This is all some sort of mass delusion or something," I exclaimed.

"It's worked many times in the past,"

"At least, so you say."

"You don't believe me?"

"I don't know what to believe,"

"Well, the brain chip works,"

"How would I even tell?"

"It works because last I checked, you didn't study Latin as an extracurricular,"

"What?"

"I've been speaking Latin to you this whole time,"

"I couldn't even tell," I said. But the more I paid attention, and really thought about it, there was a brief difference. A little delay, or fault, or whatever. It was almost imperceptible, especially if you weren't looking for it. But I could tell. My words were being translated before I spoke them.

"How do I know if I'm speaking English or Latin, then?"

"You'll choose,"

"How?"

"It depends on the circumstances. You'll be able to control it better in a day or two. Since you just got it implanted, you automatically translate to Latin when I speak to you in Latin. Soon enough, you will be able to decide which language to reply in,"

"But I can't even—"

"It's intuitive," Mattheson grinned. I didn't know what to say to that, so a silence descended upon the room. After nearly a minute of awkwardness, Mattheson left the room without saying another word. A guard walked in and escorted me back to my room for a rest. I realized that's what these people were, shepherding me everywhere. They were guards. Prison guards. It was all just so surreal. It was like a movie or a video game or something. I half-expected for some waypoints to burst out of nowhere. Objectives on the screen. None of this was real. It couldn't be. And yet here I was, getting escorted to my room after being forcibly implanted with a brain chip in a secret Turkish underground facility. Something wasn't adding up.

I got into my room and sprawled out on the bed once again. It was a nice bed, that's for sure. The alarm clock read 4:07pm. More Seinfeld. I considered watching some movies or another show, but decided against it. It was a good show, and I was just getting into it. I had never watched it before, so it was like finding a gem that was hidden in plain sight. A knock on the door. Who could it be? I answered. It was Margarethe.

"Hello." I wasn't really sure what to say.

"May I come in?"

"Uh...Sure," she kept glancing down at her feet, and her characteristic PR smile was gone. "What can I do for you?"

"Listen, I need to tell you something," Margarethe sat down on the edge of my bed and patted a spot next to her, beckoning me to sit. I obliged.

"Well.. uh," I subconsciously looked at her up and down. She was wearing a tight skirt and a blaze. She had left a few buttons undone on her shirt. I forced myself to focus my gaze on something else. She must have noticed.

"Gross! That's not why I'm here." It was like she could read my mind.

"I didn't mean to—"

"This place isn't what you think it is,"

"I didn't have high expectations for it. So it's not like——"

"It's worse than you think,"

"Are you going to help me out of here, then?"

"No,"

"Then why—"

"Just listen!" I had never heard Margarethe raise her voice before.

"I'm listening!"

"Take this," Margarethe handed me a vial with a single pill inside.

"What am I supposed to do with this?"

"When the opportunity presents itself, I want you to kill Matthias Mattheson,"

"I'm 17! Why the hell would I agree to become a murderer?"

"Because your life depends on it. You cannot go in the machine,"

"Will it kill me?"

"No, but it will do something equally terrible,"

"Does it work?"

"Yes, but obviously at a cost. If you can kill Matthias Mattheson, then you will be killing the sole driver behind all of this. They might detain you, but no one will report you to the police because this is all illegal as shit. Without Mattheson backing it, the entire project will shut down within weeks. You will be a hero."

"I can't,"

"Yes you can,"

"I'm not a——"

"Aren't you?"

"What did you just say?!"

"Goodbye, Ashton. I hope you will make the right decision."

With that, she got up

And left. I considered reporting to her, but decided against it. Better to let them figure that all out themselves. As for killing Mattheson, the opportunity just never presented itself. I spent the next few days attending classes run by my "team." They seemed like they were all just going through the motions. It all felt very much like it was nominal training. I learned little during these classes. Mattheson only appeared a couple of times a day. I never saw Margarethe again. The nightmares continued and Mattheson offered me some pills to help deal with my lack of sleep. I found it troubling that he knew my sleep patterns, but perhaps he just noticed the bags under my eyes. I refused the pills. Of course, Margarethe's visit is etched into my memory.

Nevertheless, the dreams continued.

Darkness, the eternal night seared into my faded eyes
The gray of the earth is burning my skull
I shudder fitfully on the filthy dirt, rolling around like a rabid dog.
The trees groan as they try to withstand the howling winds
Branches fly into me after a particularly violent gust
Wearing down the landscape like rust
I crawl to the lake,
To the cool of the murky waters
Only to find
It was only a mirage.

4

Chapter 4

I woke up gasping for air and drenched in sweat. The alarm clock read 7am. Eventually, I managed to force myself out of bed and into the shower. I checked the drawer and found a change of clothes, like always. It was still unsettling to think that someone was coming into my room every night and giving me my next change of clothes.

Sitting on the dresser was a pair of cloth trousers, cloth underwear, and a red shirt. They were all very basic. I changed, and my fears about the underwear were unwarranted. The cloth was actually quite comfortable. Even better than the excessively tight briefs I had been wearing earlier.

To my dismay, there were no socks to be found. I had to wear simple leather sandals. Luckily, they were the strap-on kind. Not the ones with the thing between your toes. So it shouldn't cause any blisters, as long as I wasn't hiking for miles and miles. I wasn't hiking for miles and miles, was I?

"Ready to go?" Mattheson beamed. For the first time since Christmas morning, when I was a small kid, I felt unfettered joy. It was a perverse sort of joy. I knew I shouldn't feel it, yet there it was. I had no idea what was about to happen. Yet...it seemed like I was about to experience the impossible. I was going to become a time traveler.

"Yeah. Actually, I do have a question for you," I avoided eye contact.

"Of course," Mattheson beamed.

"Do you think you could give me some of those pills, after all?" I almost regretted saying it.

"Still having troubles? I'm sorry to hear that. I'll grab you some medicine after breakfast. Trust me, the stuff works wonders. You'll need your rest for this trip," Mattheson says.

"Yeah," I mutter. Margarethe's words echoed.

He took me down the hall and after a few minutes, we entered the dining room. No one else was there. A heaping bowl of hash browns, onions, cheese, scrambled eggs, and bacon was already dished out for me. It was eerie being the only one in the entire room.

"Eat up," Mattheson said. I ate up. It was, as I expected, delicious. Mattheson left the room and came back shortly before I finished.

"The pills you requested. Take one a night," Mattheson said as he offered me a leather sac. I looked inside and found about two dozen pills.

"So many?" I asked, exasperated.

"Well, I have plenty and this way you can take them home if you like them," Mattheson declared.

I followed him down the winding hallways to the cavernous room with the big metal oval that was supposedly a time machine. The room was much more full this time; there were probably close to five hundred people scurrying about doing whatever they were doing. Some were wearing yellow construction vests, some were wearing lab coats, and others were in suits. I saw the three members of "the crew" talking to people in the crowd. They were dressed in ancient cloth clothing, like me.

"Ok, go talk to Priya. I think you can leave soon," he said. I walked over to Priya, who was in deep conversation with an older man in a suit. I was unsure whether I should interrupt, so I kind of just stood there awkwardly. She glanced over at me and told the guy in the suit that she needed a second.

"We are leaving soon. If that's why you're standing around with your cock in your hand—err, you're a kid, right? Ok, well, you've probably heard worse. Now, go wait in the Clipper," Priya rattled.

"Uh-yeah, it's fine. The clipper?" I said. Priya laughed.

"Yeah, that's Mattheson for you. He has a weird thing with nail clippers. Don't ask me why. I'm actually kind of embarrassed. I actually just called it that," Priya explained. I shook my head and smiled, and then walked over to the clipper. It was a giant metal oval, probably about 25 feet high. The door, or I guess the hatch would be a better word, was wide open. I climbed up the ladder-like steps to find four seats centered on a column with a bunch of screens, buttons, and wires. Seemingly random green scripts of numbers polluted the screens. It stunk of stale plastic. Like putting your head inside a plastic bag.

I sat down and put my seatbelt on. It was one of those seat-belts that you'd see a pilot have, with four straps conjoining in the middle chest area. I sat there for what seemed like the longest time, listening to the faint hum of machinery. My thoughts drifted towards my friends. I wondered what they were doing right now. Were they hanging out together? Playing on the PS5? I realized with growing dread the possibility that I would never return. I might never see them again. No more stupid jokes from Mike, and no more of that incessant bragging Jen would do when she won a video game. No more hearing Jim fantasize about getting Janet back, and no more—

"Hello, there," the old historian croaked. He climbed in with me, moving carefully so as not to trip.

"Hi," I replied. A ball of fear had grown in my stomach, mixed with raw excitement.

"I was nervous the first time too," the professor said. The absurd image of this old man saying that exact phrase to a young woman jumped into my dirty little mind. It took all of my energy not to burst out laughing right then and there.

"Well, I guess my concern is just like, how safe can this really be? With airplanes, I'm not afraid because there's statistics showing that very few planes crash. With cars, at least I have control over who's car I'm getting into. Whether I trust that driver or not. With this, though, I have no idea what to expect," I chattered.

"Well, I have been on fourteen trips. There was a historian before me, and he went on seven trips. So this is the twenty-second trip," Dr Charles Knotts said.

"That's reassuring, I guess. What happened to the other historian?" I say.

"Don't worry about that,"

"Okay..."

"You can call me Charlie from now on." He reached out and shook my hand. Surprisingly, his hand was extremely calloused and rough.

"Should we be worried about changing history and all of that?" I ask.

"You've watched Back to the Future, I see. No, no. It doesn't work that way. I hardly understand it myself, as it is far out of my field of study. But from what they've told me, it sounds like as long as we stay in the background, our effect will be negligible."

"How do we determine what is negligible?"

"Trust me, as long as we don't bring anything modern with us, nothing we can do will make a difference. It also helps that we are going so far back."

"Well that's good to hear,"

"Yes, this whole situation is quite beyond belief, isn't it?"

"Yeah. Do you have grandchildren?" I ask. I surprise myself with the question, but it comes out naturally. The professor smiles warmly.

"I do. Two lovely girls. One is eight, and the other is six. They are both quite interested in gladiatorial matches, I'm happy to add. No barbies for them," the old man chuckled heartily. It was the kind of deep belly laugh that was undoubtedly genuine. Just as I was about to ask about how he came to work here, Priya and the commando walked in. The commando shook my hand. It was about as coarse as the professor's hand.

"Are you ready?" He asked.

"As ready as I can be," I replied. He nodded his head and sat down, buckling up. Priya said nothing to me and started typing stuff into the screens. I had no idea what she was doing.

"ALL THE COMPONENTS ARE FULLY CHARGED!" Priya hollered.

"THEN YOU'RE A-OK TO GO. ALL GOOD FROM THIS SIDE," a voice hollered back. Priya pushed some more buttons and then sat down. A tremendous shudder filled the machine as the hatch closed, a loud clunk leaving no doubt whether the door was locked. That feeling of nervous dread, kind of like before you go on a rollercoaster, had intensified to a degree I had never felt before.

"All right, better say your prayers, fellas! If they miscalculated, we'll all be torn apart at the atomic level." Priya had the widest grin I had seen on her face yet. She pushed a few more buttons and then leaned her back against the headrest, closing her eyes. The hum of the machinery started to grow louder. Everything was vibrating more and more. I was gonna die. Torn apart at the atomic level? What would that feel like? There would be no pain, right?

Everyone was closing their eyes now, leaning back. The whirring grew louder. It was almost deafening.

I need to get out of here. I can't die yet. What will my dad think? Will Mattheson tell him if I die? Or will I merely go missing? The loss of both his children would consume my father with despair, tearing him apart. Can I ask Priya to shut it down? I don't know, maybe it's too late. Or maybe not.

Nausea overcomes me as the machine spins faster and faster. The roar of machinery consumes me. Everything blurs. The colors, the sounds, the smells. Like paint smeared all over a canvas.

"SHUT IT DOWN!" I scream, my words blending into the surrounding cacophony. I can't even see Priya anymore. It's all just a nauseating blur. My skin suddenly burns, and then freezes. Every few seconds, it alternates. It's all enormously painful, and yet strangely exhilarating at the same time. I close my eyes and suddenly see flashes of memories.

Playing with Jim in the backyard. We have water guns and I ambush him from around the tree. He laughs and sprays me back. I say he is cheating.

Studying for a test. I don't know which one. I see myself working hard. It's weird, it's like an out-of-body experience. It was recently, though, in the last few years.

Arguing with my mom about screen time. I think I was like 12 or 13. We are in the house. She wants me to come visit with my aunt who has come to visit all the way from Utah. I say I don't want to hear about my aunt polly's china collection. She says that she will take my iPad away for the rest of the month if I don't listen.

Arguing with Caleb about something. He had lied to my mom again, taking advantage of her gullibility. I was angry with him about it. Caleb tried deflecting by saying he was actually telling the truth, even though I knew he wasn't.

Eating dinner with my dad. I don't recognize this memory. My dad has gray hair and we're eating somewhere other than my house. It looks more shabby, run-down. My god, was this the future? What happened to my house?

Suddenly, the visions stopped and there was a deafening silence. Everything was still. Absolutely still. I let out a shaky sigh. My hands were warm and sweaty. The pit in my stomach remained, but not the nausea. That was gone as quickly as it had come. I opened my eyes and saw everyone slowly do the same.

"We're here," Priya declared with a pale face. I wonder what she saw.

5

Chapter 5

Priya tapped a few buttons, and the hatch groaned open. I staggered outside, following her lead. The sun was blinding, and it disorientated me even more than I already was. As I stepped out into this ancient world, the hot and dry temperatures vaguely reminded me of Mexico. I just stood there for what must have been two solid minutes, at least. Unmoving. Gazing at the rolling hills, covered in thick brown grass. Small, strange, little coniferous trees dotted the landscape. Their green pines were the only sources of color in this dry environment. There was something beautiful about it all.

Perhaps it was the fact that I had just been transported to another place. Although I now had little reason to doubt it, I could not be sure that I had traveled back in time. What I did know for certain, however, is that five minutes ago, I was deep underground in a metal sphere and now I was here. There was no logical explanation that I could come up with. I realized that no one else had said anything either. They were equally in awe. I guess things like this never get old.

"Alright, let's go," Priya said, and she started walking away.

"Wait, shouldn't we be worried about someone finding this thing?" I ask.

"No," the professor replies.

"Why is that?"

"Well, we are miles away from anything, first of all. But people have found our machine before and it has become a bit of a local legend. But that's all it will be remembered as, a legend. It doesn't change anything significantly. We just aren't here for long enough. Technically, even by visiting here we are creating a parallel universe, but it is so similar to our own that when we return, it will appear the same to us. At least that's how I understand it," Professor Knotts says.

"Isn't that a bit unethical, creating parallel universes?"

"Depends on your point of view. But it's not like we are destroying the other universe. It still continues on." The professor explains.

"Ok,"

"This stuff isn't really my area of expertise. But I can try my best. Priya would know better, but I don't think she has the patience to explain it all to you."

"Yeah, I can see that. Well I appreciate it,"

"Did you know that the city we are visiting is the third largest city in the Roman Empire?"

"Nope," I chuckle.

"Yes, a quarter of a million people live within the walls of Antioch. Only Rome and Alexandria
have larger populations. It is also the cradle of Christianity,"

"Interesting. Are there any saints here right now?" I ask. I was hardly a catholic but my mother wouldn't forgive me if I passed up a chance to meet a bona fide saint.

"Well, I believe St Ignatius of Antioch is alive right now. We probably won't have time to visit him though. Some say he is a disciple of John the apostle," Knotts croaked.

"That's a shame. My mom's a big catholic,"

"And not you?"

"No, not really,"

"Faith is very important. It doesn't matter if it's real, because that's besides the point. If you look through the lens of history, you will find that there has always been religion. People like to worship. Now, it can either be to a religion that advocates helping the poor and being empathetic towards others or it can be directed towards something else. Maybe something more sinister. And it doesn't have to be a religion. It can be a political figure, or an ideology," Knotts explained.

"You don't strike me as a religious person," I say. He laughed.

"And what makes you say that?"

"Well, I don't know. I guess I always thought scientists were atheists,"

"Isaac Newton was a Catholic,"

"Well that was the olden days,"

"Yes, I suppose. People always like to make that argument though,"

"So, are you? Religious, that is. I guess the more I ask the more it seems like I'm prying,"

"No, not prying. I'm agnostic. But like I said, I believe in the institution of mainstream religion. You know, Christianity, Judaism, Islam, Sikhism, Buddhism. They are all pretty peaceful. They are also all on the decline, in favor of atheism,"

"Well it sounds like you don't practice what you preach," I say with a laugh.

"No, no. I am a practicing catholic. I just don't believe in it, not really. What I believe in are the ethical lessons imparted by catholic teachings,"

"Fair enough. What do you say about all the religious wars and stuff that have erupted over the years?"

"They are unfortunate side effects. War will not go away with religion. Violence will not disappear. It will only intensify. People will always fight over something. Without religion, what is there to restrain ourselves?" Knotts said. He made some good points, but it didn't exactly convince me to convert.

We spent the next two hours, walking and walking. It seemed like we would never reach the city, but my boredom and exhaustion were subdued somewhat by the Professor's interesting tidbits. Priya and the Israeli military guy said nothing the whole time. Apparently, two emperors were in town right now. Trajan and Hadrian. Trajan was the current emperor, and he was resting in Antioch with his army before he continued on to invade Persia in an ill-fated decision.

Trajan was a celebrated ruler, who was especially good with military matters. He had conquered the kingdom of Dacia a few years earlier, a task that his immediate predecessors

Nerva and Nero had been unable to complete. Dacia was immensely rich, thanks to its large amount of goldmines. It was apparently mostly located in the present-day countries of Serbia, Montenegro, and Croatia.

Hadrian would succeed Trajan a few years from now, the professor explained, and his reign would be good as well. Hadrian was known for trying to transform the Empire into a Greek-centric civilization that existed in a collegial nature rather than the centralized system which he had inherited. Eventually, his efforts failed spectacularly with the Bar Kokhba revolt in Judea, but his actions in the meantime earned him praise among historians. He earned special admiration among both contemporary and modern Greeks.

The professor also told me about a bunch of other stuff, but his ramblings just glazed over as the walk dragged on. The water from the travel sac tasted warm and leathery. I took generous swigs; it was scorching outside, and I did not know how much longer we would be walking. I could always ask but Priya already seemed to dislike me and I didn't want to worsen matters by asking "are we there yet?"

So on we marched. Onward through the grassy hills of whatever region Antioch was in. After a couple of hours of talking, Professor Knotts himself slipped into what could be described as a trance caused by fatigue. I realized they wanted to take care so as not to have the machine discovered, as though it would not break reality, it could create a real headache for us on the way back. But I thought it would be like an hour hike and then we'd be there. Not the case.

The sun crept through the sky as we shuffled along. Up and down, up and down. What seemed easy at first became quite daunting, the hills seemingly becoming slightly steeper every time a new one approached.

We stopped for some breaks here and there, but generally we kept a steady pace. A bright spot was seeing a small herd of fluffy sheep approach us. I figured they would run away as we got closer, but they actually came right up to us. The professor and Priya were unimpressed, but surprisingly the soldier guy was smiling ear to ear. I joined him in petting the sheep.

"So do you like sheep...sorry what's your name again?" I ask, slightly embarrassed.

"Yes, very much so. My father had a small farm when I was growing up. I used to play with them with my little sister.

Sheep are cute, but they are also idiotic. Just like most of the women I've met!" David replies. I decided to ignore the comment about women, unsure if I should laugh or not.

"Nice. I've actually never seen a sheep before,"

"Really? Not even at a petting zoo or something? I hear a lot of schools do those now for end-of-year parties. My Canadian nephew is in junior high and he was just telling me last year about how they brought pigs and chickens and all these things. Right to the school!"

"No, I don't think my school would spend money on its students like that. They're kind of cheap. Campground outhouses have better toilet paper," I say. David bursts out laughing, maybe a little too hard.

"Yes, that sounds like my employer that I had before Mr Mattheson. I was fresh out of the Givati and this rich asshole hired me to watch his house. He was cheap like you wouldn't believe. One of my many trivial tasks was sorting through the mail for any Burger King or Wendy's food coupons. He only ate fast food from those two places, and he insisted on using coupons. The man was a multi billionaire,"

"That's crazy. Yeah, you hear about rich people being cheap. Did you ever see-"

"And he used single ply toilet paper! One time my finger popped right through," he roared. I awkwardly chuckled along.

"So, what were you going to ask?"

"Oh, nothing I already forgot,"

"Happens to me all the time," David grinned again.

"So how is it, being a time traveler?"

"Great. I never expected to be doing something like this,"

"Have you ever had to use your skills? Defend the team?"

"Once. Only once," David's face turned grim. There was

silence for a few minutes, as we walked on past the sheep after briefly petting their strange coats of wool. It was like the stuffing of a teddy bear, but as fur on a live animal. Just blew my mind. We had to keep moving if we had to make it on time, as Priya explained. My feet were aching in these ridiculous leather shoes. Professor Knotts was up ahead talking with Priya.

"So you mentioned you have a little sister," I say.

"Yes. She is amazing. She is currently a member of the Knesset. She leads the third largest party and is a minister in the coalition government," David says proudly.

"Wow, a time traveler and a powerful politician. Your parents must be proud,"

"My father passed away a few years ago. Prostate cancer. He was very proud. My mother is proud too, but she doesn't know what I really do. She knows I work security for Mattheson, but that's it,"

"I'm sorry to hear about your father. My brother just passed a few months ago,"

"Your brother? How old was he?"

"He was just thirteen," I whisper. David said nothing, but he squeezed my shoulder.

Onwards we went.

6

Chapter 6

Our walking came to a halt atop one of the many large, grassy hills that surrounded us. In the valley below lay a massive cityscape, like nothing I had ever seen. A marble metropolis, with tens of thousands of buildings dotting the landscape. I could tell from this distance that educated city planners built the settlement. It looked similar to cities from the modern day, in that the buildings were organized in something similar to city blocks. There also appeared to be enormous squares and stuff within the city, and surrounding it was farmland, including a vineyard barely a hundred meters below us on the side of the hill.

The air faintly stunk of manure and smoke, but somehow it made the whole thing that much better. I was really here. I was about to enter an ancient city and tour around with an expert historian for three days. No one could claim to be luckier than I was right now. A smile, broad and genuine, spread across my face as the full realization of my situation came into full focus.

The sun was low in the sky, and I could tell that night would come soon. Two hours, maybe less. A massive flock of birds suddenly took off from their perch on the roofs of the city slums, and they flew like a dark cloud into the hills.

"Amazing," Priya breathed.

"I.. can't believe it," I whispered. Priya smiled and patted me on the back.

"Believe it, kid. You only get three days," She sighed dramatically. We started walking down the hill towards the city.

We entered the city through what looked like the main entrance. The city was surrounded by a large brick walk. Vines crawled up the side of the weathered wall. The streets are surprisingly flat, made up of enormous stones fitted together perfectly. While I had smelled manure earlier up on the hill, that was now replaced by all the delightfully exotic scents the Antioch food market had to offer.

People bustled about on the streets, and the whole thing kind of reminded me of a farmers market. There were tents selling fresh vegetables, salted fish, fresh fish, and fruit. I didn't see any beef or pork or anything.

To my horror, there was also a much nicer looking stand selling roasted mouse, which Professor Knotts explained was a delicacy in the Roman Empire. In some ways it reminded me of a farmers market, but in other ways it reminded me more of New York. The yelling, the cacophony, the people. There were so many people. It was impossible not to bump into the crowd.

Everything, except for the mice, looked absolutely delicious. I was starving. However long it had taken for us to get there, it took a lot out of me. Hungry and thirsty for something other than hot, leathery water.

"Do we have any money?" I asked no one in particular. I had to almost yell above the clamor of the streets.

"Of course. Are you hungry?"

"Aren't you?"

"Yep. I see that was a stupid question. These stands change so much, it's hard to have a regular place to go. So just pick any place you think looks good,"

"Me?"

"Yes, you dipshit. It's your trip after all," Priya said, half-jokingly. We walked for another minute or two until we came upon some sort of fish stand. The fish was in a big pot, being kept warm by a small fire underneath it. It was immersed in a stew sauce that was yellowish and there was a strong, sweet scent coming from it. At the stand was a gray-haired man with deeply tanned skin, wearing a colorful shirt and trousers. Unlike most of the other vendors, he was not yelling trying to buy people; is business. He just was sitting, wearily staring into the distance.

"Hi-hello?" I ask. The others stand behind me, examining the food.

"What do you want?" The man grumbled.

"I was hoping to get a bowlful of that fish stew there, and I don't know about my friends, if they want any." I said. I looked at the crew and they all shook their heads.

"You got any money?"

"Yeah," Priya was already handing me a few coins. I paid the man, and he started scooping the stew.

"So, what is it exactly?" I ask. The man sighed.

"Stew," He said simply. The vendor handed me a clay bowl, heaping full of the thick yellow sauce. Inside was a wooden spoon.

"Thank you," I mumbled. The man said nothing and simply went back to blankly staring into space. The stew tasted good, although I could see some people calling it an acquired taste. It was sweet, but I had no idea what the spices were. I could tell there was some honey in it though, and maybe some basil or some other herbs. It was definitely very interesting. Maybe it wasn't that good, and I just thought it was because of my intense hunger. My biggest problem with it was the fish tasted far too fishy for my liking, but I finished the whole bowl in less than five minutes.

It was striking to see how colorful it all was. When you think about the Roman Empire, you think of pillars and beautiful gray statues. This was not the case. Even the most emaciated and clearly impoverished people wore vibrant colors. The walls of buildings were red or sometimes blue or even green. The tents themselves were colorful. Perhaps the most shocking thing was seeing the first roman statue in its prime. It was of an emperor, most likely. There was an inscription but strangely enough I could not read Latin. I could understand it and speak it, but the written words remained as foreign as ever.

"Where are we going, anyway?" I wonder aloud.

"We need to buy ourselves a couple rooms for our stay," responded Priya.

"They had hotels?"

"No, all the thousands of daily visitors and travelers just set up camp in the streets," Priya rolled her eyes. I didn't think it was so obvious; there were plenty of homeless people on the streets.

Silence. On we went. The setting sun starts glaring in my eyes, and the once-exotic scents of the market blend into something more sickening. My stomach growls and burns in pain. There must have been something wrong with that fish stew. Who trusts street food anyway? Far too romanticized if you ask me. I suddenly realize I'm not going to make it to wherever we're going.

"Are there public toilets around here?" I ask, doubtfully. I couldn't hide the urgency in my voice.

"Yes, but I wouldn't recommend going in there. Can you hold it?" Priya says.

"No," I mumble. Priya must have seen the desperation in my eyes and so we hurried just around the corner to this dilapidated building. The roof was made of rotting wood planks and the stone walls were overgrown with vines. I scurried inside the doorless entrance to find a large, rectangular room with rows of holes to shit in.

The smell!

I had never smelled something so awful. I had seen my fair share of outhouse while camping, and kind of smelled like that, but this was so much more intense. Concentrated would be the right word. It was just thick. I could practically taste it. For a second I thought the stew was going up rather than down, but then desperation made me refocus on my surroundings.

There was probably space for as many as fifty people in here, but the seats were narrowly spaced. Luckily, only a few sullen men were scattered throughout the building. I found a seat, as far away from anyone as possible, and immediately just let it out. The diarrhea was like a pressure wash, high pressure liquid. I started sweating, and my stomach burned in pain. A few horrible seconds in, I came to the horrible realization that I had no idea what I was going to do for toilet paper. There was a dirty stream of water with sticks with sponges on the end surrounding the entirety of the room. I figure they probably are used to cleaning an area. They looked surprisingly similar to modern toilet scrubbers.

Surely they weren't used for...

One of the skinny old men across from me suddenly picked up one of the dirty scrubbers and, yep, started wiping his ass. After a few big wipes, he stood up and flashed me with his shriveled little...you know. Gonna take a few days to forget about that.

A fresh wave of pain washed over me as the feces just squirted out. I felt like crying, I was shaking. I desperately wanted to avoid such a situation, as there were strangers looking directly at me. I guess the Ancient Romans didn't believe much in privacy. The inherent discreteness that should be afforded to someone undertaking something so...universally private. Everyone has to do it, King or peasant, but I think everyone needs some fucking privacy.

One of the old men groaned in pain and slumped forward and fell off the toilet, laying unmoving on the ground. Was he dead?

"Hey! Are you ok?" I called out to the man. No response. For some reason, yelling made everything worse again. Another wave of pain as the diarrhea started up again. I pinched my sweaty thigh and scrunched my eyes in pain, praying to whatever God existed for this awful moment to end. For a few scar moments, I was worried I was going to puke all over the floor. It felt like my whole body was on fire. I hadn't had food poisoning since I was a little kid. Was this what it felt like normally? Or was this something more serious?

After some unknown quantity of time, the pain subsided enough for me to become concerned for the limp body laying on the floor.

"Can someone check him?" There were only three other guys in the building, and they all had a sort of distant look on their faces. For a second, I was worried the translator had somehow stopped working. It was like they didn't hear me.

"He's dead," One man said simply, in what sounded like perfect English.

"Are you sure?"

"No, but I don't really give a flying fuck," the guy replied, his eyes locking on to mine. Was a word like fuck even around back then? Mattheson must have taken some liberties with the translator. That couldn't be a direct translation, but by the guy's tone and careless facial expression I could tell it was probably pretty close.

I didn't really know how to respond to that, so I just finished my business, scrubbed, and went on my way. I didn't check the man's vitals on my way out. I limped out of there as fast as my raw rear end would allow me.

7

Chapter 7

"Jesus, you're looking pretty pale, kid," David said.

"Yeah," I mumbled. I felt awful, but relieved that the worst was over.

"Got to be careful with what you eat around here," Dr Knotts said. No kidding. I won't be eating anything except fresh fruit and vegetables from now on. Can't trust anything.

"How long was I in there?" I ask. The sun was almost completely set. It was getting dark.

"Hard to say, probably like half an hour at least," Knotts replied.

"Are we close to the hotel?" I can't help but yawn at the thought of a nice, warm bed. A fire, some sheets. A pillow to rest my head. Everything was aching, and the last half hour took what little energy I had left over from the long hike.

"It's not exactly a hotel. More of a bed-and-breakfast than anything. But yes," Priya replied softly, looking at me with what might have been sympathy. A bed-and-breakfast sounded even better than a hotel, to be honest. More cozy. But I reminded myself not to get my hopes up. I had no idea what to expect.

To my relief, Priya was right. We walked for probably only another five minutes before reaching the "bed-and-breakfast." There was a sign in Latin posted on the beige clay building, but I couldn't read it. Like many of the others, the unremarkable building stood about four stories high. It was less busy than the big main street we had been on earlier, but there was still plenty of foot traffic. It was thinning quick though, as darkness descended over the city like a hand snuffing out the light of the candle. There were some lamps, but no standardized street lamps like today. The result was eerie and lonely. Dangerous, too, I imagine. I was happy we could reach this place when we did.

There was a big oak door, and Priya had to knock. I noticed David scanning the area, probably to make sure we weren't jumped by any thieves. A tired, middle-aged black woman answered the door, and her eyes immediately widened with joy as she saw Priya.

"Priya! What a lovely surprise! I wasn't expecting you." Once again, perfect English. Well, not quite. There was a bit of a peculiar accent I didn't recognize. I suspected she had an accent in her Latin, and that's what it was.

"Well, we were in the neighborhood," Priya said.

"Come in, come in!" We went inside. It was cozy and warm, just like I imagined. She had a little fire going in the fireplace. You could tell it had been burning all day from all the orange coals. It smelled faintly of nutmeg and some other spices I didn't recognize.

"David, dashing as ever! And Charlie...I see you changed your hair." She hugged them with genuine affection. She then looked at me, her eyes darting to my feet and then quickly back to my face.

"Hi," I said awkwardly. I wasn't sure how to put my arms. Cross them? Too strict-looking. Behind the back? Too butler-ish. On the hips? Too sassy. After a brief attempt at each, I settled on letting them dangle helplessly on my side.

"And who might you be?" The lady smiled and extended her hand. I shook it.

"I'm Ashton," I said. The woman burst out laughing. It was a warm, deep belly laugh.

"Another strange name! Did you all have the same parents? I suppose David is a normal enough name for a Jew. But Priya? Charlie? And now Ashton! My, oh my,"

"What's your name?"

"Well, it's not as unique as you folks. Decima is the name. A true Roman name." Was that disdain in her voice?

"Nice to meet you, then," I say. Decima's face suddenly lights up, somehow animating more than when we first walked in.

"You all must be totally exhausted! I'll show you to your rooms."

"Thank you," Priya says.

"Have you all eaten yet?" Decima asks.

"Oh yes, I've eaten. It was no good, though. Made me sick," I reply. The others say they didn't eat at all, perhaps wisely so.

"I see. Then I'll prepare some bread and grapes. You can have the two rooms on the third floor all to yourselves. Two to a room, unfortunately. Business is good tonight. They should be plenty spacious though," Decima eagerly sputtered. She seemed incredibly excited to see Priya and the others. I wonder if she knew about the time travel thing. Once again, the question of why Mattheson would keep sending people here time and time again when they can go to any point in history came to mind.

I pushed it aside for later. Whatever the reason, here I was in an ancient bed-and-breakfast talking to a person who has been dead for two thousand years. If I died right now, I could say I lived. I'm not sure people who make it to 80 nowadays can say that.

The stairs were narrow and uneven, but they were solid stone. Priya and David just sort of went into the room on the left as soon as we got there.

"Guess that means we're bunking together," Knotts chuckled.

The room was surprisingly spacious for such a seemingly humble establishment. There were two small beds with thin sheets. Just like out on the streets, it was exceedingly colorful inside as well. The sheets were red, and the walls were an intricate blue and gold pattern. So colorful I would even go so far to say ugly. This stuff all looked way better, gray and faded. It was definitely refreshing, though.

The smell of spices remained. I wondered if it was because of the candles or something else. Probably the candles. There were a lot of candles. A fire hazard, for sure. I guess they didn't have much of an option. Fireflies? No, that's cartoonish. How would they get them? Well, maybe—

"Which bed do you want?" Knotts asked.

"I don't care," I sighed. All I wanted to do was sleep. My legs were shaking, and I began to doubt my ability to continue standing up. I briefly considered staying up in the room and not coming down to eat, but decided against it. The fact of the matter was that I was too weak to continue on without eating, and who knew when we would stop for another meal?

"Well, this is lovely," Professor Knotts mumbled, sitting down on his bed.

"Yeah," I agreed.

"So, how are you holding up? I know this can be a lot. Especially for first-timers such as yourself," the professor asked carefully.

"It's crazy. I mean, everyone here is dead. But you know, it's exciting. I would never have imagined this. As a historian, this must be your dream come true!" I exclaimed.

"Of course it is. It really doesn't get old," Knotts said quickly. His eyes drifted down to the floor.

"Seriously though, you can tell me. Why here? Any time and place in history, that's how it works, right?" I sat down on the other bed.

"Any time and place. Not that we'd know for sure. This is the only place we've gone," the professor spoke slowly and methodically. He kept making eye contact, which made me uncomfortable. I couldn't help but glance away at the floor.

"So you won't tell me then?"

"No, I can't tell you. Mattheson tells us where to go. He funds the whole thing. What are—-" Knotts burst into a coughing fit. It was a loud, terrible cough that just kept going.

"Professor? Are you okay?" I leapt up from the bed and ran towards him before realizing I had no idea what I could do. It was like he was choking. What was I supposed to do? Go get Priya? He probably just needed some water. Luckily, there was a pitcher with two glasses on a table in the corner. I hastily poured him a glass, spilling some on the table, and scrambled over to him. His face was practically purple from all the coughing. The old man drank the water in big gulps, some of it running down his chin.

"Thank.. thank you," Knotts whispered hoarsely. The remainder of his water was tainted with blood.

"Have you seen a doctor about that?" I said, looking at his bloodied water glass.

"I already have," Knotts sighed, rubbing his eyes.

"Oh,"

"It's lung cancer, stage four,"

"Oh,"

"I have about four or five months left,"

"Oh, I'm so sorry,"

"Don't worry about it." He let out a hearty chuckle, and I couldn't help but be worried it would turn into another coughing fit. Luckily, it didn't.

"Do the others know?" I felt terrible for the guy. He was so nice. And what about his grandkids?

"Yes, but please don't bring it up. This is my last trip."

"Oh,"

"Yeah.." I had no idea what else to say, so I changed the subject.

"So does our host know about the whole time travel thing? You guys have obviously been here before," I ask. He once again burst into laughter.

"No, no. She would throw us out onto the streets as lunatics if we ever tried to tell her that!"

"So then, what does she think you are?"

"Meet Charlie Knotts, industrial fish sauce salesman," Knotts smiled. I laughed.

"What?"

"Yep, that's what we are here for. On previous visits, we set up a business and we have factories. It helped that we could bring gold from the future, of course,"

"But why? Why wouldn't you just go incognito? Why make such a name for yourselves?"

"Don't ask me. Mattheson keeps sending us back here, and I guess if we are going to be doing that we needed a career,"

"But how do you keep it going in your absence?"

"We hire people. There's a Greek fellow named Ajax, and he runs the day-to-day business. But keep in mind that we have a time machine and so while our trips may be months apart, we can come back only weeks or even days after we left."

"I didn't know they had factories in the ancient world,"

"Oh yes, at least in the roman empire they did. China as well. Things kind of fell apart in the middle ages,"

"Cool," a terrible thought crossed my mind.

"Yeah,"

"You guys don't use slaves, do you?" I knew little about the Roman Empire, but I knew that there was slavery. I had Russell Crowe to thank for that.

"No! Of course not. Ajax would likely love that, though. Always trying to cut costs. He's harmless though. Slavery is actually not very common outside of Italy and the western provinces, so luckily it isn't the norm," Knotts explained.

"That's good, because I don't know if I could dine with slaveholders. Should we eat?"

"I think that is a fantastic idea. The others should be ready. Let's go," Knotts exclaimed. He grunted as he got up, another reminder of his age.

Priya and David were all ready when we knocked on their door. We went back downstairs and Decima was in a room to the left of the lobby. It must have been the dining room. There was another fireplace and an enormous oak table. Two large platters of grapes, fresh bread, and some cheese filled the table.

There was a bottle of wine and a pitcher of water. Once again, it struck me as more elegant than you would ever expect, looking at the building from outside.

"Enjoy," Decima said simply. We sat down and devoured the food in silence. The bread was delicious. Soft and warm. The grapes were juicy and sweet. They were about half the size of the ones you'd buy in the store, but I suppose that's just because we add all those GMOs and shit to our food nowadays. There were seeds too, which I hate but at the moment I didn't care at all. I was just scarfing it down. I felt a little rude, grabbing big handfuls onto my plate like I was, but such thoughts were firmly in the back of my mind.

The cheese tasted kind of strong, even in my hungry state, but I ate it anyway. Was it goat cheese? Or something else? I had no idea. Eventually, the silence broke.

"So how are the grandkids, Charlie?" Decima beamed.

"They are doing great, thanks for asking," Knotts replied.

"How old are they now, anyway?"

"Eight and ten,"

"A wonderful age. Same age as my nephews,"

"Really? Why don't you ever visit them?"

"Well, they are going to school in Greece right now. I finally scraped together enough money to send them to private school."

"How marvelous!" Knotts exclaimed.

"Their father is a goat farmer, you see. That's where I get my cheese, actually. He makes very little money,"

"I'm sorry to hear that."

"Actually, I've been looking for you all these last few days. You see, I've run into a bit of trouble with the creditors and—" Decima began.

"Again! Decima, we can't keep bailing you out. You need to get your spending under control. I thought you said you were making investments in those apartments on the other side of the city," Priya cried.

"I know, I know. I'll be better," Decima scrunched hair thick eyebrows in shame.

"It's fine, of course. We'll take care of it," Charlie smiled.

"Hold on—Charlie, can I talk to you for a minute?" Priya said to charlie. I noticed that David was just quietly eating, avoiding eye contact. Priya and Knotts excused themselves and left the room, leaving just David, Decima and I. An awkward silence briefly descended upon the dinner table.

"So.. Ashton, is it?"

"Yeah,"

"So, how did you get involved with these dumbasses?" She laughed. I had no idea what to say; no one gave me a cover story.

"I-I don't know," I stuttered.

"What do you mean you don't know? Speak sense!" She cried.

"I guess you could say I'm on vacation," I said.

"How vague of you," Decima squinted. David looked up from his plate and gave me a look. I decided to change the subject.

"So, how do you know everyone?"

"Everyone? No one knows everyone, boy."

"Well—"

"HAHA!"

"What—"

"Got you there, didn't I?" It wasn't very funny.

"I guess..."

"Well, let me tell you something, I'm not on vacation,"

"How long have you lived in Antioch?"

"About twenty-odd years now,"

"Nice," Nice? Really? I needed to get better at small talk.

"I am the child of slaves, you see," she said grimly. Things just took a dark turn.

"I'm sorry to hear that," I said uncomfortably.

"They were household slaves in Carthage,"

"Oh,"

"Named me Decima to try to improve my chances as a freedwoman,"

"Oh,"

"At least I assume so,"

"Why do—"

"They gave me up to my uncle when I was a baby,"

"Oh,"

"'We lived on a farm in a small village near Hippo Regius,"

"What kind of farm?" I asked. It was kind of random that she was just telling me her life story, but I didn't mind. David was just sitting quietly in the corner, dipping his bread in wine.

"Wheat,"

"Good crop," I said stupidly.

"My Uncle was a great man, a kind man. The closest thing to a father I ever had. He always made sure we were well fed. I had a great childhood. There weren't a lot of other children in the village, but I was friends with the few who were stuck there with me. My wonderful uncle even had enough money to get me a tutor while growing up. Mathematics, rhetoric, poetry. Studying those damned Cicero speeches," she reminisced.

"Well, that sounds nice,"

"It was until I was around your age. Raiders came to the farm and stole all our wheat. While they were at it, they broke my

58

poor uncle's legs. He couldn't walk again,"

"Oh.. I'm so sorry,"

"We would've starved, so I went to Hippo Regius and prostituted myself. Eventually I made enough money to get some other girls on my payroll,"

"Oh,"

"We didn't starve, but my uncle caught the plague and died that spring,"

"I was 17 the summer when I moved here to Antioch,"

"Oh," I mumbled awkwardly. I really needed to think of something better to say. David suddenly sprang to life.

"Decima! Take it easy on the poor boy, will you? If I have to hear that sob story one more time, I swear to God I'm gonna slit my wrists with this bread knife," David exclaimed. Did he really just say that? I looked at Decima, unsure of how she would react. She just laughed.

"David, you're such an asshole! Relax, Ashton. I was just trying to make you uncomfortable. It's all true though, of course," Decima said. I was surprised at how normal she seemed. Like a modern person, almost. Once again I wondered how exact the translation was. Priya and the professor suddenly walked back into the room.

"What's going on here?" Priya asked.

"Decima's just trying to make the boy sweat," David chuckled.

"Well, I need to talk with Decima one on one," Priya said. David's smile faded.

"Alright, well, I'm ready for bed anyway," I declared. It was true; my eyes were getting heavy and the fireplace and wonderful aroma didn't help matters.

"I could use a good sleep as well, I think," Knotts said. So we thanked Decima and headed upstairs to our little room. Knotts didn't say anything after we got into the room. He just stripped down to his cloth underwear and climbed into bed. He was asleep within five minutes of walking in the door. A heavy snorer too, I might add.

I sat down on my lumpy bed and tried to process the events of the past day. I had traveled back in time for almost two thousand years. I hiked probably at least ten kilometers in the desert, only to reach the city and eat some nasty fish stew. I had chronic diarrhea in a public toilet and witnessed a man die (maybe or maybe not.) Finally, to end up here, in this strangely colorful bed-and-breakfast in a strangely colorful city with a host whose personality was most colorful of all.

Deciding not to strip to my underwear, I pulled the thin sheets up to my neck and let everything start to fade away.

The pills!

After everything, I had almost forgotten about my nightmares and the pills Mattheson gave to help me with them. I reluctantly reopened my eyes and pulled the little leather bag out of my pocket. Balling up some spit, I swallowed one of the little capsules; I fully realized I had no idea just exactly what kind of drug I was taking, but I figured considering how much trust I had already placed in Mattheson, this was nothing in comparison.

I closed my eyes again and relaxed. All the events of the days suddenly seemed very distant. Darkness enveloped my mind, and the last thing that went through my head before drifting off into a dreamless slumber was the eager wonder for what could happen tomorrow.

8

Chapter 8

I woke to the desperate, viciously angry screams of Decima. It was still dark out. The professor was already awake.

GET OFF MY PROPERTY, YOU INBRED SON OF A BITCH!

"What the hell is going on?!" I cried. Knotts looked as confused as me. Suddenly someone started pounding on our door.

"IT'S DAVID, OPEN UP!" David demanded. I scrambled out of bed, blessing myself for deciding to stay dressed. I opened the door to see David's wild eyes staring back. He was not his usual self. The man looked deranged. I looked down to see a sword in his hand.

"What's happening down there?" I asked.

"Look, just stay up here. Don't leave. I'll deal with this." He gritted his teeth and muttered something under his breath. The professor had already dressed himself somehow. I closed the door behind David and—-

I'll GET THE MONEY! STOP! PLEASE!

Her cries were getting more desperate. Suddenly there was some loud clanging...sword fighting, probably. Must be David.

"Should we help them?" I ask the professor.

"Do you have a weapon?"

"No,"

"Do you know martial arts?"

"Well, I took Karate for a couple years—-"

"Oh, shut up!" The professor said incredulously. Fair enough. More clanging. A man's voice I didn't recognize started barking orders, which was interrupted by more clanging. Something crashed and fell over.

GET THE FUCK OFF ME!

Decima screamed at the top of her lungs. It was an awful wail that could probably be heard for blocks away. There was no more clanging. What the hell was going on down there? Was David dead? I grabbed one of the bigger candle holders and held it as a weapon. It probably wouldn't do much good if there were more than one of them, but I figured it was better than nothing. Decima abruptly stopped screaming. There was silence.

"What should we do?" I whispered to the professor. Suddenly, footsteps slowly crept up the stairs. What the hell? No, No, NO. I was not going to be killed. I'm too young. Too young to die. I need to see my dad. And my mom, I have to make that right. My friends, what will they think? I won't just die, I'll go missing. No one will find me. Mattheson's not going to say anything. No one's going to say anything. Legal liability, that's what I am. I want to eat again. I want to tell people about my trip. I want to go to college and get a girlfriend, maybe get married. A kid or two, retirement, all that shit. Those grapes last night really did taste nice, maybe——

A big man with a bloodied arm suddenly kicked the door in. He was bald and bulky and way too big for me to take on. Two more men followed him inside, including a rather slight man with curly brown hair and deeply tanned skin. He had a nasty little grin on his face. The other man was white with a buzz-cut and a forgettable face.

"Ajax!" Knotts gasped.

"Ajax, indeed," the tanned man said. He then pulled out a big, bloody knife and stabbed Knotts in the throat, right under the Adam's apple. Knotts tried to scream, but all that came out was this horrible wheezing sound. Blood started gushing from his neck and mouth, a crimson river of death that quickly stained his clothes. He collapsed to the floor.

Kuhhh, kuhhhh, kuhhhhhhhhhhh, kahhhhhh, koaa, kuh, kaaa, kuh, kuh,

Knotts grunted as he started convulsing on the floor, a pool of blood surrounding him. His eyes were wide and bulging, and they were looking right at me in an expression that I couldn't recognize. Ajax, as I assume the tanned man was, decided not to remove the knife. To prolong the suffering, I suppose. I could only watch, paralyzed in fear, as the wonderful old man known as Charles Knotts lay dying on the floor. I could feel cold sweat on my skin. My heart was pounding, but I couldn't move. I sank to my knees, clutching the candle holder like my life depended on it.

I knew that I wasn't going to use it. It would be futile. I was dead, just like Knotts. Finally, the old man stopped breathing, and there was total silence. Just the sound of breathing. I felt my eyes welling up. Almost against my will, I forced myself to make eye contact with the murderers.

"So, who might you be?" Ajax said, brushing his long hair out of his eyes. His voice was nasally and unpleasant.

"Why?" I sobbed.

"Why? Why?!" Ajax exclaimed, skipping wildly around the room. The other two stood stoically. I could only nod, afraid of provoking him.

"I deserve some *fucking* respect, first of all. These pieces of shit seemed to think that I was just quiet and lovely.. Well look at me now, Charles!" Ajax cried, kicking the professor's limp body. Tears started streaming down his face, that crazed look fading away into deep sorrow. I had a sudden and foolish urge to say, well, you won't have to worry about people mistaking you as lovely anymore, but I restrained myself.

"Oh," I mumbled. I felt like there was a big rock in my throat. It took everything in me not to just start balling right there. I had to be a man. Die with dignity, as they say.

"They never stopped to wonder what was going on in my life. I needed more money. It's not greed. It is a necessity. It is survival. It is business. They just couldn't understand. We needed to turn to slavery, and I know they wouldn't have it. So I did what I had to do. Do I like it? NO! But we do what we must make it in this world, so stop FUCKING LOOKING AT ME LIKE THAT," Ajax screamed. He stomped towards me and slapped me hard with the back of his hand. For the first few seconds, it just felt numb, but that quickly transformed into a burning wave of pain that radiated deep into my skull.

I tried my best not to grunt, but a little one came out, nonetheless. The tears abated, replaced by shocked fuzziness.

"Well, whoever you are, you look young and strong. You'll make a good slave alongside that bitch Priya. She's smart, I'll give her that. All the more money for me!" Ajax exclaimed, almost as if he was convincing himself of his own murderous course of action. I had no response to that. My hand loosened and let the candle holder roll away. The big bald guy shuffled towards me, obviously injured. With considerable effort, he carefully pulled a powdered cloth out of a bag. As a last resort, I jumped up and tried to smash the candle holder across his face. Unfortunately, I was too slow. The man grabbed me by the wrist, squeezing so hard I was worried he would shatter the bone. I squirmed as he placed the powdered cloth firmly against my face. Everything went black.

9

Chapter 9

<u>Before</u>

Winds thrashed against the snow-covered window of the Sunshine Village ski lodge. It was late in the day and my aging parents had already skied more than enough for their liking. They were ready to drive back, but Caleb and I kept begging them to do one more run. It was not to be. My dad had bad knees and my mother was vegetarian so that meant she had little energy on the best of days. I know, some vegetarians have plenty of energy. They do just fine. Which is good for them, but all I know is personal experience and from what I can tell eating no meat is bad for sports endurance. Perhaps she just wasn't eating enough Tofu. It's hard to tell.

The only other person I know who was vegetarian was my cousin Micheal. Well, he wasn't really my cousin. I guess he was my uncle's friend's kid. But my family knew Michael's family well enough that I was told to call Micheal a cousin. You see, Micheal was an unfortunate soul. He had been diagnosed with bone cancer at the age of 11, and his mother Carol got some wacky ideas about "juicing" and natural remedies after the doctors gave Micheal a discouraging prognosis. Their beliefs intensified after Micheal's cancer went into remission two years later, but my dad and I are pretty sure that it was the extensive chemo and radiation rather than the carrot juice which saved his life. Either way, to this day Micheal won't eat meat, dairy, or gluten. Which means that my cousin Micheal is a gluten-free, Vegan cancer survivor with a wack job for a mother. If that's not piss-poor luck, I don't know what is.

My mother talks with other mothers, as mothers do. Carol convinced my mother to join her Vegan diet but my mother could not convince the rest of us to join the fad. I like my bacon and my steak and my BBQ chicken. She can't take that away from me. Maybe I'll die a few years earlier. Who really cares? At least I'll die happy and warm with an extra layer of fat on my bones. Die with a smile, that's what I always say.

I could never understand those melancholic assholes. I get it, you're sad. Get over yourself. Do you understand me? Look, we've all had our troubles. Parents can be really irritating sometimes, and that can drive a man insane. You hear what I'm saying? At the end of the day though, you push through. You get up and continue on because what else is there. Besides, there's always something one hasn't done. Like skiing down a double black diamond, or eating chocolate dipped bacon. Always something! Suicide is the most selfish act known to man, and I'm not the first to say that. But I truly do believe it.

My family does have a history of depression. Apparently my grandfather had depression, and that's why he killed himself. I think he was just afraid to face the world after the way he treated my grandma. Nevertheless, we mourned him because that's what you're supposed to do when someone dies. Isn't it? I never understood why people can't speak ill of the dead. I suppose it's because they are here to defend themselves. But it's more than that, isn't it? We sort of have this superstition. People have a lot of superstitions, some more silly than others. All of them are nonsense, nonetheless.

Besides, it doesn't matter if they aren't here to defend themselves. If they were an asshole, and they knew I thought that they were an asshole, then I'm gonna talk about them the same way I would if they were alive. It's that simple. My grandpa was not a good man. He was rude, cruel, and demeaning towards my grandma. She never deserved that. Every time I visited her she would bake me raisin and oatmeal cookies. I never really like raisin and oatmeal cookies. But when she made them I ate those things up as fast as I could. They were delicious. I don't know what she was putting in them, but whatever it was I couldn't ever get enough. I wonder what she is doing right now. She lives alone now, sitting in solitude in the only good thing my grandfather ever accomplished; the house he built nearly sixty years ago is large and beautifully designed.

Caleb and I shivered as we slowly ascended the mountain aboard one of the longest chairlifts on the resort. It kept halting for unknown reasons, the icy winds swaying the chairs on the cable. A few weeks earlier, I had read a news story about a chairlift in BC that broke down, leaving skiers trapped for several hours. Exposed to those icy winds with no protection other than the clothes on their backs. I realized that my clothing wouldn't provide enough protection against frostbite if a similar situation arose here.

"Looks like another little kid fell down," I said after we stopped the second time. We weren't even halfway up. Caleb was the only other one on the quad chairlift, as it was nearing the end of the day,

"Yeah," Caleb muttered, *"Hey, did you see the news?"*

"What news?"

"Avengers Endgame should be out in a few months,"

"That's hardly news,"

"Well, are you excited?"

"Of course,"

"What's the hottest Marvel superhero girl?" Caleb asked. I burst out laughing.

"What? I don't know," I knew, of course. It was Black Widow. We continued talking about marvel for the next five minutes or so. Marvel was one of the few things that we shared in common, and it was nice talking about that stuff with him.

"So what do you think you want to be when you grow up?" I asked Caleb. I had probably asked him this question before and as a brother I probably should already know. But young kids change their minds on this sort of thing all the time and I wanted to see what answer he would give me this time around.

"An astronaut," Caleb replied. I laughed, but he didn't laugh along with me.

"An astronaut? Aren't you a little old for that?"

"No. It's possible,"

"There's like a few hundred people in total who have ever been to space,"

"That's gonna change soon though with commercial space-flight,"

"Are you going to be a Mars colonist?"

"Why not?"

"Well, first of all it's barren and cold. There's nothing there. If you could even get there, you would probably never return. Live in little habitats with a few dozen other people under the ground to protect against radiation and the elements,"

"So?"

69

"I'm just saying a person who would want to do that must really hate other people,"

"I don't hate other people but I just think it would be cool,"

"You know what? I agree with you. If there is ever a chance for us to go to Mars, then I'll go with you,"

"Really?"

"Yeah, you're my brother. Of course I'll go with you. I might want to kill myself by the time we get there but whatever. That's fine. What else are brothers for?" I cleared my throat. My lips and mouth had become dry because of the cold weather. We reached the top of the lift and disembarked, beginning our silent ski down. We raced each other down a blue run because our parents were in a hurry and neither of us wanted to upset them. Hopefully my dad would agree to stop at the candy store on the way out of town.

I really wanted some toffee and also those weird chocolates. Oh! Fudge as well. I think the store sold chocolate crickets and stuff. A couple years earlier I convinced my mom to buy me one of those boxes of chocolate crickets but I never ate them. I tried convincing my friends to eat them once we got home, but I never had any luck. They ended up in the garbage.

Upon our arrival at the candy store, we had to park seven blocks away as all the paid parking stalls alongside Banff main street were already occupied. The store was practically bursting at the seams in every way imaginable, from the people to the volume of items to the very courageous color palette. Strange foreign candies, chocolates, cereals, and other unhealthy so-called foods covered every square foot of the place. The sweet, thick scent of fresh fudge wafted through the warm air. I saw an all-blond family and chuckled to myself.

"What's so funny?" Caleb asked.

"Look...Nazis," I gestured to the blond family. They had blue *eyes as well. There was no helping their case. It was a lost cause. Caleb laughed. We shared a sick humor.*

My Dad gave us five more minutes to get in line. So far all I had managed to pick out after what felt like forever was a bag of sponge toffee. There was just too much selection. I quickly grabbed a bag of gummies and hovered over an absurdly overpriced single gummy bear. It was the world's spiciest gummy bear that was made with California Reapers. It was red and looked normal. I called Caleb over and asked him if I should buy it. He concurred with my plan to give it secretly to my friend Jim among other gummy bears once we got home. I had to buy it with my own money, though. My dad refused because it was twenty dollars for a single gummy. Jim's reaction a few days later was worth it though, Caleb and I later decided.

The drive home was long and boring. Due to the fact that my iPad was dead and Caleb had the only charger. More reason to get an iPhone. My parents were against it, but I was sure they would get me on any day now. After all, most of my friends had one already. It was normal! They just didn't understand. Maybe if I could convince them that I would only use it for communication. Problem for another day, I suppose.

I found myself thinking about my crush, Jennifer. We had been friends for years now, but it seemed like we might be heading in a different direction. A spicier direction, if you will. Although I didn't feel intensely attracted to her, I thought I might as well seize the opportunity if it presented itself. I was a junior in high school and being a taken man might relieve certain social pressures and allow me to be more myself. Besides, Jen was a great person who I enjoyed spending time with.

Who knows where it could go? Just because I don't find her crazy hot right now doesn't mean that might not change with some time. Don't they say personality is more important than looks? Although, my motivations for all this are pretty bad. I know that. I'm ashamed of myself, but at least I know what I am. I don't deny it to myself. Once you start lying to yourself things start to go downhill.

Sometimes I wondered to myself what kind of person I was. Everyone likes to believe that they are the good guys. I think it's a survival mechanism, really. It's a cliche to say that but I think it genuinely does reflect my personal beliefs. You know, people try their best and even when they don't they try to come up with excuses. Things they tell themselves to sleep at night. It's not like I was a murderer or anything but I have my fair share of flaws and I'm not sure if I am aware of all them. That's why I always found it interesting to hear what other people's opinions are of me. It's not that I care, exactly, but more so it is a way of doing a sort of diagnostic on my behaviors and people's perceptions of those behaviors. That sounds kind of mechanical but essentially it's true.

10

Chapter 10

bizzzzzzzZUH bizzzzzzzzzZUH bizzzzzzzzzzzzzzzzzZUH

I woke up with an awful headache that thundered deep within my brain, tearing apart my brain tissue. Stretching and compressing it again and again in an unforgivable cycle of agony. With each beat of the heart came another cyclic burst of pain. Within a few seconds of gaining consciousness, I reluctantly examined my surroundings.

Four men surrounded me in a circle. The one directly in front of me was drooling and making a buzzing noise every few seconds, which contributed to the blitzkrieg of pain unfolding underneath my poor skull. Next to the drooling man was an older fellow with gray hair and striking black eyes. To my left was a brown-skinned guy with a wooden cross around his neck. And to my immediate right was a skinny bald black man with yellowed teeth. Actually, come to think of it, they all had awful teeth. But the black man was missing a few, so I noticed him first.

They sat in silence, staring at me. Well, as silent as they

could be with all the buzzing. It looked like we were in a prison. There were bars on the doors. It stunk like rotten fish, and it was clearly daytime because it was boiling. Sweat drenched my skin; I could taste the salt on my lips.

"Where...where am I?" My voice was raspy, and I coughed violently. Thick, bitter phlegm sprayed into my mouth; unwilling to spit, I swallowed it.

"Apollo's mansion, uh course!" The drooling man snickered.

"What?"

"Ignore him. He gets bored in here—we all do," the guy with the cross said.

"That's uh.. that's fine. I'd just like to know where we are. Is this a prison?" I mumbled. All the men except the christian chuckled.

"In a sense, I suppose. You've been enslaved,"

"Oh,"

"This is the slave housing for a fish sauce factory,"

"Oh,"

"Yeah, I wouldn't know what to say to that either," the christian smiled. I tried a dry chuckle, but it just turned into another coughing fit. It stunk really bad. Almost as bad as the public toilets I was at earlier, which I didn't think was possible.

"It stinks in here," I groaned. They laughed again.

"I like you. The name's Paul," Paul reached out to shake my hand. I shook it. He had a firm grip.

"Ashton," I replied.

"I'm Marcus," The skinny black guy said, and I shook his hand. It was warm and sweaty.

"Samuel," the older guy said. Another firm handshake. I turned to the drooling man, but he just laughed.

"What? You think I'm gonna—buzzzzzzAH—shake your grubby hand?" The buzzing man shook his head dramatically with his thick tongue flapping about.

"That nutcase over there is Felix," Paul chuckled with affection.

"Nice to meet you Felix," I said. My head pounded even more when I dipped my head. Not going to be doing that again.

"No, don't—-buzz—lie. It isn't nice to meet me. You're a slave now. Meeting me confirms that you are truly fucked," Felix hissed. Despite his harshness, he had a certain twinkle in his eye that convinced me he was a good guy.

"So how did you end up here, Felix?" I asked.

"Parents sold me," Felix said quickly.

"He doesn't like to talk about it," explained Samuel.

"Sorry, I didn't know," I muttered.

"Well, what did you expect? It's not exactly a pleasant topic. How did you get here? You're the freshman, after all," Samuel said. I realized what he meant. Just thinking about what happened was traumatizing. Knotts on the floor, choking on the knife plunged into his throat. That wheezing noise. That awful noise was permanently etched into my memory. It was the sound of death.

Kuhhhh, Kuhhhhhh, kuhhh, kuahhh, kuhhh

"I see what you mean," I said simply.

"So! What are your skills?" Marcus asked. He suddenly grabbed my arm and started massaging my muscles.

"Uhhh...could you stop that?" I pulled my arm away, unsure

how he would react. He just laughed and sat back.

"I see you keep in shape," Marcus said.

"I try,"

"That's good. Very good. For hunger. It would be better if you were fat, but athletic is the next best thing,"

"What?"

"Notice how we're all scrawny? It's the lack of food. We get two meals a day. Breakfast and supper. But they are small portions and the food is often spoiled,"

"Oh,"

"Don't worry, at least you won't——bizzzzzzAH — suffer alone," Felix said with that twinkle in his eye.

"So, skills?" Marcus pressed. I didn't know what to say. What were my skills? I was an excellent basketball player. Not that basketball would do anyone any good here. I was smart, which is useful I guess. Besides, I was pretty sure that I was better educated than most people in the city. Whether my 2023 high school education was applicable as an ancient slave is another question altogether.

"I'm educated," I said simply. Their eyes widened.

"How educated? Are we talking primary school or tutoring?" Marcus asked eagerly, leaning over.

"Well, I got my latest lesson a few days ago," I said, smiling a bit at their surprise.

"You're lying!" Felix cried.

"What happened? Seriously. You must be rich!" Samuel exclaimed.

"I don't want to talk about it, but no I'm not lying," I said.

"Doesn't make much difference here, though," Marcus chuckled.

"Then why'd you ask?" I crawled back a bit so I could

lean against the hard wall. It was made of stone or clay or something. There were pieces missing from it.

"Just curious," Marcus mumbled.

"So how long have you guys been here?" I wondered aloud, only half-willing to hear

the answer. They all sighed, except for Felix who kept on buzzing. I smiled a bit as I remembered the yapping man from the bus. Hope he's doing alright.

"I just got here about a week ago," Paul muttered.

"But unlike us, he sure as hell won't be here for long!" Marcus boomed.

"What? Why?" I asked.

"Cause he's one of those...Christians!" Felix screamed. I jumped back a little, surprised at the sudden change of tone.

"A cult is all it is," Marcus declared. I wasn't used to people dismissing Christianity as a cult. It was strange.

"I won't have you speak ill of the Lord in my presence!" Paul cried. He stood up, glaring at Marcus.

"Yeah, yeah. What's your dead God going to do? Smite me? He was crucified like 200 years ago, right? Isn't that the BIG story? How would—-" Marcus hissed.

"It was only 100 years ago. And he rose again to save the living and the dead," Paul interjected.

"Do you hear this guy? 'Rose to save the living and the dead.' Gimme a break," Marcus said, exasperated.

"I pray for your soul every day," Paul whispered between gritted teeth. Marcus and Felix just chuckled. I noticed Samuel was staying silent through the whole thing. I wondered if he was secretly a christian as well.

"Mars and Jupiter spit—BizzzUH — on your God!" Felix screamed. Just as a furious Paul was about to reply, a door down the hall swung open and someone thundered towards our cell. Everyone immediately went quiet. The person who came down the hall was that big bald man from earlier. He glared at us through the Iron bars with unconcealed contempt. I expected him to yell at us to be quiet or something, like you'd see in the movies. He certainly looked the part of an angry slave-master eager to use a whip. Instead, his face softened, and the contempt faded away

"Is this guy in on the plan?" The big man asked, glancing at me.

"No," Samuel replied.

"Fill him in. He has soft hands; never worked a day in his life. Feel them for yourselves. That means he's an aristocrat of some sort. He has money and probably an education," The big man rattled.

"Yeah, he told us about that education bit, we didn't really believe him," Marcus said.

"Speak for yourself! I believed him," Samuel cried, nodding at me.

"Whatever you say," Marcus said.

"Look, the time to go is in five days. I've already got the timing lined up," The muscular guard whispered.

"Good," Marcus said.

"I would like to add that I don't approve of this," Paul declared.

"Oh, save me the lecture," Marcus groaned.

"Thou shalt not steal," Paul said solemnly

"We've been enslaved, dipshit!" Marcus yelled.

"Yeah, wha——bizzzzUH——what do you expect us to do?" Felix mumbled.

"I'm fine with the first part of the plan, but not this," Paul said.

"Wait, what's going on?" I asked.

"We'll tell you later, kid," Marcus patted me on the shoulder.

"Anyway, this is important...half the guards will be gone in three days time. Ajax has to settle a dispute with the Prefect. He wants a show of strength," The big guard said, glancing down the hall as if he expected someone to burst in.

"It's actually taking place, then," Samuel murmured.

"We'll be ready," Marcus said. The gargantuan guard nodded and left. What was happening? They must have some kind of arrangement with the guard so they can escape! Best of all, it seemed like I was going to be a part of it! All I had to do was...find Priya. In a world without cell phones. Or any knowledge whatsoever of the people or the culture or anything at all. That was a problem for another day. I had hit the jackpot here. Well, not exactly. It was still not an exceptional situation.

Actually, it was awful. I was a slave. A fish sauce slave. That's me now. I expected to be thrown into a gladiatorial ring or maybe forced to haul bricks or something. Like the Israelites in the bible. They already built the pyramids, right? What was that movie? The 'prince of Egypt.' Was that Disney or DreamWorks? I think it was DreamWorks. Come to think of it, they must have already built the pyramids because Jesus was dead and he was in the New Testament. So the old testament was...older. Right? Yeah. I should really focus on the situation at hand.

Why am I thinking about 'the Prince of Egypt,'? People have died. Good people. Knotts, who I never really called Charles. Why didn't I call him Charles? Or Charlie? He would've loved that. I guess I just liked calling him 'the professor,' or "Knotts' because it seemed cool. Like I was in an adventure novel or something. Well, here I am. Here's the adventure. Not as exciting as you'd think. More disgusting, really. Terrifying. And David, was he dead? He seemed like such a nice guy. Maybe a little reserved, but I was getting along with him. And Decima! She had such a personality. Had. Should I be speaking in the past tense? I guess I don't know anything for sure, other than Knotts was dead, and Priya was enslaved somewhere else. As a household slave, I think. Probably better off than me, though. Household slave.

God! That's kind of sexist, isn't it? She gets to like, fold laundry and shit while I'm here doing whatever the hell you have to do to make ancient fish sauce. Absolutely that's sexist. I thought the ancient Romans were supposed to be all socially progressive. Where did I get that idea? Maybe it was true, what do I know? I wish Knotts was here to tell me. I guess I could just ask——

"Ashton? Hello?" Marcus pushed me on the shoulder. I really need to stop zoning out like that.

"Hello," I mumbled. My head was still throbbing, but it had reduced to a dull thud.

"Did you hear what I was saying?" Marcus asked, exasperated.

"No," I whispered, embarrassed. Nasty situation like this, and I wasn't paying attention! Marcus sighed and squeezed my shoulder.

"It's alright, kid. I know it's a lot," Marcus said. Why does everyone call me 'kid?' These aren't sixties western. Would an ancient person really talk like that? Guess I have no other way to tell. It's not like I could lip-read Latin. It was really strange, by the way, how I could hear what they were saying but their mouths didn't really line up. It was like a badly dubbed tv show on Netflix. I always preferred subtitles. People who like dubbed shows are crazy. Somehow I didn't notice it before. I could see that over time, it would become quite irritating.

"Thank you," I said simply. Marcus took a deep breath.

"So, as I was saying...we have a plan to escape" Marcus said. The others nodded their heads in excitement. Felix scowled at me. I figured he didn't know of my inclusion into the plan.

"Yeah, that's what it sounded like," I said.

"In three days' time, we will meet at the southwest stairwell and fight our way out. Our friend on the inside had hidden swords for us under the third and fourth stairs. Do you know how to use a sword?" Marcus asked, making direct eye contact. He had a steely gaze. I decided it was best to tell the truth.

"No," I sighed. Paul winced.

"That's okay, we have time. I will get an ax placed there for you instead. They are much easier to use. You look strong, as well. You have to be careful though...slice, don't chop. If you get your ax stuck, you will be in trouble," Marcus said. I almost felt like bursting into laughter. It took a lot of effort to contain myself. Me? Ashton Beachum, ax murderer. I guess it wasn't murder, but still. Chopping—sorry, slicing—-people up with an ax is not exactly what I had in mind when I agreed to go on this godforsaken 'vacation.'

"I don't know if I can kill someone," I whispered.

"Nor should you have to!" Paul exclaimed, shaking his head.

"You can...and you will," Marcus said carefully, his haunted eyes staring back at me. I expected him to say more, but he didn't. A silence fell over us. I had no idea what time it was. The once lively Felix closed his eyes, apparently resting. The others just stared into the walls. We sat there in silence for what felt like forever, but it was probably only twenty minutes.

Was it morning? Lunch? Late Afternoon? Lunch...were they going to feed us? I was starving, but at the same time I was terrified of what they might serve. Just as if they read my mind, a scraggly boy no older than fourteen came down the small hall carrying a tray of food. Was he a slave too?

"Breakfast," The boy said simply. He slid us the tray of five small bowls of what looked like some kind of oatmeal and walked away. There were little clay cups filled with murky brown water. It was warm, of course. I wondered if even rich people could have cold drinks, given the lack of freezers and such.

"It doesn't taste very good, but you need to eat it. It's all we get until tonight," Paul told me. I nodded and scooped some of the oatmeal into my mouth. It was coarse and dry, but at least it wasn't rotten or anything. I could tell they used water instead of milk, and there was no milk. I don't think it was oatmeal, either. It was some other type of grain. In any other circumstance, I would've gagged.

I licked the bowl and washed it down with two big gulps of dirty water.

11

Chapter 11

"ALRIGHT YOU SCUM, LET'S GET TO WORK, SHALL WE?" the big, bald guard hollered, clanging on the bars. He laughed. We jumped to our feet, and Felix jolted out of his nap. I tapped Paul on the shoulder.

"What do we do, exactly?" I whispered.

"Just follow our lead. They like to keep cellmates together. It's easy. Don't worry," Paul replied.

The big guard, whatever his name was, herded us out of our cell, down the little halfway, and out a door leading outside. Turns out, our cell was a building all on its own. There were probably twenty-five or thirty cell-houses just like ours in the field. They were surprisingly well-maintained on the outside. The walls were painted a shiny hue of reddish orange. Before us was a large open-air building with hundreds of emaciated people working outside.

There were plenty of guards, and the whole compound was surrounded by a manned wall at least 12 feet high. I couldn't tell how far we were from the city; or if we were even in the proximity of Antioch anymore. For all I knew, we could be in Egypt or Spain or wherever. There was no way of knowing how long I was out. A fresh wave of panic washed over me. Nevertheless, any panic was quickly replaced by the attention that the situation required.

The smell intensified, somehow. It was utterly repulsive. I wouldn't have been that surprised if I could actually see fumes from the stink, like in a cartoon or something. The big bald man led us to a massive vat, one of many. It was half as tall as me, and at least ten feet wide. There was also a table with about a hundred strange empty jars strategically placed underneath it. To the right, people were already labeling jars that were packed by other stations in front of us.

"Alright, you'll tell him what to do," the big man said. Marcus just nodded. The big man walked away.

"Okay, so basically we have to scoop this fermented Garum into these jars here. It's very important that you seal the jars properly, otherwise it will spoil during shipping. The guards keep their distance, but they are watching," Marcus almost had to yell above the bustle of the factory floor.

"Sounds good," I said. Marcus quickly showed me how to seal a jar, and it looked pretty simple. I grabbed a ladle and began scooping. As a way to try to enjoy myself a bit amid an obviously monotonous job, I decided to keep count of how many jars I filled.

After an hour or so, I had filled eighty-two jars. I just kept scooping and scooping, and people kept bringing more jars. The heat beat down upon us, desperate to kill us. The heat and the stench eventually caused me to throw up after I had packed my 107th jar. One of the guards noticed me throwing up. He approached with a clay jug of water. At least someone was concerned about my health!

"Thank you, sir," I said, unwilling to upset him. The guard, who had salt and pepper stubble, smiled. I noticed he didn't have any glasses. A little rude, but I supposed drinking from a jug was hardly a hardship, given the circumstances.

"My pleasure," the guard snickered. He suddenly raised his arms and smashed the clay jug against my head. Everything went numb, and despite my instinct to fight back, my body did not answer my commands and instead I collapsed to the ground, my face getting smothered in my own vomit. The warm water drenched my clothes and diluted the vomit of the stone floor. Everything was ringing. I felt a dull pain at the back of my head. A warmer, almost hot liquid was running down my neck. I realized it must be blood. The headache had just been starting to go away. This was much worse than anything before. I hoped he didn't do any damage. I groaned. The pain and the stench were making my nausea worse.

"Get up, slave," the guard grumbled. I forced myself onto my hands and knees, but the guard just kicked me in the ribs. A sharp burst of pain reverberated throughout my stomach, and I threw up again. My face was soaked in vomit and blood. I could see black dots in my vision.

"Clean up your mess first. Boss likes a clean environment," the guard demanded. Unable to argue, I forced myself back on my hands and knees and started pushing the disgusting fluids onto the grass with my bare hands. The guard's hard foot slammed into my ribs again. I gagged twice, but nothing came out except a little stomach acid. My throat was burning.

"Lick it up," the guard hissed. I heard a few audible gasps. It sounded like everyone had stopped working. Reluctantly, realizing I had little other choice, I started licking up my own blood and vomit. I had to force myself to swallow it. It was bitter, and it burned. Worst or all, it was kind of chunky too. That grain meal I had a couple hours earlier for breakfast came up surprisingly intact. The guard laughed.. and laughed...and laughed. It was completely silent at the factory save for the sound of me choking down my vomit and the sound of his laughing. I thought I had felt hatred before. I hadn't. I had never hated anyone more than I hated that evil man at that moment.

"WHAT IS GOING ON HERE?!" Ajax screamed. I rolled onto my back, unable to get up. Everything was too fuzzy. Hopefully, he didn't cause any serious damage.

"I'm sorry, sir, I was just— -" the guard started.

"I was just, I was just.... USELESS! GO SCRUB THE SHITTER! EVERYONE GET BACK TO WORK!" Ajax gave the guard a hard slap with the back of his hand. The guard scurried away.

"You! Samuel! Carry this kid back to your cell and clean him up. I want him working again in a few hours, or else he is of no use to me. I'll send over some bread and clean water. There will be no doctor," Ajax said, briefly glancing down at me before walking away.

Samuel helped me back to my feet and, with his help, I managed to limp across the field to our cell. A guard was waiting there to open the door for us. I collapsed into the corner with a heavy sigh. My muscles were still kind of sore from the day before, but that was irrelevant now. The entire right side of my ribcage was bruised. That guard probably kicked as hard as he could. It felt like a rib or two was broken, but maybe they were just very badly bruised. I had never broken any ribs before. Come to think of it, I had never broken any bones before. I suddenly remembered Mike in his cast at the hospital. That seemed like it had happened years ago. Something that was very distant. From another life.

"Are you alright?" Samuel asked finally.

"No,"

"Fair enough," Silence. Suddenly that skinny kid who served us breakfast earlier came in with a fresh loaf of bread and a big jug of water...just like the one I had been assaulted with. There was a cloth as well.

Samuel dipped the cloth in the water and washed off my face. This guy barely knew me, and here he was, washing my face for me. I decided right then and there that I could probably trust him. After he finished scrubbing my face, he poured the remaining (uncontaminated water, he didn't double dip) into a cup. I chugged it down greedily.

Realizing that Samuel was probably hot too, I offered him some of the water. He graciously accepted. We ate the bread together as well. Unlike the strange oatmeal, or whatever the hell that was this morning, the bread was delicious. It was warm and fresh. Crusty on the outside, and warm on the inside. My headache subsided a bit. I realized that asking for a bandage was probably pushing it. Although I doubted it was out of any sort of compassion, I was surprised that Ajax had already given us this much.

"Has anything like this happened to you?" I asked.

"Yes," Samuel whispered.

"Is it just that one guy?"

"No, but he's one of the worst ones. He's also one of the more stupid guards, so Ajax doesn't like him," Samuel said.

"Oh,"

"His name is Albus" I chuckled. Like Albus Dumbledore?

"What's so funny?" Samuel asked, confused.

"It's just that I know someone named Albus," I said.

"Oh," Samuel raised his eyebrows.

"So, how well do you trust this plan?" I asked.

"It's risky, but it's our only chance,"

"Fair enough,"

"Who was the big bald guard that's helping us?"

"That's Titus. He's helped us a lot so far, but I still have some small doubts about him. He's only helping us with the promise of money. I am quite wealthy. A man who only fights for money can never be fully trusted. Titus has no honor, only greed. What's more, I heard a rumor that he's a deserter from Dacia," Samuel seethed.

"Wouldn't the army be looking for him, then?"

"Of course they would be. The army crucifies deserters, and rightfully so. We are far away from Dacia, though. Nevertheless, it's just a rumor, and it's not like we have much choice either way."

"I suppose so,"

"Where are we, exactly? They put me out when I was taken. Last place I remember being was a small lodge in Antioch,"

"Oh, then you haven't gone far. From what I've heard, most of us are from Antioch unless they were slaves beforehand. There's a couple who are Persians, captured from the war. But they are exceptions. Ajax prefers Latin-speakers," Samuel explained.

"So, how were you captured?" I inquired. I realized he didn't want to talk about it earlier, but I figured he would be more willing now.

"I was just discharged from the army. My twenty-five years of service were over, and I was free to serve out the rest of my life on a farm. See?" Samuel showed me an SPQR tattoo on his arm. Once again, I found myself thinking of Russell Crowe and his Gladiator movie.

"What went wrong?"

"Nothing. Not at first, anyway. I farmed for a couple of years in Macedonia. It was rough soil, not great for growing food. Very Mountainous. Even more so than here. Regardless, I raised some animals, and I was doing well. I was upset that they couldn't get me some land here, where I grew up and where my sister lives. But you know, I had my wife and a couple of kids, so it was bearable. Unfortunately, my wife was rather depressed. Not that I could tell! I hated myself for not figuring it out sooner." Samuel wiped away tears with the back of his hand.

"Oh," I said. Memories of Caleb came flashing back.

"Anyway, she killed herself. Didn't leave a note or anything. So it was just me and our little daughter, Cassandra. She was only ten months old,"

"I'm so sorry," I said, and not for the first time on this trip.

"So, basically, I was too devastated to stay on that farm all by myself. She was the love of my life. And she killed herself. We were so happy. But after the pregnancy, something happened to her. She became bitter and reserved. Almost like she didn't like our daughter. I'll never know for sure, but I think the pregnancy was too much for her. She couldn't handle it,"

"That sounds like postpartum depression,"

"What is that?"

"Sometimes women can become depressed in the year immediately after a pregnancy. I don't know for sure, but maybe it's a hormonal imbalance or something,"

"Hormones?"

"Nevermind,"

89

"Well, how do you know this?"

"It's just something I learned a few years ago in passing,"

"Oh," Samuel sighed.

"Yeah.."

"Anyway, after her death I couldn't stay there, so I sold the farm as soon as I could and moved back here with my sister. Luckily, my legion was stationed nearby, and I convinced the commander to grant me a five-year contract as a cook,"

"That sounds nice,"

"It was, I renewed the contract three times and I've been working for the last 16 years as a cook. Then, suddenly, about six weeks ago, I was kidnapped by thugs and taken here,"

"So, are people looking for you?"

"Probably, but I'm not waiting around,"

"So, this whole operation is illegal?"

"Yes, technically. The enslavement of Roman citizens is illegal. God knows I earned that citizenship. Nevertheless, Ajax probably is bribing all the right people. As soon as I get out of here, I'm bringing in the army and freeing everyone here," Samuel said through gritted teeth.

"I'd like to see that," I said.

"You will," Samuel assured me.

"So, are you an officer?"

"Back in my fighting days, I rose to be the Primus Pilus. In case you aren't familiar with military terminology, that meant that I commanded the most elite of the ten cohorts in the legion. 480 highly skilled soldiers under my direct authority. As a cook, I retain my rank as a matter of respect, but I obviously don't fight in any battles anymore."

"Cool," Cool? Really?

"So, what about you? How did you end up here?" Samuel

asked. I suddenly realized I couldn't be completely honest if I wanted him to believe me.

"Well...I was in town with my friend and his aunt. She was on a business trip...with her husband, of course. He was meeting us here. But suddenly, while sleeping at a hotel, Ajax and his thugs broke in and murdered my friend and his father. Ajax said he was going to enslave me and my friend's aunt, and then he put a powdered cloth over my face. Probably just like the one they used on you," I said, rather proud of the half-truth I just invented.

"I'm sorry to hear about your friend. Don't worry, though, we'll be out of here soon enough. You're lucky you ended up bunking with us," Samuel said.

"Yeah, really lucky," I agreed.

We talked for probably another hour. I asked him about his time in the army, and where he fought. He loved talking about past battles. Samuel was one of those natural storytellers. His face would just light up, and he would do voices and move his hands about in all sorts of ways. One of those people who would make a great drinking buddy, not that I'd know. I'd never been to a bar. But from what I knew from TV, I guess. I asked him about the meaning of his name. I thought to myself that Samuel seemed like a surprisingly modern name to be found among the ancient crowd. Paul was pretty normal, too, but I suppose that was because of the whole christian thing. Marcus was not too uncommon nowadays, either, but I remembered from Gladiator that there was an emperor named Marcus Aurelius. So it couldn't be that uncommon.

Samuel, though. Strange. Turns out, Samuel's parents were Jewish, and it was a common name among the Jewish community. I asked him if it was uncommon for Jewish people to join the army, and he said that it wasn't. Apparently, joining the army was a common way for provincials such as himself to gain citizenship and earn some degree of prosperity for themselves, albeit at the considerable risk of death in battle. He was a Roman now, Samuel explained, and he believed in the Roman Gods. Nevertheless, he maintained his respect for other gods, as he believed that as long as enough people worship them, then they must exist to a certain extent. How else, he wondered, could the Egyptians have been so great?

Just as he praised the army again, a guard I didn't recognize came inside and forced us back to work. Despite my throbbing headache, I reasoned that my ribs weren't broken, after all. So I reluctantly agreed to go to work.

The sun had moved to the center of the sky, and the heat was even worse than before. I limped over to the canning station to find my exhausted cellmates still laboring away, desperately trying to keep up the unrelenting work pace.

I noticed someone had cleaned my little mess up. We worked for probably at least another ten hours, long past dusk. There were no more breaks. There was no more water. Just work.

When we finally scraped the big barrel of garum clean, I hoped we were done. Nope. Just another barrel. And another. We did three barrels that day. The pace was relentless for fear of being whipped. Only one person received a whipping that day, but that incident, along with my own experience, was enough to keep people on track.

Scoop, seal, repeat.

Scoop, seal, repeat.

Scoop, seal, re—-

"Alright, all done for the day! Let's go!" One of the guards abruptly called out from somewhere. Everyone in the factory immediately laid down their tools and shuffled back to their cells, more or less in an orderly fashion.

For the second time that day, I found myself happy to be back inside a cell. I crumpled to my corner of the wall and closed my eyes. Everything hurt. The urge to cry was once again overwhelming, but I managed to control myself.

"What do we get for supper?" I asked, unwilling to open my eyes yet. There was silence for a few seconds, so I reluctantly opened my eyelids and glanced around the room.

Paul whispered something under his breath.

"What?" I groaned.

"Cereal," Paul muttered.

Sure enough, out came that scrawny little boy with the small bowlfuls of the disgusting dried out oatmeal or whatever we ate in the morning. "Cereal" as Paul called it. Luckily, we each got an apple too. The water was still warm and dirty, but at least we got an apple. It wasn't rotten or anything either. The others seemed surprised to see the apples, and they devoured them almost as quickly as me. It was so juicy. Unspoiled, as well. Perfectly fresh. Sweet. Ripe. Perfect. I loved that apple.

That apple was everything to me. I would have given anything for another apple. After consuming it right down to the core, I forced myself to eat the grain mixture in the bowl.

It was flavorless and hard to swallow, but at least it filled me up. Besides, I was able to wash it down with the dirty water. It was a little gritty, but that was fine. With this escape plan, I would only have to endure a couple more days of this. It was going to be tough, but I was sure I could do it.

I was careful to preserve some of the water to help me swallow one of Mattheson's pills. Things were bad enough; the last thing I needed was for nightmares and a lack of sleep to be added to my long list of troubles.

"That was surprising," I blurted.

"What? The apples?" Marcus sighed.

"Yeah,"

"They give them to us once a week. As a 'treat',"

"Oh,"

"One time they gave us oranges. That was nice,"

"Yeah, I wouldn't mind an orange right now. Or a banana,"

"A what?"

"A banana,"

"Speak sense, boy! Banana. What is a banana?" Marcus exclaimed.

"It's a type of fruit," I suddenly realized bananas were from South America.

"You really are rich! Ha! Banana. Must be some sort of exotic fruit from India or someplace. At the edge of the earth,"

"Have you ever been to India?" I asked. Marcus laughed.

"No! Who do you think I am, Alexander the great? No, I've never left the Empire,"

"What about the rest of you? I mean, I talked to Samuel already. He has traveled far and wide with the Army. But what about you, Felix?" I asked. One day with these people and I was already comfortable with them. That was probably the only good thing about a situation like this. It was easy to make friends. Shared trauma, and all that.

"I was...BizzzUH...sold. My parents didn't want me. So they sold me. All I've done is travel. From town to town. City to city. I've been to Persia. India. Even...BizzzzUH...China," Felix blubbered.

"You see, Felix is a merchant," Samuel explained.

"What do you sell?" I asked.

"Anything. Mostly spices, though. And silk," Felix said. I looked over at Paul.

"I've lived here in Antioch all my life. Never left," Paul said.

"And he never will," Marcus mumbled solemnly.

"Why is that?" I wondered aloud.

"Well, I don't think we ever got to explain why Paul is here in the first place," Marcus said.

"I'm to be executed," Paul blurted out.

"What? Why?" I exclaimed.

"I'm a christian. Ajax hates Christians," Paul said simply.

"Is that legal?" I asked stupidly.

"Look around, buddy. None of this is legal," Paul sighed. I realized he might actually be my age. I couldn't tell before because he was so disheveled and rough-looking. I supposed I probably looked similar by now. However, in this moment of fear, I could see his youth shining through all that.

"When?" I asked.

"The day after, we are supposed to escape," Paul mumbled. Cutting it close, then.

"We'll make it out. Samuel here is an elite soldier, and the rest of us are young," I assured them, reading the creeping doubt in the room.

"Of course we will," Marcus agreed. With that, he sighed

and crumpled his thin body into a ball.

I waited until everyone had fallen asleep so I could take one of the pills. I was lucky that no one stole them from me while I was unconscious. I curled up into the fetal position like the others. The ground was cold and hard. I put my arm out as a cushion, which was uncomfortable. I was surprised me how cold it was, actually. It wasn't freezing or anything, but it was pretty damn chilly. My arm started to fall asleep, so I switched arms. After that, everything sort of faded away. I let my mind drift, desperately trying not to think too hard about how much trouble I was in.

This could really be the end of me.

12

Chapter 12

I woke up in a cold sweat. My throat was sore and my body was aching. Not just from the usual pain that is associated with a day of hard work, either. I was sick. These were sick aches. The kind that you could feel right down to your bone. The kind that made you shiver and crave fuzzy blankets and hot chocolate. Sure as hell not getting anything like that here.

I just couldn't believe it. All of this and now I'm sick too? My headache was gone, but the sore throat was a new and unique issue that more than made up for it. I decided to avoid telling my cellmates about my new condition for as long as possible. They seemed nice, but I had only known them for a day and I watched enough prison break movies to know that the group will always try to cut out the weak ones. Or perhaps just one rogue, dangerous person in the group. I had no idea who that dangerous person would be in this situation, or if there was one at all, but I kept the sickness to myself nonetheless.

The disgusting oatmeal, as I'm going to call it, was served around the same time as the day before. The sun was already up, and it was already sickeningly hot. The fishy smell was omnipresent, but I was slowly getting somewhat used to it. Don't get me wrong, it was awful, but I was starting to tolerate it much more than the day before. I don't know if that's a good thing or not.

We mostly ate in silence, except for a brief war anecdote from Samuel, which was entertaining as ever. Felix was much quieter than usual.

"So we are leaving tomorrow?" I asked.

"If the Gods...BizzzUH..smile upon us," Felix said. I nodded and stood up, stretching my back. My spine gave a satisfying crackle before Titus sprung the door open to take us out to work.

"Let's go," Titus said softly. Just before we walked out onto the field, Titus whispered something into Marcus's ear.

The work was simple, but I hated it. It stunk, and being so close to the source of the stench made me realize I would probably never get used to the smell anytime soon. If I ever did, it would be because my nose had become so desensitized that it could no longer smell anything remotely subtle. I'd be like one of those people who has to eat spicy food because it's all they can taste. Another reason I couldn't stay at this godforsaken factory.

After the first couple of hours, I considered spitting in the jars. After all, whoever is buying this stuff is supporting slavery. They deserve my sickness. Nevertheless, I decided that was too nasty. People were just buying a bottle of sauce. If I was still here in a week, maybe I would reconsider.

Suddenly, Marcus tapped me on the shoulder. He looked anxious.

"Follow me," He whispered. We picked up some of the jars

and somehow made our way all the way to the far side of the factory floor. There were so many people scurrying about that the guards didn't notice; They were probably exhausted from the heat, just the same as us. Standing there in that leather armor, doing nothing.

There was a wooden staircase in the corner. It was a strange building. One of those sorts of things that is built around a hill. This field must be the peak of a small mountain, though it was hard to tell from here. We handed off our jars to some labelers nearby.

"Is that the staircase?" I asked.

"Your ax is under the third step down. The step is loose. When the time comes, walk your way over here with the rest of us. Try to act natural like we just did. Once we bend over and try to remove the steps, things are going to happen quickly. Luckily, there will be only half as many guards on duty tomorrow. Still, it will be a tough battle. Hopefully once we get things rolling, the other slaves will join in the fight," Marcus explained so quickly I could barely understand him. But I understood. I was ready. A fat, ugly guard approached us with suspicion.

"Hey, you two get back to work! Your station is way over there. What are you doing?" The guard demanded.

"Just handing off some jars," Marcus said. Surprisingly, the guard was satisfied with that weak response.

"Get over there or you'll each get five lashes," the guard grumbled. We obliged him without any complaint, and back to work we went.

Unlike in the cell, there was little conversation between us, which made the day even longer. I could have broken the silence, but I figured it was there for a reason. Maybe the guards didn't like it. Maybe the others were too focused on the job at hand. Maybe they just preferred silence. I don't really know for sure. All I knew was that somehow the second day was longer than the first, despite the lack of a beating. Nevertheless, I made it back to my cell without any trouble.

There wasn't any fruit this time.

13

Chapter 13

Despite the sleeping pill, I woke up throughout the night. I was coughing horribly. It was a phlegmy cough that burned my sore throat. My nose was running, too, and there was nothing to clean it with except my dirty sleeve. As a result, the skin on the edges of my nose became red and sore from all the snot. The chills and aches worsened as well, and I realized that I was in no condition to fight.

The others realized it as well, as I could no longer hide my sickness from them. However, it's not like anyone has a choice. The day to go was tomorrow. Everyone knew it. They were going to do it without me. I was just a happy coincidence. If I came along, so be it. If not, oh well. That's the subtext I received from my cellmate's tired glares throughout the night. Breakfast came. Revolting, as always, but I was eager to get some food in my system.

"Can you fight?" Samuel asked, concerned.

"I'll have to," I say, between coughs.

"Damn right! Don't be b—b—bizzzUH, backing out just because of a little cough and runny nose!" Felix cried. He was drooling more than usual. As usual, he didn't seem to care whatsoever.

"I.. I won't," I said. I meant it, too. Titus entered the building.

"Titus! What news do you bring us? Is Ajax leaving as expected?" Samuel asked.

"Yes, he has already gone," Titus boomed.

"All the weapons are in their place?" Samuel inquired.

"Yes. Payment?" Titus demanded.

"Of course. You have done well, Titus. Thank you. I have some gold buried under a massive tree next to the estate off via Lucio. It should be more than sufficient," Samuel said, carefully.

"Pleasure doing business with you, then. I should let you know once again that I will not fight for you. I plan on leaving immediately, in case things go wrong," Titus said. Felix scoffed.

"Well, you've done what we asked. Thank you," Samuel smiled. Titus left.

"Can he be trusted?" Felix asked.

"Time will tell," Samuel replied. Paul sighed.

"Do you trust him?" I asked Paul.

"No man is born without sin," Paul proclaimed.

"Yeah, ease up already buddy," Marcus scoffed.

"I trust him, though," Paul told me.

"How did you come to be a christian?" I asked. I was curious as to how he would respond. I had never met an early christian before, obviously. Most Christians nowadays become Christians because of societal pressure; their parents, community, etc. Here was a guy who was doing it on pain of death.

"Here we go," Felix sighed.

"As a young boy, my parents taught me to worship the traditional pantheon of Gods. When my mother was pregnant with my little brother, she sacrificed a goat to Juno. When we faced tough business decisions, my father and I would turn to Janus in prayer. When I found the girl of my dreams, and she did not love me, I sacrificed a chicken to Cupid and prayed to Him every night. But you know what? My mother died in childbirth. We buried the unborn baby with her. My father had terrible business acumen, and he died buried in debt. That girl married a rich farmer. Why did this happen? How could things go so wrong? Why would the Gods turn their backs on me and my family?" Paul said.

"Did you think Cupid would personally assist you in getting laid?" Marcus chuckled.

"No. Because I had not yet found the beauty of the Lord," Paul said dreamily, as if in a trance. I see why people talk about it as a cult.

"Listen to him, beauty of the lord. What a dumbass," Felix exclaimed.

"After my father died, I was penniless and alone. I came upon one of the christian congregations. They gave me food, shelter. Helped me back on my feet,"

"Yeah, quite the enviable situation your Lord has put you in," Marcus snickered.

"God's plan is a mystery to us all," Paul declared. I noticed that once again Samuel was staying out of the whole conversation. I wondered what his position was, being Jewish and all. It's the same God, technically. Isn't it? Jesus was a Jew. But different somehow, because Jesus was not divine in Jewish eyes. That's the splinter point, isn't it? I don't really know. I

103

know very little of the various religions that people adhere to.

"Go on," Samuel said suddenly. Despite all their groanings, I wondered if Paul had ever actually told them the full story. This could be our last day alive, after all. If things went bad, then there's not really much we could do to control the situation. We were slaves.

"I became indebted to the good people of the congregation, but I wasn't fully converted until I witnessed the preachings of Bishop Ignatius. He was so eloquent. When he spoke, his speeches actually seemed completely relatable, unlike the myths and legends of the Imperial cult,"

"Whoa! Come on, buddy. You're the cultist here," Marcus cried.

"Imperial cult. Nevertheless, I truly believed in the positive messages the church was putting out. The message of charity, forgiveness, and nonviolence. So I changed my name and named myself after one of the Lord's twelve disciples," Paul said.

"Good for you," Marcus rolled his eyes.

A guard came inside our hut and led us outside towards the factory. As expected, there were much fewer guards. Probably only a couple dozen for the whole compound. There were still far too many for us to take on alone, but a fight would likely incite a general uprising and the guards would probably be overwhelmed quite quickly in such a scenario. They no longer had the numbers to actively suppress the hundreds of us.

A cloud blotted out the sun, reducing the light but doing little to reduce the thick, humid heat. Once again I found myself desperately trying not to throw up from the repulsive stench of the fermenting fish.

We worked just the same as the last two days. I scooped that nasty sauce with mechanical efficiency. Even after just two days, I was very good at it. Scoop and seal. Scoop and seal. Very simple. But the whole time I couldn't help but wonder when Samuel was going to give the signal. When we could finally get out of here. Although I didn't mention it, as talking was largely informally forbidden while working, I figured it was probably a good idea to get going as soon as possible. There was no benefit in waiting. The longer we waited, the higher chance that Ajax could return with the rest of the guards.

"Let's go," Samuel whispered finally. He was old, but I had no doubt he could kill three of me, no problem. Maybe it was just the way he carried himself. Maybe it was all the army stories he told us. Either way, I felt comfortable following behind him.

As we started making our way across the factory floor, I noticed a couple guards looking at us. After all, it was incredibly unusual for an entire station to abandon their post and just start walking to the other side of the building. I kept expecting them to yell out at us, but luckily, confused looks were all we got. It would be far too suspicious to run, but that's exactly what I felt like doing. We were about halfway there, and the guards weren't the only ones who had noticed. The others were looking at us, as well. Hushed whispers permeated the air.

I was sure we were going to be caught. At any moment, the guards would rush towards and drag us away to be whipped. They would laugh as they did it, just like that whacko from the first day. However, none of that happened. We made it to the stairwell.

I loosened the third step down and sure enough, there were swords and an ax. The second step had swords underneath it, as well. I picked up my ax, to find that it was strangely heavy. It had a wooden handle, which was shorter than the wood chopping axes that I was used to, but it was still longer than a hatchet.

"KILL THEM!" Ajax suddenly screamed from somewhere. Wait, how was Ajax back already? I turned around to see a swarm of guards slowly flooding towards us. There was way more than before. Titus was in the crowd of guards, sword in hand. And the other slaves were doing nothing! They just surrendered and slipped away.

"Shit," Marcus grumbled.

"I guess this answers whether we could trust Titus," I chuckled nervously. Paul sighed. There were so many guards. We weren't going to make it. They were going to kill us. We probably wouldn't even be able to take very many of them with us. We were just going to be overwhelmed. Simple as that. There was no hope. I was dead.

The memory of my mom screaming at me in a blind rage came rushing back to me. She hated me. I was the reason Caleb died. I knew it, she knew it. He hated himself because of me. Because of how I treated him. Just because I loved him deep down, it didn't matter. Actions matter. Not intentions. Not sentiment. Actions matter. Truth matters. And the truth was that I killed my own brother, and my mom knew it. I was going to hell. I was going to hell. I WAS GOING TO HELL. I WAS A MURDERER. I DESERVED THIS.

"GRAAHHHH," I wailed, swinging my ax wildly as I ran out into the crowd of guards. The guard closest to me managed to widen his eyes before I sunk my ax into his neck.

Kuhhhhhhhhhhhh

The guard choked, sinking to the ground. Another guard

swung his sword at me, but I ducked and slammed my ax into his stomach as hard as I could. It was much sharper than I expected, sinking in deep.

"FUCK!" The guard screamed. His eyes were watery and desperate, and I didn't care. I sunk the ax in deeper and ripped it out the same way it came in. It was a good thing I was strong, because otherwise that thing could have gotten stuck inside him. His guts spilled out all over the brick floor, and the man fell to his knees, still alive.

"Ashton!" Samuel cried. The others followed me, fighting like their lives depended on it. Because they did. There was no more fear. Fear was gone now. There was no time for fear. All anyone could do was kill. Don't think. Kill.

After gutting the second guard, another one came from the seemingly endless mass and lunged towards me. I swatted his sword out of the way, and it was dangerously close to impaling me. Doing a false step to the left, I leapt forwards from the right and tried to sink my ax into his shoulder. Instead, the guard parried my attack and then rapidly swung at me. He almost knocked the ax out of my hand. Luckily, I was able to keep up, and on one of his swings I counter-attacked and cut his wrist. The man screamed and scurried back to the safety of numbers.

"There's too many!" Marcus yelled. They were closing in on us. After my initial success, they had recovered their bearings and were staying together, making it very difficult for us to do anything except retreat into an increasingly small radius. There were guards by the stairs as well, so it's not like we could escape that way.

Fear, which had been briefly suspended, started to return. We were finished. There was no way we could win this fight. It was over.

"It is time to surrender. You've done well," Titus boomed.

"Traitor!" Paul screamed.

"Actually, betraying Ajax would have been treasonous. I never had any obligation to help you people," Titus said. Ajax appeared through the crowd and smiled.

"You thought you could escape me? Did you really?" Ajax grinned like a Bond villain. I suspected he enjoyed all of this.

"You...you —-bizzzUH—-you are a cruel Son of Hades!" Felix scowled.

"You..you...you ha! Insufferable! I have had enough of your fucking stutter," Ajax growled. One of the guards suddenly fired an arrow at Felix's head. It went right through his eye. Felix crumpled to the ground, never once making a sound. Paul fell to his knees in despair.

"The army will find out about this eventually and they will crucify you!" Samuel bellowed. Ajax produced a feigned frown.

"Crucifixions! How I love them! Which reminds me; I have prepared a nice cross for you, my lovely little christian. Oh, how I love to see Christians suffer like their God once did. You should probably be thanking me, really. To face the same fate as your Messiah must be a great honor for you," Ajax said.

"Burn in hell," Paul grumbled, tearfully glaring at Ajax from over Felix's dead body.

"Take him away," Ajax said indignantly. Two guards came through the crowd and dragged Paul out of sight. Suddenly, Marcus sprung forwards with energy I would have never expected from a man so skinny and malnourished. He sprinted towards Titus with incredible speed. Titus got himself into a ready stance, his eyes widening in surprise as Marcus leapt up and slammed his sword into the top of Titus's skull. I was surprised Titus was unable to parry in time. With a small moan, Titus collapsed to the ground, face first. Yet another pool of blood began to grow.

The stench of fish had now been combined with the horrible stink of blood, shit, and piss. I heard somewhere that when people die, they lose all muscle control and all of their bodily wastes are released. I could never imagine it. And when I thought of death, or saw it in a movie, I never imagined it would stink like it does. Now I didn't have to imagine.

Marcus managed to exhale before another guard slashed his neck with their sword. He too, fell quickly and relatively silently. Well, mostly silent aside from a few loud gurgles, which were awful.

My mouth was dry as sandpaper. I couldn't believe it. All that's left now was Samuel and I. In a matter of minutes I had become a killer. Well, maybe I already was a killer at heart. That was an internal debate for another day. But I had never outright killed someone with an ax. Now I have killed two. Watched the life drain right out of their eyes. Dead. Just like Felix. Or Marcus. Probably Paul, as well.

"Would you like to watch your friend's crucifixion?" Ajax said with his evil Cheshire grin. It was a rhetorical question. His thugs seized us and dragged us across the factory floor to the field. The other slaves were nowhere to be seen. I figured they must have been sent back to their housing. Screw them. And sure enough, there was a big cross in the field. I didn't see it walking in, so they must have dragged the thing there in the five minutes we were working. How did we not notice?

"PLEASE GOD!!!! FORGIVE ME!!!" Paul tearfully pleaded as some guards hammered giant nails into his wrists and feet. Blood oozed out of his wounds. I looked over at Samuel and found a distant, empty face. Samuel was a broken man. I could tell already he was unlikely to recover from this, even if he did somehow survive.

"Now for the fun part," Ajax giggled. About eight guards had to hoist the cross upright. Paul screamed so hard I was sure his vocal cords would burst. The veins on his neck were bulging, his face was cherry red. Everyone was drenched in sweat. The sun was still nowhere to be seen, but the humidity was more intense than ever.

"Oh my god," I muttered under my breath.

"Now! As for you two. Samuel. *Primus Pilus*. I know for a fact you are worth quite a bit of money. There are those who will pay handsomely for your release. The trick is arranging it so I remain anonymous. Nevertheless, it will be arranged. So you will live," Ajax said, turning towards me. Oh no. I was done for. Who would pay for me? No one. I had no one. I was in an ancient world. I was going to die here. My parents would never hear from me again. Neither would my friends. I would just disappear. Forever.

"I have forgotten your name, but you are young and strong so I will keep you alive. I need fresh slaves who know their Latin. You will live as well," Ajax said simply, and then he walked away with some of the guards. The rest of the guards forced us back to work. We scooped and sealed for another eleven hours, the corpses remaining untouched. Rotting in the heat. That night, I cried in my cell, all alone. Samuel was somewhere else. I cried and cried and cried. There was no one to hear me. My silent sobs bounced off the walls, exacerbating the overwhelming sense of helplessness.

14

Chapter 14

before

It had been a long day at school and I was glad to be back home at last. Squid Game was waiting for me and I was planning to go out with my friends later that night. However, it was not to be. When I got home that night, I was greeted by a teary-eyed Caleb and two very concerned parents. This incident was the first of many to come.

"What happened?" I asked as I grabbed myself a glass of water from the kitchen. The ice machine hadn't been working lately, and no one had any idea where the ice cube trays were. So I was drinking lukewarm water. Great.

"Ask Caleb," my dad responded. So I did. Apparently, someone was claiming that

Caleb only washed his underwear once a week. Which was disgusting if it was true, but I was fairly certain that it wasn't given the sheer volume of laundry that he went through on a weekly basis. It just didn't make sense. So whoever was saying this about him was just doing so to spread misinformation and create beef. I told Caleb as much, but he was still upset. Which makes sense.

It was humiliating, and although nothing quite so bad had ever happened to me, I knew what it was like to walk into a room and everyone stopped talking because they were gossiping about you. I wouldn't wish that feeling on my worst enemy.

Both of my parents were furious, and rightfully so. My mom was especially angry because Caleb was her favorite and because mothers get really protective in these sorts of situations. So we marched down to the school first thing the next morning and protested to the principal. Well, not really. My mom did. I just went to school as usual, and I had to explain to my friends why I had to stay at home and watch Game of Thrones with my brother instead of going to the trampoline park with them.

This was fine with me as I enjoyed watching Game of Thrones. It had everything a teenage boy could want—gratuitous sex and violence, mythical creatures, political intrigue, and cultural clout. We spent hours down there, wasting our time. Peak brain rot, as they say nowadays.

Too bad it turned out to be that Caleb was lying about the whole thing just to get that poor kid in trouble. Caleb was suspended instead, and those little lies that we had all started noticing started getting bigger from there. I tried to convince him to change his ways, but Caleb never admitted fault. I wonder what would have happened if I had pushed harder in those early days. It was clear something was deeply wrong, but I did very little. The bare minimum, really. Bare fucking minimum. That's what I did. That's the kind of brother I was.

15

Chapter 15

By the morning, sickness had consumed me. My nose was running ceaselessly, and every five minutes or so, I would spiral into a violent coughing fit. There was no kleenex or rag or anything to be seen, so I had to just wipe it away with my hand. It was absolutely disgusting. Sores started to form on my face. Fever consumed me, and I shivered so much I was afraid I was going to chip my teeth from chattering them so hard. The heat made it worse. That horrible feeling of hot and cold made me nauseous—but I couldn't throw up. It just didn't stop. Throughout the night, as the symptoms worsened, so did my despair. They were dead. Paul. Marcus. Felix.

Dead, just like that chance of getting out of here. Gone. I was stuck here, in this place, without kleenex. Left to die alone in this filthy cell, probably from this disease. What if it was something my immune system was unaccustomed to? I was two thousand years in the past. Who could know what sort of diseases were floating around? Maybe it was for the best. Better to suffer for a few days from a fatal sickness rather than suffer for years as a slave.

Paul screamed for the first few hours of the night, but eventually, there was silence. I imagined that he had finally died, either from asphyxiation or perhaps one of the guards impaled him with one of those big spears. Either way, he was done. Just like me.

Turns out, I was wrong. Despite my sickness, the guards forced me to work. On the way, I noticed Paul was still nailed to the cross. To my horror, he was still breathing. I suppose he had just tired of screaming. No more energy. We made brief eye contact, and I could tell that he had lost all hope. Perhaps I had lost all hope as well, but at least I wasn't in the same situation as him.

Paul survived for the entire work day, but by the next morning, crows were pecking at his already decomposing body. They kept him up there for two weeks. I know because I counted the days. The sickness had faded away on its own, despite the darkest days where I feared for my life. By day 57, I had stopped counting.

A routine started to take shape. I was actually getting used to it, somehow. Get up, eat the awful porridge. Get to work. It sounded so bizarre, calling it "work." It wasn't "work". It was labor. Forced labor. But I would go to work and I would do my 12 hours dutifully, silently. Instead of grouping me up with my cellmates at the workstation, they grouped me up with some random people that I never talked to unless I had to. They avoided talking to me, as well. They had a strict rule against engaging in unnecessary conversation during work time. I guess everyone had decided it wasn't worth the beating. And despite my newfound relatively subservient disposition, there were beatings. Nothing quite as bad as that one from the first day, but five lashes here and five lashes there. Why? I don't remember. Maybe I looked at a guard the wrong way. Maybe I grumbled a little too much at the morning wake-up call. Maybe I was working too slow.

Whatever it was, the solution was always the same. Five lashes! Five lashes will straighten them out. After all, we need discipline in the workforce. Efficiency, efficiency, efficiency. That was all they cared about. Whenever Ajax was around, we worked a little harder, a little faster. He wasn't as cruel as some of the guards, because he regarded unnecessary cruelty as an impediment to efficiency. I suppose that made him even worse than the cruel ones.

At least the cruel ones might have an excuse; maybe their daddy beat them when they were a child, maybe they are having a bad day and their unusual power gives them the unusual opportunity of taking it out on helpless slaves. Awful people, but maybe they aren't quite evil. Evil implies a lack of humanity. Rage and childhood trauma were distinctly human things. It wasn't an excuse, it was an explanation. Emotional cruelty has an explanation. It makes sense to me. Ajax made no sense to me. It was like he was inhuman. Perhaps he was a psychopath. He always seemed to be cool-headed, even when he was dishing out awful punishments like when he crucified Paul.

One time, someone tried to escape on his own. He was a feeble man—-he wasn't that useful to Ajax anyways. So Ajax saw fit to tie his arms and legs to four horses and pull him apart. It was awful. His intestines stretched all over the field. It was a bloody mess. I had seen such a punishment on tv before. You know, a couple of movies. I don't remember which, But I knew people used to do that to other people "way back when." However, whenever they showed it on the screen, they would always cut the camera to a different shot right when it happened. Seeing it in person was something else, let me tell you.

They never replaced my cellmates. I spent all of that time alone. The nights were long, very long. I realized I was going to run out of pills, and the thought of the dreams coming back was something that terrified me. One day 15 or something like that, I started biting the pills in half to ration them for as long as possible. They still worked, luckily. But I realized my efforts were merely an ill-fated attempt to delay the inevitable. Eventually I was going to have to face my internal demons. Just not yet.

Samuel was nowhere to be found. I assumed he was being kept somewhere on his lonesome, or he had been sold back to the army anonymously. If he was free, then I was happy for him. Despite my numbness, there still remained a vague hope that Samuel would come marching back at the head of a legion, ready to rescue us. Yet I knew that such hope was in vain. In all likelihood, no one was coming. The consistent failures of others, and the resulting punishments constantly tempered ideas of escape. Somehow, Ajax always came up with new and refreshingly disgusting forms of execution. OK, maybe they weren't new exactly, but he rarely used the same method twice. He decapitated people, gutted them, made the rest of us stone them to death, impaled two people on a pole, and one time he even slammed a sword up someone's asshole.

Since people tried to escape every week, there was no short supply of victims. Some were, of course, spared. Especially if they were "young and strong," like myself. However, any old slaves looking to escape better make damn well sure their plan is airtight.

Once in a while Ajax would "reward" us for our hard work. If he felt production was going well, he would give every slave a delicious feast comprising fresh bread, an entire fish, seasonal vegetables fried in olive oil and herbs, and an enormous glass of wine. It usually happened every couple of weeks. I yearned for those feasts. It was the one bright spot in my miserable existence, despite the demanding nature of the whole thing. Waiting for my "reward." Fuck them. Doesn't mean I'm not going to eat the fish. No, I'll do whatever it takes to keep myself sane.

Eventually, Ajax expanded the business. We started making clothes as well. Tunics and trousers. The sowing was difficult, at first. My hands are pretty shaky, and that kind of thing requires coordination. Nevertheless, I got pretty good at it after a few weeks. The person who taught me was a scrawny Parthian man named Frahāta. My conversations with him were the only ones of any substance during this period. Since he was instructing me, the guards were much more lax in enforcing the "conversational rules," or whatever.

Frahāta was from the city of Qumis, where he was coincidentally a carpet maker. Apparently he was drafted into a war which was currently being waged against the Roman Empire. According to Frahāta, Emperor Trajan had unjustly invaded Parthian territory in an attempt to expand Roman hegemony further to the east. Frahāta was a scout. He explained that he was captured in a small skirmish between a Roman detachment and his own unit. After being captured, he was swiftly enslaved and after a few weeks of being passed around from market to market he somehow ended up in Antioch, where he was purchased by Ajax. Ajax was looking for Parthians of a specific skill set in his attempt to broaden the factory's output.

To Frahāta, embroidery was not a profession or a skill; it was an art. Even in slavery, he took great pride in his work. So our job was to take the plain fabric and decorate it with intricate patterns and colors. We would do about a third of the work, and then we would pass it down to the next station, who would do the next third, and so on. It was much slower than the fish sauce, but I think it was still pretty efficient considering there wasn't any machinery at all. Despite our conversations, I never really got to know him. He was very reserved. And after a week of instruction, Frahāta was gone. Off to the next person. I was no Parthian embroiderer, but I came to be somewhat proud of my work. It was much more rewarding than that godforsaken fish sauce canning job. At least with the embroidery, I was creating something that wasn't there before. I was actually doing something, even if it was in horrible conditions and against my will.

As I worked alone, stitching my colorful threads through that fabric, I found my thoughts listlessly drifting from one thing to another. In the mornings I would sometimes hum some song from the past. When you are really bored, random sounds can seem almost musical. Familiar. It's like when you see faces in random objects. You know what I'm talking about. Like those craters on the moon or Mars or whatever, and people on the internet are like, "Martians are the true inventors of the smiley face emoji, LOL. Just look closely enough. You'll see it, trust!" When really, there is nothing there. No pattern. No smiley face emoji. Just some rocks and boulders and shit. Just like the howling wind is NOT screeching "Never gonna give you up," by Rick Astley.

The fish smell remained, of course. So did the heat. I

remembered the heat of one summer back in the city. It was some years ago now. Maybe five or six. I was a lot younger, I know that. So was Caleb. We got along back then. We were playing with water guns at someone's house. My dad was barbecuing hot dogs and burgers. A few steaks for the parents, of course. How I loved hot dogs. What would I do for a nice hot dog now? I didn't want to find out. But he was barbecuing, and we were playing with water guns, and there was one of those lawn slides. I don't know whose house it was. There were other kids there, I think it was a birthday party. I didn't know the kid that well, and none of my friends were there, so it was just me and Caleb.

There was one of those lawn slides. You see, the kid had a massive lawn, he lived out in the country. It was an acreage, I think. So put up one of those plastic lawn slides that people jump on and slide with their knees. And I sprayed Caleb, and he laughed, running away. The water was cold, but the sun was already scalding so it didn't really matter. The other kids were having their own water gun fight, and we would join them soon, but right now I focused on attacking Caleb. So little Caleb, giggling, ran and ran. He tried to escape by jumping on that plastic slide. Instead, he broke his nose. There was blood everywhere. We had to go to the hospital. I remember my mom yelling at me, telling me how it was all my fault. How I should have been more careful, and kept him away from the slippery slide. Caleb was my responsibility, she said.

My fault. His nose was my fault, just like everything else Caleb did. Just like when he killed himself. It was my fault he did that. She made that very clear. I could see the hate in her eyes. The rage. The disgust. I always knew my mother loved Caleb more than me, but I had never expected she would

119

resent me in the way she did after what happened. The thing was, she was right. I was responsible for what happened. I treated him like shit. He was just a little kid. Being grumpy and bratty was well within his prerogative. Yet I treated him like he knew better, instead of applying a lighter touch. I should have watched out for him. That last argument at the campground was part of the problem, but it was only one component of a cycle of rejection. He died thinking that I hated him. He died without knowing that yes, I loved him even though I didn't like him. It was my fault. It was. Perhaps all of this, this entire situation, was some sort of cruel divine punishment for my misdeeds. My penance. Maybe I deserve all of this. Maybe it's just karma, after all.

Can't be thinking like that.

Sometimes I wonder why. Why do I keep going? My mom hates me. My own mother! There was no way I was getting out of here, anyways. I was stuck here. There was no escape. I was going to die a slave. Making clothes and fish sauce. Whether it happens 3 years from now, or three hours should make little difference. At least it'd be over with quickly. Put myself out of my misery. Even if I somehow did escape, they would probably track me down. Even if they didn't track me down, I would somehow have to find Priya. She may or may not be alive, but by now she could be halfway across the Mediterranean. Who the hell knows. I didn't even know her last name. It's not like I could go and ask the police for help, or look her up on fucking yellowpages.

Can't be thinking like that.

Late at night, as all the dark thoughts seep in, sometimes I would fantasize about women. You know, sexually. There were some female slaves, and sometimes I thought about them, to my deep shame. I was a virgin. But you know, it was never enjoyable. You'd think that given the situation, I would spend lots of time doing stuff like that. After all, birth rates among the impoverished are sometimes quite high. It's because they have nothing better to do. When your life sucks, it makes sense to turn to sex as a brief respite. The "desires" consumed such people with an intense fire, only to gradually fade into a cold, emotionless apathy.

I was a teenager, and I was used to engaging in such acts before going to sleep. Nevertheless, the longer things went on, the less I thought about girls. After a while, I stopped altogether. There was just no pleasure from it anymore. I felt completely drained and occasionally even parched. They tried to give us enough water, but it wasn't always enough. Especially on the hot days. So those "solo sessions," as I would call them, faded into a distant memory after a few weeks. What was once a delightful distraction from my perils had dissolved into nothingness.

Instead, I increasingly spent my nights daydreaming about my "other life." I would fantasize about the most arbitrary things. Mcdonalds. Soccer fields. Raspberries. Raspberry jam. I didn't even really like raspberries, yet for a few days there I couldn't stop thinking about them. They had raspberries in the ancient world, didn't they? It wasn't one of those things exclusive to North America, was it? Maybe on one of his generous days, Ajax would give us some raspberries as a treat. I hoped so. In fact, I prayed so.

I didn't really believe in God, but I prayed anyway. I figured it couldn't hurt. I needed all the help I could get. Situation like this was something that my Uncle Hermann would consider to be divinely fucked up.

One cloudy day, Ajax summoned me to his office. I had no idea why he would ever do such a thing. I hadn't spoken to him at all since the failure of the escape and the execution of everyone I knew here. I stopped counting on day 57, but I knew it had been a very long time since then. Weeks, months? I couldn't be sure. I had a full, thick beard. I was not normally a hairy guy. In my other life, I only had to shave once every ten days. And that was only to remove a little stubble. So either something had changed dramatically in my hormones and shit, or I had been here for a very long time.

The office consisted of a desk and a couple chairs. There was little else, aside from a fruit and cheese platter on the desk. Ajax was smiling.

"Ashton, is it?"

"Yes," I muttered hoarsely.

"You've been a busy little bee," Ajax declares. I could just strangle him. What was the worst they could do? Execute me? Who gives a shit? He needs to die.

"I suppose," I say, keeping my head down. There's silence, and Ajax examines me. I look up awkwardly, and then quickly return my gaze to the floor.

"Your friend, Samuel, has petitioned for your release," Ajax said suddenly.

"What?"

"Yes, it seems after being returned to the army, he has made it his sole focus to destroy me and this establishment. Unfortunately, for him, no one knows where we are. However, he has offered money to buy your freedom," Ajax said, inspecting his nails. I only knew him for a couple days. Would he really do that? That's amazing.

"Have you agreed?" I asked, unable to conceal my excitement.

"Well, I wouldn't have brought you here otherwise. Now, is there anything from your cell that you would like to bring with you?"

"No,"

"I thought as much. You're free to go. Arcadius here will take you to the home of your savior. Of course, he will have to blindfold you so you don't reveal the location of this facility. I hope you understand."

"Yes, of course,"

"Good, good. On your way, then," Ajax waved me away, like it was nothing.

The muscular guard supposedly named Arcadius led to a carriage, where he then placed a dark bag over my head. I couldn't see anything. Just darkness. I didn't care at all. I was free. Finally free. No more beatings or 12 hour work days. No more shitting in the same room I sleep in. No more sleeping on a filthy concrete ground either, with only my arm as a pillow. I was free, not from an escape or anything from my own initiative. It was just luck. Pure luck. I couldn't believe it.

As the carriage drove away, I laughed so hard my face hurt, and then I laughed some more. It was just all so hysterical, wasn't it?

16

Chapter 16

"Get out," Arcadius commanded. Arcadius took the bag off my head, and I happily obliged. It had been a relatively long ride, and I was sore as hell. I instinctively stretched, as if I had just finished a long car ride or something. We were deep within the city. Samuel was standing there with a hearty smile on his face. He was in full uniform, sword and all. He didn't have a helmet on, though. A beautiful woman stood next to him. She was young, probably the same age as me. She had the most sheepish smile I had ever seen, and it was amazing.

"Ashton! It's great to see you, my friend!" Samuel cried. I focused my attention back on Samuel, and was immediately overcome with emotion. I sank to my knees, suddenly unable to stand. Arcadius took off.

"Thank you, thank you, thank..." I mumbled, tears streaming down my face. I could feel a lump in my throat. Samuel's smile faded, and he came over to me, kneeling down.

"My only regret is that I can't save everyone," Samuel said solemnly. He helped me to my feet and introduced me to the woman.

"Ashton, this is my daughter, Livia." Livia extended her hand. I shook it. Her grip was strong, her olive skin was soft. She looked me directly in the eyes.

"I'm so sorry," she whispered.

"At least it's over now," I said. She nodded and glanced down at her feet.

"I'm sure that you're starving," Samuel said. I nodded, and he led me inside his massive house. I was sure that it was worth even more because of its prime location in the city; Samuel was rich. Must have been all those spoils of war. He led inside the kitchen, where he had practically a full team of servants hard at work. It smelled delicious. There were so many unique, exotic spices permeating the air. It was about as colorful as the streets of Antioch.

We sat down and I devoured what they served me. Some sort of chicken in a spicy sauce, fresh bread, wine, fish, lobster, and steamed vegetables. The grand dining room table was full of food. Anything I could want. They were there. Even raspberries! They also had roasted mice, which apparently were a delicacy?! I decided not to partake in mice, but I tried just about everything else. There was even some of the garum, the fish sauce that we made. I decided to try some on the plain chicken drumsticks. It was delicious. It didn't taste at all like the fish sauce I was used to, like from the Vietnamese restaurants back home. It was sort of fishy alright, and it had an umami taste, but it was also unique to anything I had ever tasted before.

"I'm sorry it took so long," Samuel said.

"Don't even think about it. I'm surprised you remembered me," I exclaimed between mouthfuls.

"We weren't cellmates for long, but I remember how well you fought. You were sick at the time, as well. Weren't you?" Samuel inquired.

"Yeah, I was sick. It got much worse in the days right after the escape attempt. And Paul was up there for quite a while. It was terrible," I muttered. Samuel grimaced.

"They reserve crucifixion for the most sick criminals. To use it on a good man like Paul is an abomination," Samuel grumbled, his face descending in hardened resentment. I simply nodded along, trying to crack open the lobster shells. The butter mixed with garlic and herbs was irresistible to me. They didn't starve me at the slave camp, exactly, but the food was generally so awful I was relieved to have something over-the-top for once.

Some servants came in and cleaned up some of the empty dishes. They kept their heads down.

"What's your name?" I asked the female servant, cleaning up an empty dish near me.

"Duccidava," the woman replied. She was middle-aged, her long brown hair speckled with gray.

"She is one of our best," Samuel explained.

"Employees?" I asked.

"Slaves," Samuel said, with no hint of irony.

"What?" A pit of dread filled my stomach. How could this be? How could he enslave others after being made a slave himself? In what world was that right?

"Legal slaves, of course. Duccidava was bought from the Dacians. She has been very good," Samuel smiled, and reached out his hand. Duccidava squeezed it and smiled. The other slaves left.

"I don't understand. We were slaves. How can you—-"

"Who do you think you are?!" Samuel exclaimed, slamming his fist against the table. Duccidava left the room.

"I—I didn't mean..." I stutter. His sudden change in tone shocked me.

"Don't you dare compare me to a slave ever again. I am a Roman Officer, and you will treat me as such,"

"Father, I don't think he meant any harm," Livia interjected.

"Yeah, I didn't mean to offend you. That's what I was trying to say. I was just surprised, is all,"

"Surprised? Where do you come from, boy? Everyone has slaves. Even poor folk,"

"I'm sorry." I wasn't sorry, but I had little choice but to say otherwise. I wasn't starving.

"Do you want me to show you to your room?" Livia asked, as if reading my mind.

"I think that would be great." Samuel threw his napkin on the table in frustration.

I got up and followed Livia. We didn't have to go far. The room was on the first floor. While the house was sprawling, it comprised only two floors. Her white dress was thin and airy. The ornate drawings of various mythological characters covered the walls of the house with a disorienting array of colors, breathing life into them. I didn't really know what the hell was on the walls, but that was my best guess.

My room was small, but much nicer than the cell I was used to. There was a bet with sheets and a pillow, probably feather-stuffed. There was a window and green curtains, which went sort of strangely with the red walls. Almost christmassy, except it wasn't christmassy at all. If that makes sense? I suppose it doesn't really have to.

' "Thank you," I say. She gives me that sheepish grin again.

"Sorry about my dad. He's sort of traditional,"

"I see that,"

"I assume you probably want to rest," Livia says. I did, of course, but I knew I couldn't sleep. I only had six half-pills left. I couldn't waste one on a nap.

"Well, it's still daytime," I say. Livia looks surprised.

"What would you like to do, then?"

"What do you usually do?" I asked.

"My father lent me some money, and I started a store about a year ago. We sell fresh fruit and vegetables. Some trinkets as well. Aelia, and I, that is. She's my best friend," Livia explains.

"You run a shop?" I was mildly surprised. I figured women had very little rights. Owning a shop isn't precisely congruent with that view. Nevertheless, her wealth could possibly explain it away.

"Yeah. My dad wants me to get married. Settle down and all that,"

"I see,"

"But you know, I don't really want to fuck an old dude," Livia bursts out laughing, and I laugh along.

"Ok, should we go there then? I'd like to see this shop of yours," I ask.

"No, no! You're new to town, right? If you don't want to rest, should we go have some fun!" Livia insists, playfully pushing me. I was surprised at how comfortable she was talking to me. There was no awkwardness, or whatever. She was definitely an extrovert.

"Sure, I guess. I don't know what you mean by that, but ok," I say.

"Follow me, then," Livia says. I followed her outside to the streets. Samuel was nowhere to be seen. The streets were bustling, as always. Most of the people seem to be walking in the same direction. We follow them. I was still kind of shocked that I was finally free. I couldn't help but smile at my drastic change of situation in the last few hours.

"So, what brought you here, originally?" Livia asks.

"I was enslaved——" "I begin. Livia frowns.

"No, I'm so sorry. No, I meant what brought you to Antioch originally. My father never told me,"

"Well, I came with some friends. They were on a business trip, and I guess you could say I was on vacation. Most of them were killed, except myself and Priya."

"Ashton and Priya. What strange names," Livia muttered.

"Yeah, well. I guess our parents wanted us to have unique names," I said. I never really did like the name Ashton, to be honest. There were women named Ashton. But whatever. It was my name. A modern one, at that. I wonder if Priya was a common name in Ancient India. I had no idea. We were in the middle east, right? There must be some Indians around here somewhere. I knew that they traded spices and stuff with the Romans.

"Mission accomplished,"

"Where are we going, anyway?"

"Oh, just the arena. They put on a good show. It's not the coliseum, obviously, but one can't set their standards too high. We can take bets, if you like."

"Bets? I don't have any money,"

"I'll give you some betting money. Don't worry about it. You were a great help to my father when he was locked up. Some of us were giving up hope. We believed that he had been killed.

"Our escape attempt failed, though,"

"I know, but the effort counts. Have you ever been to the

coliseum?"

"No," I decided against telling her that I hadn't been to any "arena" at all.

"Well, if you ever get the chance, it's amazing. And the Circus Maximus! 250 thousand people were all packed in, watching the chariot races. It's so exciting. The roar of the crowds, and all that,"

"Do you prefer the chariots to the gladiator stuff?"

"Nope. Chariots are better. But Gladiator stuff is what's going on today. I guess it's ok, but it doesn't have the same thrill as a race. You know?"

"Yeah, I guess I can understand that." I didn't understand it. I guess their gauge of what was acceptable was different back then.

"Where are you from? You have a strange accent," Livia said. I suddenly realized I had to idea what to say. I paused for a few seconds, and Livia gave me a look.

"Somewhere very far away," I said vaguely.

"I see. I'll just have to figure it out all on my own, then. Is that it?" Livia laughed, a pretty laugh that made you feel warm inside.

"Yep." We reached the arena. There were probably about ten thousand people there, sitting in the open-air seating. There were two bloodied corpses in the sandy arena. The victor was raising his sword in triumph, to thunderous applause. People came in and dragged the bodies away. The sand was soaked in blood, creating an almost muddy environment in certain areas. There were attendants walking up and down, serving drinks and fresh fruit.

"That guy is great. He's a Celt. Great fighters, those Celts," Livia mumbled.

"He looks terrifying,"

"Should we make a bet? I think we should. Over here!" Livia called out to one of the attendants.

"Yes, ma'am?"

"I'll bet five sestercii on that Phoenician there,"

"Of course, ma'am. You'll have to register your bet at the office first, of course."

"Oh," Livia seemed embarrassed. The attendant walked away.

"Haven't you been here before?" I asked. Livia went beet red.

"Nah, I usually go to the comedy shows, to be honest. Just tryna be cool," Livia chuckled awkwardly.

"Oh," I said.

"Yeah, but we can still watch. I've been a couple times, you know. But never to bet. Lots of people like it,"

"Do you like it, though?"

"Nah, but that's ok. I'm sure you'll like it."

"Well, no. Let's go see a comedy show. Why not?"

"Okay!" Suddenly, a tiger leapt out from the floor of the arena and growled. The celt gladiator tried his best to keep the tiger away, but since he didn't have a spear, it was a rigged game. Within a few seconds, the tiger lashed out his claws and slashed the gladiator across the chest. He screamed out in pain and flailed his sword, only grazing the agile beast. The tiger lunged forward and tackled him to the ground. He fell like a sack of potatoes, screaming as the tiger sunk its teeth into his soft flesh. Blood oozed everywhere. The crowd oohed and awed. He screamed even louder. How was he not dead? Livia seemed uncomfortable.

"Let's go," I said.

"Yeah, screw this place," Livia agreed. She led me to a quaint little open-air theater in a small corner of town. There were probably about 60 people filling up the stone bench seating, which was quite uncomfortable.

The first play was rather strange. It was about a young man who falls in love with a slave girl named scamps, only for his father to become infatuated with her as well. The second play involved an old man getting tricked by his personal slave, who managed to keep fooling the old man into humiliating himself in front of others. The third and final play was a version of the death of Julius Caesar, and it was much less comedic. People weren't laughing, although I thought the production design was pretty cheesy. I recognized it though, and I was surprised they were already making plays about it only a hundred years later. I wonder if any of them knew how famous his death would become. Getting stabbed to death by dozens of old senators. I guess there's not much you can do when you get swarmed like that.

Perhaps the strangest thing about the plays, aside from the bizarre humor and underlying fear of some sort of slave disobedience, was the masks. They were all wearing these big wooden masks with exaggerated expressions. I guess people found them funny, but to me, they just seemed weird and antiquated. Honestly, they were creepy. Like something you'd find mounted on the wall inside a haunted house or something.

"How was that?" Livia asked me.

"I liked it," I lied. Livia smiled and hugged me. Surprised, I jerked back a little, but then hugged her back. Why was she being so nice?

"I think we're going to get along really well," Livia said.

17

Chapter 17

I woke up the next morning excited to start my day. Every day, for the longest time, consisted of 12 hours of non-stop labor. For the first time in a long time, that wasn't the case. I could spend my time with people whose company I enjoyed, (putting aside the whole kitchen slavery thing and the bizarre behavior of Livia.) I could confidently say that Samuel and Livia were good people, at least in the context of the time period. Most importantly, they were being incredibly kind to me. I had no right to judge them. Samuel even agreed to begin searching for Priya, after I told him last night that she was likely enslaved by a military officer.

Nevertheless, despite my sudden immense luck over the past 24 hours, the situation remained quite dire overall. Questions over my origin, in jest, were slowly becoming more serious. I realized I would need an answer pretty soon if I expected to stay here for more than a few days. I also realized that locating Priya, even with the help of the powerful Samuel, was going to be an arduous task. She could be anywhere. At least her name appears pretty unique for the time period, assuming she told people her real name, which was far from a guarantee.

On top of that, I also had to contend with the fact that my pills were quickly running out. It wouldn't be long now before my supply was completely gone, even with the half-pill rationing I had instituted ages ago. I had no idea if the nightmares would return without the pills, but I knew that if they did, my already stressed psychological state might implode on itself.

All of those things are a worry for another day, maybe tomorrow. For now, it's time to enjoy myself a bit. As awkward as she could be, I found Livia to be incredibly endearing. She was also perfect. I think I have a crush on her. Oh well. That's fine. She's hot, alright? What can you do? Nothing's going to come of it, anyway. She would never go out with a guy like me. SHe's way out of my "league," as they say. Mind you, she was being pretty nice to me yesterday. She hugged me! Who does that? A great hug it was, too. Warm and tight.

Just what I needed, actually. You know, emotionally. I was kind of emotionally unstable because of the whole slavery thing. And also because I might be stuck here for life. Also, there's the whole issue of my mother disowning me and getting sent to an institution because she blames me for my brother's suicide. That's nice. REAL FUCKING NICE. See what I was saying? Unstable. So back off. A little crush is harmless. Doesn't mean I'll act on it. She was probably just being nice because I helped her dad out when we were enslaved together. Or maybe that's just her personality. Damn it! I need to stop thinking about her. I've got some bigger issues going on, don't forget it. MUCH BIGGER ISSUES. I'm really going in circles now. Great. Fan-fucking-tastic. Wow. Why am I swearing so much? That's so foul. My mother would be disappointed in me. Screw her! NO, FUCK HER. I CAN THINK AND SAY WHATEVER

I——–

"Master?" a woman whispered.

"What?" I ask, startled. The kitchen slave walks in. What was her name?

"Breakfast is ready. The others are waiting for you." Duccidava, that was it. Strange name.

"I'll be right down. Thank you," I said. I was going to tell her she didn't have to call me master, but I hesitated and she left. I decided I could just tell her that the next time I saw her. It was all so awkward.

I crawled out of bed and put on some new clean clothes Samuel had lent me. I still hadn't had a shower or bath or anything since I had left the "real world" way back when. I smelled disgusting, and it was kind of embarrassing. While enslaved, I had almost gotten used to it. Sure, I got itchy and stuff. I was aware. But there was almost a sort of complacency that I developed during my time there. It was terrifying, to be honest.

Last night at supper, Samuel promised to take me to the baths today. I wondered why we didn't do it yesterday, but I didn't complain. I was eagerly looking forward to it. Breakfast was wonderful. Fruit and oatmeal. Unlike the oatmeal from the slave camp, it was quite tasty.

Livia was not at the breakfast table. Samuel explained she had left early to go open up shop. That brought another question to mind, which was how did they know when to wake up? Did they have clocks? I decided against asking Samuel because it was one of those questions that would draw too much attention to myself.

When we reached the baths, the sun was high in the sky. I estimated it was probably close to noon. I guess that's how they knew. Wasn't there like sun clocks or something? Where do you place a stick on the ground and watch the shadow change? I remembered doing a science project in grade six, and that was the primitive clock. Surely they had something a bit better.

I remembered that they created the modern calendar. Or Julius Caesar did. The Julian calendar. 365 days, a leap year every four years. It was the basis of the modern Gregorian calendar. My Grade 8 social teacher told us that. He was a bit crazy. Hey, I guess the education system didn't totally fail me after all.

"Alright, here we are. It'll be nice to get clean," Samuel said.

"Yes, thank you,"

"Yeah, don't worry about it," Samuel paid the attendant a few small coins, and we entered the bath complex. It was very steamy, humid. We entered the change room. There were about a dozen men from all walks of life. Skinny, fat, white, black, brown, old, young, some wearing rich clothes and others wearing poor clothes.

It suddenly dawned on me that I was supposed to strip down completely and bathe naked with a bunch of strangers. Looking over my shoulder, I noticed Samuel had somehow already stripped down to his underwear, and he was.... Oh no. I just saw his wrinkly penis. Damn it. That's disgusting. Ok then.

"Are you ok there, Ashton?"

"Yeah, yeah,"

"Come on then," He said. I stripped down. Completely naked. It was embarrassing, but I guess it helped that everyone else was naked as well. I was mostly worried about accidentally getting a hard on. Not that I was in conditions that would facilitate such an action, but sometimes they just happen. I'm young. What can you do?

Luckily, the pool was kind of cloudy. Which was good in case my fear ever became reality, but it was also kind of sketchy. Why was it cloudy? I guess I couldn't complain. I needed to clean off, and this was probably the best I was going to get. It would be incredibly impolite and, above all, reckless to decline Samuel's hospitality. I wondered if it was a hot spring or if they heated it from a fire underneath the floor. We entered the water, and it wasn't very hot. It was basically lukewarm. Like a kiddy pool at a recreation center.

"Do you know how they heat the baths?"

"Of course. You don't?"

"No," I said, somewhat embarrassed.

"There are some furnaces beneath the floor, and they regulate the temperature by allowing colder water from reservoirs to enter the bath,"

"That makes sense,"

"So, I remember you saying that you are an educated man,"

"Yes," That was a very relative term. "Educated." I hadn't even finished high school yet. I mean, maybe I was educated relative to everyone else. Probably not.

"My daughter could use your help. She has run into some debt. Poor management. Women are not always the brightest creatures. I try to get her to marry, but what can you do? She's very willful, like her mother,"

"Would you rather have a weak daughter?" I asked. Samuel gives me a look.

"Of course not. I love her, but there are some things that she's going to have to do. It's her duty as a woman of high standing. Maybe if we were just regular citizens, but I have worked hard to get us up to where we are."

"Well I'll do my best," I said. My mathematical abilities

without a calculator were seriously in doubt. Also, if he was so rich, why didn't he just hire someone for her? Or buy an educated slave?

"Why me, though? Surely you can get someone better,"

"Two reasons: firstly, it's going to be awhile before I can locate your friend, Priya. So You're going to need something to do. I can find another job for you, but you seemed to get along with Livia. Didn't you?"

"Yes,"

"Good. So you two get along. Secondly, I don't want her to know that I'm sending you to help her out. Alright? She's very independent and all that. She would be furious if she knew I sent someone to fix up her mess. I'm an old man, and I don't want to fight with her unless absolutely necessary,"

"Makes sense,"

"She'll be mad enough once I force her to marry,"

"What?"

"Don't worry about that. That's a problem for another day."

"Sure," I muttered. I suppose arranged marriage was just a common occurrence around here, but it still seemed awful.

"So, how are you settling in?"

"Very good, thank you," I decided that saying thank you as often as possible was a good habit to get into, given my situation. There was silence for a few minutes.

"You seem uncomfortable with the household slaves," Samuel said.

"A little, I suppose. After being a slave for so long,"

"You're a Roma citizen, though? Right?"

"Yes, of course," I said quickly.

"If you are a Roman citizen, and educated Roman citizen at that, then how did you become so anti-slavery?"

"I guess I have a new perspective now." I wasn't lying, exactly.

"Fair enough. You need to understand, though. What happened to us was illegal. You can't enslave Roman citizens. It offends God. Ajax was also cruel. I would never beat my slaves. There are laws against that,"

"I see,"

"I never did ask, where is your sister?" I ask. I remembered him telling me about how his sister was the one who still lived in Antioch when he moved back from Macedonia. Samuel rubbed his eyes.

"She's dead," He says simply.

"What?"

"She died when I was away. Livia is devastated, of course. That's probably why she was acting so strange. That's also probably why her spending is out of control. She's giving away too much stuff. Someone comes to the store, gives her the fakest sob story you can imagine, and she just lets them have what they want! Word has spread, it's completely out of control," Samuel explains.

"That's awful. Are you ok?" I ask.

"Don't even worry about it. It was her time. But you know, this is why you can't have women running businesses! They are too emotional," Samuel exclaims. I decided not to respond to that.

We probably spent another three hours at the baths. After the warm pool, we transferred into what was essentially a hot tub. That was my favorite part. It was super nice on my sore muscles, but we could only stay for like ten minutes. We then transferred to a big, cold pool. The water was actually pretty cold. I wondered how they kept it that way, considering the sweltering Mediterranean climate. Surely, it should be lukewarm like the first pool. But it wasn't. It was hard to get in the cold water at first, but it felt truly great after the hot pool. After the cold bath, we were massaged by some slaves (yep.) They rubbed some sort of oil on us, and they managed to get most of the knots off of my back. Afterwards, they scraped the oil and sweat off of my back with some sort of metal tool. That was kind of gross. They also shaved me, which was long overdue. Apparently a beard was long out of fashion. Samuel said I looked much younger without facial hair.

There were also some people working out in a courtyard, playing athletic games with leather balls and lifting weights. To my bemused horror, they did all of this butt-naked. There was even a little theater, which people thankfully witnessed covered by towels. We caught one of the shows, and it was one of the same ones from the previous night with Livia. It was the one about the slave who kept tricking the old man. It sure felt good getting cleaned up, though. I felt totally refreshed and rejuvenated. The whole naked thing got easier with time, as well. I became more comfortable in my own skin, and although I probably wouldn't go to a nudist beach if I ever returned to the modern world, for the first time I saw the appeal.

I found myself re-thinking Livia and her behavior. She was just grieving. That's why she was being so nice. I felt ashamed of thinking otherwise. The question was whether I should bring it up the next time I saw her. On one hand, it would be good to be a "shoulder to lean on," especially amid all the sexist and toughen up attitudes that were surrounding her. Conversely, I didn't want to be subconsciously taking advantage of her vulnerable emotional state. This wasn't an opportunity to get a kiss, this was a grieving human being. I knew that, I knew.

Despite that, I couldn't trust myself. Also, I didn't want to interfere too much in family affairs, when I was so very dependent on her father's charity. I guess I could say something, but not right away. Only if it was natural. Besides, what would I even say? Maybe it was better to say nothing at all. Isn't that kind of cruel to say nothing at all? What's the social expectations here? What social expectations should I be following? Those of modernity or the classical roman social expectations, which I actually knew very little about. Maybe my modern sensibilities would prove to be a breath of fresh air.

The real question was: why did I care so much about social expectations. Just do what is natural and be done with it. I had bigger concerns here. Bigger fish to fry, as it were. I hadn't mentioned Priya once during that visit to the baths, and I didn't later that day either. But it was on my mind, nonetheless. I just didn't want to push it. The next morning, I spent breakfast with Livia. This time, it was Samuel who was gone.

"Good morning," Livia smiled wearily.

"Morning," I said. Oatmeal and fruit again. Duccidava was standing in the corner, holding a jug of water.

"So, I hear you went to the baths yesterday with my father. Sorry I couldn't catch you. I was very busy with the store. We've had a lot of business lately,"

"Yeah, your dad told me you've run into some financial difficulty lately,"

"Did he? How prudent of him. Tell him that I don't need his help,"

"Maybe I can help. I'm good with money," I was really getting used to lying through my teeth. What did that say about me?

"Did he send you?"

"No, no. I mean, he told me about your problems...but...he told me not to interfere,"

"And you decided to do the opposite of what he said?"

"Well, we got along pretty well the other day, and I figured might be friends,"

"Maybe,"

"So, what do friends do? Help each other out,"

"I suppose," She conceded. I knew I was making a big jump with the whole friend assertion, but I figured she was the type of person who would agree, given the way she was acting with me earlier. I felt awful. I was lying to a grieving person because their father told me to.

With that, she led me to her store. It was small, but well-stocked. There were a wide variety of fruits and vegetables. Another woman about my age was already there, working with a customer who wanted some cabbage. The customer bought the cabbage. Livia introduced me to the short woman.

"Ashton, this is Aelia," Livia said.

"Hello," I reached out my hand. Aelia shook it. She had sweaty palms, and a sweaty little face too.

"Ashton? What a strange name," Aelia muttered nasally.

"That's what I said!" Livia exclaimed.

"So you two are partners?" I asked. Aelia winced dramatically.

"No, I have sixty percent control," Livia said.

"To everyone's detriment!"

"Aelia!"

"No, she keeps giving away our shit. Look around, see any crowds? No! Because Livia hasn't been working yet. Once word gets out that she's here, the vultures will come circling,"

"That's not fair!" Livia laughed. Aelia just scowled.

"How can you laugh? Easy for you, I suppose, with daddy's money to fall back on," Aelia grumbled. Livia's smile faded away. I decided to interject.

"That's why I'm here. I can help with the finances," I say.

"Really?" Aelia said doubtfully.

"Yeah, I'm an educated man,"

"Man," Aelia chuckled.

"Aelia, that's enough," Livia whispered.

"What? What are you going to do? Fire me? You need me!" Aelia cried.

"Geez, could you not have some compassion?" I said.

"Why? Why would I have compassion for her? I'm sorry about this Ashton, because you're probably a great guy and all. I don't know. But she is—"

"She's been nothing but kind to me,"

"Kind. That's exactly the problem!"

"Ok, maybe she's—-"

"Can you guys stop talking about me like I'm not in the room?" Livia demanded. Aelia took a deep breath. I looked down at my feet.

"I'm sorry," I said quickly, glancing up at her.

"Can you show him the books, Aelia?" Livia ordered.

"Sure, thing...ma'am," Aelia said resentfully. She showed me the books. Or scrolls, rather. I couldn't read them, because they were in Latin. I could only translate words once they were spoken. Not a text. The numbers I could kind of read, because I knew the basic roman numerals. But the numbers were way too big for me to understand. Whoops. Didn't think that one through. I pretended to read the numbers.

143

"Hmmm..." I said, nodding as I pretended to read.

"Yeah, it's not good, is it?" Aelia said.

"Nope, not good at all," I declared.

"Can you fix it? Livia asked desperately.

"I think that, if you stop giving away free stuff, and really try to boost your sales through some sort of promotion or something then you might be able to make things right,"

"Really? Is that your big solution? Be better?" Aelia said, exasperated.

"Um—-"

"I think it's a splendid plan," Livia says.

"Can you stop giving away stuff?"

"Yes, yes of course. I have self-control,"

"Good," I said. I was kind of worried, because I had no idea exactly how much money they needed, or by when, or anything. Aelia was right, all I could really offer was common sense financial advice. Really general stuff.

They set me up, showed me the ropes and all that. It was pretty simple, really. I didn't really need to know anything about the products to sell them. It was mostly just fruit and vegetables. A few trinkets and souvenirs, as well. After the brief tutorial, people started to appear. Aelia seemed to be right; people sure really did seem to flock here once Livia appeared.

The place was practically deserted when we first arrived, and within no more than fifteen-twenty minutes there were dozens of people crowding the little store. Most of them didn't want to talk to me, but I still managed to sell over 130 sesterce worth of products. I overheard some of the conversations that these customers had with Livia. They did indeed give sob stories about whatever, but Livia seemed to be refusing them.

I'm so poor I had to eat my neighbor's dog last week. He doesn't know what happened to him yet. Please don't say anything!

Livia, dear, don't you know about my father? He's so sick he can't get out of bed.

My son's got the pox, so I haven't been able to work lately

Please, I know I owe a lot of money but I'm good for it, I swear!

My brother was killed just last week by some thugs, I'm just devastated

OH MY GOD, PLEASE LIVIA, YOU KNOW ME...I'LL PAY YOU BACK!

Time after time she reluctantly turned them down. Some of them bought something anyway, but most of them left once they realized they weren't getting any charity. There was one customer she didn't refuse right away, though. I approached to overhear the conversation.

"... and look, Livia, you know I wouldn't be asking you for help if I didn't need to," Some guy was saying.

"I know, but I just..."

"Listen, if it makes you feel uncomfortable, I'll just go,"

"No...you can have all the cabbage and carrots you want. It's only money. You need to help your mother. You're a good guy, Heraclius," Livia smiled gently. I looked around, hoping Aelia would stop this. But she was busy with another customer.

"Hold on," I said, tapping the guy on the arm.

"Yes?"

"Umm...you can't just take that,"

"Livia said it was ok,"

"It's ok, Ashton. I trust him. He's family," Livia said.

"I know, but you wanted my help with the finances and—-"

"SHH!" Livia forcibly put her hand on my mouth.

"Help with finances?" Heraclius asked, concerned.

"Don't worry about it, honey," Livia said, taking her hand off of my mouth and giving Heraclius a sloppy French Kiss, pulling

145

him close. I looked away awkwardly. Damn it! Of course she was taken, what was I thinking?

"Hold on, though, what is he talking about?" Heraclius pulled away from Livia.

"We've been having some trouble lately, but it's nothing——" Livia said quickly.

"It's not nothing," I interrupted. Heraclius looked at me up and down, as if seeing me for the first time. His face was stony and painted with concern. I wonder if it was genuine. Who was I to ask if it was genuine concern or not? I didn't even know the guy. I was slipping into outright jealousy, and jealousy is not—

"If you can't afford it, I can't take these," Heraclius said, trying to hand back the vegetables. Livia refused.

"A few won't hurt. I've been turning everyone else down, so it's fine," Livia explained.

"Are you sure?" Heraclius asked.

"It's..it's probably fine if it's just him," I said reluctantly after a long silence. Livia smiled at me, which made me feel good.

"Alright, then. If you're sure. I'll see you tonight, Liv," Heraclius said. A nickname. Oh no. Yep, I stood no chance.

"Thanks for that," Livia said, squeezing my shoulder. She walked away to attend to another customer. Aelia approached me.

"Was that Heraclius I just saw scurry out of here?" Aelia grumbled.

"Yeah," I replied.

"Did she give him free stuff?"

"Yeah,"

"Fuck!" She exclaimed. I looked over at her.

"What? Is he a bad guy or something?"

"He's just always taking advantage of her. They've been on and off since they were kids. She always gets mad at him when he cheats, but somehow she always forgives him,"

"Oh,"

"She wants to marry him, last I heard,"

"Which can't happen?"

"Which *won't* happen, unless she runs away with him or something stupid like that.

No way in *hell* I was allowing that to happen.

18

Chapter 18

Over the next few weeks, I became more comfortable with everyone. Once again, a routine set in. The whole thing was still exceedingly bizarre, of course, but I was almost getting used to living in an ancient city with another family. I would wake up, eat breakfast, mainly with Livia (and Duccidava standing in the corner, of course.) Samuel would sometimes be with us, but he was usually gone. I only saw him at supper time, and at supper Livia was commonly over at "Aelia's house," which I knew to be a lie since Aelia and Livia were still on bad terms. They might have been best of friends once upon a time, but they were almost always antagonistic towards each other. It was sad to see, really.

Aelia came to be a good friend of mine, more so than Livia. Livia was beautiful and kind and innocent, but she was also gullible and deeply in love with another man. So our connection was limited, despite my best efforts. Livia was always easy-going with me from day one, and we became closer with time, but it became clear that she behaved that way with everyone. She was just a kind-hearted person. Aelia was super ironic, and I enjoyed her quips. She was like a sarcastic comedian or something, and she shared my concern for Livia's increasingly reckless behavior with Heraclius.

Not that it was really my place to be concerned. I had only known them all for a few weeks. Nevertheless, it was hard not to feel sympathy for a girl who lost someone so close to them. I still didn't know how her aunt died, but I decided I would ask her sometime later. Maybe I could relate to her through Caleb. Maybe not. Maybe I needed to stop thinking about Livia. Time to move on. It was not healthy. I thought about her almost all the time. The way she smiled when I made a joke. The way she pushed her long, brown hair behind her ears. The way she kissed.

I spent most of my nights furiously masturbating, thinking of her. It was bad. I had never been so attracted to a girl before. Sometimes she would wear a dress that was a little higher on the legs, and I had to force myself not to look for more than a few seconds.

She had such long, perfect legs. And her breasts were big too, but not too big. Very firm. Sometimes, with her thin fabric dresses, I would see her hard nipples poking through. I was so dirty, it was disgusting. I hated myself for it. There were so many better things that I could be thinking about instead Why would I...Why was I being like this? When I had a crush on Jen, it was different. Of course, I was no stranger to my sexuality, but this was a whole new level of intensity. I truly understood the word lust now.

I suppose part of the reason I did...the reason I did that at night was a fear of a return to the nightmares that I re-membered so very well. My pills had long since run out, but luckily, the nightmares did not return. My nights consistently remained dreamless, and sometimes I wondered if the pills had done permanent damage. Not that I dreamed a lot before taking them, but usually I would at least have one hazy dream a week or so. Now—there was absolutely nothing.

On the rare occasion that I wasn't thinking of Livia, I would find my mind drift towards increasingly dark places. Was Priya dead? Was I ever getting out of here? What would my mother do once she decided I was never coming home? Would she collapse even further into despair, or perhaps even worse, would she not care at all? What about my dad? I was gone for what must be months now. They would have filed a missing person's report and everything. My friends would be worried, too. Samuel said he was still looking, but I knew that with each passing day, the odds became smaller and smaller.

The memories of the slave camp were still etched into my memory. I had almost managed to push it back into my memory until the other day when someone whipped a donkey. The memories just came flooding back. That hard whip, slapping against my skin. The feeling of the warm blood running down my back. It was numb for a split second, and then the pain came like a burning inferno. I stopped in my tracks, and Livia had to shake me out of it. I was shivering. Actually shivering in fear. I had never experienced anything like it. It hasn't happened since, but I still think of my time there.

Of the fish that they would serve us as a treat. Smug sons of bitches, they were. Especially Ajax. He was so cold. So cold. Other times, the feeling of sleeping alone in that cell. The sheer boredom that would fester in such conditions. The cartoons that I would imagine in the moonlight-formed shadows on the wall. I would see all sorts of things. Or I would imagine songs or melodies that would form from random, distant sounds that had no rhyme or reasons.

I would think of Titus, the traitor. How we all trusted him. I would think of how they pulled that man apart into four pieces using four horses. The sheer mess of it all. I would think of how they crucified Paul. He screamed for hours and hours until he couldn't anymore because the weight of his body was suffocating himself. The man was up there for more than 24 hours. Big Ass nails right through his wrists and ankles. Some of the guards laughed with glee. I thought of how I killed those guards in the escape attempt, how I made them bleed. I watched the life drain from their eyes. I can still hear the kuhhhh kukhhhhhh kuhhhhhhhhh sounds of that one guard choking on his blood. I could have never known how familiar that sound would become. Knotts. Felix. Jesus Christ...I was a damaged human being. I knew it. I knew it. I knew it.

I eventually decided that I needed Livia. I wanted her so badly, it wasn't even funny. So I devised a plan. It was cheesy, I know. I had no idea if Aelia would agree to it, or if it would even work. But I was willing to give it a shot. I was so miserable, there was just so much trauma and uncertainty. I had no idea what the hell I was going to do to get home. I could very well be stuck here. More reason not to create drama, but you only live once. Right? Right.

"Aelia, I need to ask you something," I said in a hushed voice one day when Livia was away at the market. We had been working at the store all morning, and Aelia seemed to be in a relatively good mood.

"If you want me to jerk you off, the answer is no," Aelia deadpanned. She never even looked up from sorting vegetables.

Even now, she caught me off guard sometimes.

"What—no. Well, not exactly. Do you want to pretend to date?" I asked, looking over my shoulder. It sounded so ridiculous when I said it out loud.

"I'm sorry?" Aelia laughed.

"You know, to make Livia jealous," I responded unevenly.

"Why would that make her jealous?" Aelia shook her head in disbelief, still smiling ear to ear.

"Forbidden fruit?" I offered.

"You're such a fucking dumbass,"

"Well, you always say you hate——"

"Wait a minute. So you *do* have the hots for Liv?"

"I guess you could say th—"

"You horny beast! I thought you were better than that."

"And what gave you that idea?"

"I don't know. You're educated. Respectable,"

"I was a slave,"

"Yeah, whatever. So was Samuel. It was an illegal slave camp,"

"I guess,"

"Which reminds me, you'll have to tell me your history sometime. You always seem to avoid answering questions about your past. If I didn't know any better, I'd say you're an undercover praetorian!"

"Please. I'm far too young,"

"I suppose that's true. Now, what is it you love so much about Livia?"

"I don't know. She's just so kind—"

"Debatable,"

"She is! You can't deny it. She's beautiful too,"

"Yeah, that's the real reason. Everyone loves beautiful Livia.

She's always so immaculate. Always getting the hot boys,"

"As if! You aren't jealous,"

"No, I'm not. Got me there." Aelia threw her hands up in mock surrender.

"So, are you going to help?" I took a step closer to her. I was thankful that no customers had come into the store.

"Someone's got to deal with that parasite," Aelia grumbled.

"Did you just— -"

"Heraclius, not Livia, She's many things, but not a parasite,"

"I was going to say! Now, how do we go about this?" I rubbed the back of my neck. It was sore for some reason. I must have slept weird the night before.

"We kill him, of course," Aelia broke out into a terrifyingly broad smile..

"Very funny," I chuckled nervously, always unsure when she was joking.

"No, we'll have to disgrace him. His father is a member of the baking guild. If we can frame Heraclius for stealing flour, then his family will be disgraced,"

"That seems a little extreme." I was uncomfortable with the prospect of ruining an

innocent man's life just to get a girl. I had enough on my conscience already.

"Oh, they have lots of money. They'll figure something out, but they might have to move," Aelia sighed.

"Wasn't he just here begging for money?" I furrowed my brow.

"Only because his daddy won't give him enough spending money to afford all his booze,"

"Oh. It still seems kind of extreme,"

"I was going to do it, anyway. You can help me or not? It's

up to you. But if it works, then I promise to help push Livia in your direction once the dust settles,"

"Really?"

"Maybe. Now, what do you say?" Aelia squinted. I considered the potential fallout and then decided to just go for it. If we were discovered, it could jeopardize my chances of finding Priya by removing me from Samuel's favor. Additionally, I had to worry about how Livia would feel if she knew we were manipulating her like this. Even if she never knew, it was highly immoral. Even beyond that, I didn't actually know Heraclius that well, and even if he was a bit of a douchebag, it didn't really warrant what Aelia and I planned to do. On the other hand, though, I was desperate for Livia and Aelia said she was going to do it, anyway. So did it really matter what I did? It's not like I could stop her or anything.

Livia never showed up to work that day, and so after closing up shop, Aelia and I walked together through the crowded Antiochene streets towards her apartment. I never ceased to be amazed by the colorfulness of the city. It was such a contrast with the gray concrete jungles that I was used to. Everything was so vibrant; no matter where I looked, it was clear there was life and a long history behind it. From the buildings to the market to the people themselves, I couldn't help but be in awe, even after being stuck there for so long already. People were chattering loudly in various languages. Hebrew, Latin, Greek, and who knows what else. It was like a cultural mosaic. I was learning that the Romans seemed to generally accept other cultures so long as they were loyal to the Roman State. Otherwise, watch out. They did like to call everyone who wasn't Italian or Greek a "barbarian", though, which wasn't very nice.

Aelia navigated the streets like a pro, knowing every little nook and cranny. I was still getting used to it, but I thought that I was slowly gaining some sense of direction. I could probably find my way back to Samuel's villa from the shop, but that was probably it. I was proud of that. After all, I had only been here for a few weeks.

We passed by a small stage with actors. It was a crude comedy involving a giant black dildo and lots of weird masks. The thirty or so audience members gathering around from the streets were roaring in laughter. I couldn't help but chuckle at the absurd audacity of it all. Aelia stopped by a street food stand to buy a roast mouse, but I refused her offer to buy me one as well. It looked exactly how it sounds. Absolutely disgusting. Aelia couldn't get enough of them. Apparently, they were a delicacy.

Eventually, we arrived at Aelia's apartment. It was like what you'd imagine a modern European flat to be today. One of many crammed along a busy street that has lots of foot traffic. It was definitely much smaller than Samuel's massive villa, but it was cozy enough inside. I imagined that it was better than what most people had. There was a small dining room, a living room, and a kitchen. The walls were colorful, but the house lacked the decadent decorations found in Samel's villas. It smelled strongly of nutmeg and cinnamon, and it was quite stuffy. Aelia felt it was uncomfortable as well, so she opened a couple of windows. The warm breeze blew the red curtains in a dancing pattern that entranced me for a few seconds.

"Wine?" Aelia asked. I decided it would be a bad idea to get drunk in my situation.

"No, thank you," I said, sitting down on one of the couches. It was very comfortable. Aelia offered me some bread as well, and I accepted. It was kind of stale, but I ate it anyway, dipping it into some spiced olive oil.

"So the flour is located in the guild granary,"

"Wait, how would we even frame him? It's not like there's a photo we can take or..." I stopped myself. Whoops. Gotta watch out for that stuff. Sometimes it can just come out.

"What's a photo?" Aelia asked, confused. I scratched my head.

"Nothing, nevermind," I said quickly.

"You're very strange,"

"I know. It's part of the charm," I smiled. Aelia was still confused.

"No, it just makes your strange," she declared

"Anyways, my question still stands," I said.

"What? Oh. Yeah, we'll just steal the flour and then pay off a couple of prostitutes to say that they saw Heraclius do it."

"That doesn't sound like a good plan,"

"It's not like the guild needs a high burden of proof,"

"Is the flour not under guard at night?"

"Yeah, but there's only two guards and I can distract them."

"How?"

"They're men. I'll just seduce them,"

"What? No—that's awful. You don't need to do that."

"It's fine. I'm not gonna fuck them or anything."

"You have a very dirty mouth,"

"I'll bet a hundred sestertii that you have a dirtier mind,"

"That's probably true,"

"So, what do you think?"

"It's possible, but how do you know the prostitutes will deliver?"

"I'll pay them triple their rate,"

"That sounds expensive,"

"It's really not," Aelia sighed. We spent the next few hours just talking. It's not like we were plotting the whole time. Aelia was a fun person to talk to. Very foul-mouthed, kind of like Priya. Unlike Priya, though, she seemed to genuinely like talking with me. I felt I could tell her anything, except of course my true history. I don't think she would believe me. Me, Ashton, from the future? How ludicrous! Yes, ludicrous is the right word. Ludicrous, ridiculous, hilarious, impossible, bullshit.

But I told her what I could, adapting some stories from my past into a sort of Roman lens. Some of them didn't make sense because of these ad hoc changes, and Aelia had questions. I noticed I was getting pretty good at brushing those questions aside. It wasn't hard, really. I would just change the topic. The longer I was there, the more comfortable I got. All of these weeks (months?) and I had never been to Aelia's house. I suppose that was normal. Who would I have been to her house? It was very cozy, that's for sure.

Eventually, I folded and shared some wine with Aelia. It was not my first time drinking, but it was definitely my first time drinking something so strong. I was shocked at how strong it actually was. When I started coughing, Aelia laughed and explained that she never cheated out on wine. That watered down stuff was for peasants, she said, and one thing she was not was a peasant. I agreed even though I had no idea what qualifies as a peasant in this world.

I wondered if I was a peasant back home. Middle class, happy enough, or at least I thought I was. Most of all, if my socioeconomic status were ever to change, it's because I would be moving down the ladder, not up. Whatever. That all seemed like a fever dream now. This was my reality, at least for the time being. What a strange realization that was. Look at where

I was sitting! Talking to a wonderful woman who has been dead for two thousand years.

Apparently, Aelia was a big fan of a certain board game called Tabula. It kind of reminded me of backgammon in the way in which the board looks, but the rules were different. I tried to understand how to play and I think I did a couple rounds of rounds with her, but I was drunk and I lost every time. It all seemed so complicated, but maybe it wasn't. I really don't know.

The whole night smudged into a blur. Aelia started singing something and Greek, and I started humming along. I smiled, and my whole body was warm and fuzzy. My breath stank. I didn't care. Aelia got some more wine, and we started dipping some stale bread into the crimson alcohol. She told me about her favorite chariot racer, who she had had a crush on when she was little. His name was Licinius, and I made fun of her for that.

Licinius. What a name! According to Aelia, Licinius was absurdly muscular and back in his heyday he won almost every race, which of course made all the girls go wild. Especially Aelia. By the time he retired, Licinius had recorded 238 wins with only 16 losses. I asked if he was still around and Aelia said she wasn't sure, but the way she grinned afterwards made me think she knew exactly where he lived.

We talked about my opinions on perfume. I was firmly opposed to it, as they usually gave me a horrendous headache. Aelia agreed, but she said that there were exceptions. She stumbled to her feet and shuffled into the next room. Some stuff clattered around and Aelia reappeared a couple minutes later with a metal bottle of fragrance. She asked me to smell it and I did. I must admit, it wasn't too bad. It smelled kind of fruity, like pomegranate or something. Also, I suppose part of the issue with modern perfumes is all the chemicals and stuff. This was the real deal.

Aelia put the bottle away, but on the way back tripped on her dress. I quickly helped her up, and she said she was fine. Just a minor scrape on her palm. She licked it off the blood, which I thought was a little weird, but I knew that I would probably do the same if no one was around. There was something about her quirkiness that made me drunkenly suggest we go find this Licinius. To my surprise, Aelia agreed. She said she knew exactly where he lived.

"I knew it," I smiled broadly, my vision blurry. We staggered outside. It was late now. How long had we been pent up in her apartment? It didn't seem like it had been that long. The fresh sea breeze blew against my face. I loved that smell. That slightly salty, fresh smell. It was really so fresh. The day time it stunk a bit more, because of all the spices and body odor and perfume. Pomegranate perfume, what a thing. Who could have thought? Maybe it was normal, I have no idea. It's not like I spend my time wandering the halls of shoppers' drug mart. Shoppers drug mart. I wonder if I will ever enter another shoppers drug mart in my life. Or a Rexall drug store. Or London Drugs. I would probably be fine going without. They were never my favorite stores. Mind you, I might need some of that modern medicine. It definitely would have come in handy when I was sick at the fish sauce factory. God damn, that place stunk.

After a bizarre fifteen-minute walk through the dark and narrow Antiochene streets, we appeared at a house only slightly more grand than Aelia's. The door had gold lettering that read Licinius the Champion.

"I guess this is it," I chuckled. We both knocked very loudly. There was no response at first, but just as I was about to say we should turn back, we heard a voice boom from the other side of the door.

"WHO KNOCKS AT THIS UNGODLY HOUR?" The man bellowed. Aelia and I struggled to constrain our giggles. We didn't answer him. I could barely breathe. The man opened the door. He had a massive beer belly and a scruffy gray beard. He reminded me of that time when Thor was fat. Which movie was that? It was one of the Avengers.

"Hello," Aelia said awkwardly. Licinius just scowled.

"What do you want?" He coughed. We tried not to laugh, but the giggle came out, anyway. This just made Licinius even more angry.

"I—I'm—I'm a big fan," Aelia struggled to speak. Licinius tried to punch me, but even in my drunken state, I could duck quick enough. We ran. I could hear him hollering after us, calling us stupid hooligans. It was hilarious.

Eventually, we had to catch our breath. I made a fat joke about Licinius and Aelia laughed along. Somehow, we had reached the docks. It was strange looking out onto the Mediterranean at night. The moon and the stars were unexpectedly bright. There weren't many lanterns or anything, so it was still much darker than I was used to as a city boy. But the night sky was so unbelievably bright. It was unbelievable. Aelia and I sat down on a gray brick sea wall and gazed out into the distance. A dog was barking somewhere far away, and I could hear laughing from a party a few blocks away. Otherwise, it was extraordinarily peaceful. We passed out there, staring into the mysterious night sky.

19

Chapter 19

Before

"Get the fuck out of my face before I knock your teeth in, boy."
My brother was beaten quite a lot while he was growing up. There
was a group of guys who picked on him because he had stubby
fingers and a rather short stature. They liked to make fun of his
exceptionally large forehead as well. My mom always defended
Caleb. The thing was, after all the bullying, Caleb was pretty cruel
as well. I might feel inclined to experience empathy for him had he
not been so cruel to me and others. I suppose he was just lashing
out, trying to gain control of a situation. Any situation. Caleb took
what he could get. Which was fine, I suppose. But it didn't make
me like him much. He was kind of an asshole, in my opinion. After
12 you kind of lose the age card, don't you? Caleb was 14 now,
and he was irritating as shit. He whined about every little thing.
You see, some people are complainers. They just can't take care of
anything on their own. So all they'll do is make sure everyone feels
miserable along with them. Yes, there are good complainers too.
Those are the types of people who can talk about their troubles and
make people laugh at the same time. Caleb was not one of those

people.

Anyways, back to the quote. So basically last week Caleb got himself into some trouble again. The ringleader of bullies targeting Caleb decided it would be a fantastic idea to call Caleb Megamind in front of Caleb's only remaining friend, Jakob. This was a serious miscalculation on behalf of Enzo. Yes, the bully's name is Enzo. No, he is not a crooked pizza delivery man in his free time. He is thirteen years old, although I suppose it's possible. (Caleb's main bully is a year younger than him. It's pathetic, I know.)

So, Caleb gets insulted like this and instead of firing back with a witty remark, Caleb stayed quiet and plotted his revenge. Typical Caleb. Always plotting. He's a sneaky son of a bitch, he really is. So anyways Caleb took a dump in a paper bag and lit it on fire, leaving the burning bag on Jakob's doorstep. I did see someone do something like that on a TV show once, but it was dog poop. Unfortunately for Caleb, he was caught sneaking away by Jakob's father. So that's the "knock your teeth in '' line. Yeah, Caleb could have been beaten that day. There's no telling what a drunk, washed-up accountant might do when he catches a whiny 14-year-old boy leaving a bag of burning human excrement on his doorstep. Just a recipe for disaster. Caleb was lucky he wasn't hospitalized that night.

Jakob's father did manage to control himself, though. He did the rational thing and let Caleb go without touching him. Probably for the best. After all, it doesn't look good to your employers when the police call saying that you've been arrested for assaulting a 14-year-old. At least it's not sexual assault. Whoa! Better watch out for the priests and boy scout leader. That was a rough one there. Better tone that shit down for you young readers out there. I hope there are no young readers. Although that would be amusing to me if there were.

Jakob's father called the school the very next morning and informed them what had happened. Despite my mother's protestations, there was nothing anyone could do. Caleb was suspended from school. Instead of punishing him, we decided to spend September long weekend at a campsite about two hours outside the city. It was an awful campground. We had come here once before and I had assumed we would never return. The amenities were catastrophically un-maintained. There was no beach. No fish in the lake. Worst of all, no ice cream shop.

At least that's what I remembered best about the campground from when we had last been there. I was ten at the time, and I wanted ice cream and fish and a nice sandy beach to make my sandcastles. Don't judge me. Alright? Is that clear? Good. Now, when my father suggested this campground, I was not enthusiastic. Nevertheless, there were some good hiking trails and I could not argue with going to get some fresh air and peace.

School was terrible so far this year. It had only been a week and my girlfriend had left me because she had to focus on her schooling. We are both academically inclined. That's why we got together a few months into grade ten. Regardless, I saw it coming for some time. We had only kissed once, and it was gross, if I'm being honest. She had eaten tuna for lunch that day and we should have considered eating some mints. There was no attraction there at all. Of course, we enjoyed each other's company. She was one of my closest friends. It just made little sense to date each other if we didn't have the "animal attraction," as they say.

I enjoyed the status that being a taken guy gave me. I'm not ashamed to say as much, either. It is just a fact of life that, without that status boost, I probably would have experienced some degree of bullying. My high school was a typical high school. We lived in Canada, in Edmonton. So it wasn't that bad. Not like the United

States schooling system, at least. That was something us Canadian teenagers always liked to say. "At least we are not as bad as America"

Come to think of it, a lot of Canadians liked to say that. It made us feel better about ourselves. Like we were special. Like we were good people. People lie to themselves all the time. It's just a survival instinct. I know that. Most people know that truth as well. Yet they do it anyway. Why shouldn't they?

The first day of the trip went well. We unpacked relatively smoothly. Back when we were younger, there was a big fuss over keeping the camper clean, but nowadays, even Caleb helped out with setting it up and things went fairly quickly. No more basins of water to rinse our feet before going inside. We were cleaner than that now. More careful, I suppose. Was that a good thing? I wasn't so sure. In a lot of ways, I missed my childhood innocence. The days when I could go play hide and seek with dozens of kids in the forest. Just run around and hide, desperately trying not to get tagged. The days when I didn't care when I got a little dirt in my shoes, when I returned home with blackened socks. When I had to rinse my feet before entering the trailer after our barbeque dinner. I miss those days, because I know they will never return. Sure, new unique memories are on their way. I will always be me. But I will never be a child again. The young Ashton Beachum is dead forever and there's nothing I can do about that. All I can do is move on.

"Come on, Ashton, let's go play some ball," Caleb asked me that first night.

"Ball?" I replied, in disbelief. Caleb never asked me to play ball. He resented the sport. What was he up to? Nothing good, I imagine.

"Yeah!" Caleb was beaming like a small-headed dog.

"What are you, a rapper?" I grumbled.

"That's what people call it, right?" He grinned.

"Yeah, they do call it that," I sighed.

"Well, so why are you making such a big deal about it?" Caleb narrowed his gaze.

"I'm not making a deal about—"

"Yes you are,"

"If you want the truth, it's kind of cringe how you speak like that,"

"Speak like what?"

"Play ball. You my Brutha. Things like that,"

"'Are you suggesting it's racist?'"

"I'm suggesting it's cringy,"

"Why are you using the term cringy, anyway?"

"Because I'm a teenager and I can."

"There's ya answer then," Caleb snickered. Such a menace.

"Fine,"

"So?" Persistent as ever.

"Fine." I rubbed my eyes and resigned myself to his demands.

We played ball, or rather, we tried to play. Caleb didn't know what the hell he was doing. It was embarrassing. Some people on the half-overgrown pavement court gave us looks. Why were they giving us looks? After all, it was just a campsite. They didn't have to be so serious. Maybe that sounds hypocritical coming from me. You readers are hearing my nasty internal dialogue. I assure you, though, I'm pleasant enough. No side eyes from me just because you play like an arthritic grandma.

After about an hour, we quit and headed back to our campsite for the first dinner of our three-night stay. My father was angry with Caleb, but my mother was not. Neither was I, honestly. The whole thing was rather funny to me, if I'm being honest. Of course, I couldn't tell anyone that aside from my closest friends.

I wonder what those friends are up to now. One problem that I don't have is an inability to socialize; I do talk with plenty of people, and I even joined the badminton team back in grade ten. Unfortunately, I had to quit last year to focus on my academics. At least that's what I told myself. I broke up with Jennifer around the same time. We called her Jen, of course. Jennifer has far too many syllables for us teenagers. After all, we were the same people who brought you rizz (charisma) and suss (suspect.) By comparison, the nickname Jen was nothing at all. Oh and apparently the low down is no longer the low down. It's now known as "lore." I found that out when Jen first broke up with me. I started telling people it was mutual, and I mentioned a couple of stories about our relationship. Even though it was mostly mutual, that was somewhat misleading.

Although I didn't have romantic feelings for her, it kind of sucked for her to ask to break up. No more status, and no more guaranteed conversations with Jen. She was a good person to talk to. An active listener, they call those types of people. I hope I'm an active listener as well, but I know deep down I'm probably not. Anyways, when I told these classmates if that's what you want to call them, when I told them these stories they said "ooh, the Ashton lore." That's when I found out what lore meant. I'm always behind on these things. People say it makes me strange. I say it makes me...a rizzler.

My friends. I wonder what is happening to them. I suppose they are studying or playing Xbox, or with Jim, neither. You see, Jim had a real controlling girlfriend. Real bad. It was like nothing I've ever seen, and I haven't seen a lot. Yes, you read that right. I haven't seen a lot. But from what I do not know, it was a deeply unhealthy relationship and plenty of people agree with me. Unfortunately, Jim's still stuck up on her. She literally flipped on him like a coin, and he can't bring himself to hate her. I don't understand that.

The story is, his girlfriend was being all nice to him and they were having a great time. They had dated for a few months. One day, they were out on a date to the mall and she flipped like Jekyll and Hyde. It was unbelievable. One minute everything was fine and the next she received some texts and she changed her tune and broke things off. She walked away like it was nothing. Jim was left sobbing in the mall, feeling devastated. He almost drove home, but luckily some strangers managed to stop him and help with his breathing. He probably would have crashed if no one did anything. I had to drive him home. I've never seen him that distraught before, at least in recent memory.

Jim is my best friend, I've known him all my life. Or since I was five or six or whatever. No one really knows what happened, but she blocked him and sent him the most cruel and demeaning text message I've ever seen. He couldn't respond because she blocked him right after sending the message. They listened to the same music and apparently she even unfollowed him on Spotify and deleted their mix. How petty can you get? I don't think he did anything, but he must have. However, I saw the text, and she didn't really accuse him of anything. She just called him hard to look at and a "charity case from the start." Apparently, he also had "bad manners" and was "disgusting", and that's why she wanted to break things off. I've seen her in the halls joking with her friends like nothing happened. Like he was nothing. So I felt terrible for him.

Anyways, he is not my only friend. We are part of a close-knit group of friends that I've known for a while. There's Mike, John and Roger. Jen was a part of the group for a while, but after what happened a couple of weeks ago, her position is unclear. I'm sure in the end she'll still hang out with us. We've had too much fun.

We arrived at the campsite. My dad had cooked up some spicy Italian sausages. They smelled delicious, and the faint scent of smoke in the air from the increasing amount of campfires in the area really completed the feel. It was comforting to be back in a campground, even one as dull as this particular location. For all my resentment of Caleb's complaining, I sure do a lot of it myself. At least I keep my mouth shut, though. That's the way it ought to be, as far as I'm concerned.

"Where have you two been?" My mom grinned.

"Just playin' ball," Caleb exclaimed. I sighed.

"Yep," I affirmed.

"Well, you are just in time," my mother sat down at the set table. Paper plates and red solo cups, plastic cutlery, and plenty of love. Just the way I like my campground dinners. We had the sausage with rice and boiled carrots. It was delicious, aside from the carrots, which were bland due to overboiling. I did not complain, though.

My dad sat down last, with a loud grunt. His beer belly sagged over his belt, and when he sat down, this unhealthy reality became ever more apparent. Apparently, my dad was an athlete in his formative years in high school and college (yes, college), but he hadn't set foot in a gym for the better part of two decades. He was a hard worker, though.

"Hey there bucko," my dad would sometimes call me bucko. Especially when I was younger, not so much now. Whenever something was wrong, or I had a hard day at school, I was no longer Ashton. I was Bucko.

"Yeah?" I replied.

"Pass the salt, would ya?" I passed the salt. We ate in relative silence, and following the clean-up, I built the fire. Cabin-style. I never understood those who made their fire teepee style. It just doesn't burn as well. A good cabin will always outperform a

teepee.

As we sat by the smoky hearth, the crimson sky slowly fading into darkness. Heat blurred my vision, like ripples on an untouched lake. The distant chatters of fellow campers drifted in and out of focus as the sometimes tedious family conversations hit a wall and silence descended upon us.

Eventually, fatigue set in and we all went to sleep. I always slept better while camping. My bed at home was more comfortable, of course. Maybe it was just all the activity, or maybe it was the relative lack of worries. But whenever I was out in nature, I always slept well. It was a deep, dark, dreamless slumber that consumed the night and transformed my world into one of light.

The sound of birds chirping in the distance and the faint scent of bacon-grease fried pancakes nudged me back into consciousness. Briefly, I didn't know where I was. There was a split second of panic before I realized what was happening, and I couldn't stop myself from smiling a bit in amusement. Early onset dementia. Hopefully not, although you can never really know for sure.

After getting changed, it became clear to me that I needed a shower. My hair was getting greasy. It was not nearly as long as some of my fellow teenagers. A lot of them seem to like the puffy mushroom style. Mike and Jim jumped on that train. They can't seem to comprehend why no man under the age of 23 has the same haircut; could it be perhaps that it's ugly as hell? They call me weird. Fughettaboutit! Get outta here! You know what I mean?

We ate breakfast, once again mostly in silence. The solemnity of the feast was punctuated by the occasional inquiry from my mom about various mundane things. How did you sleep? What will you two do today? How is your schooling going? Those types of questions. The types of questions that exemplify boredom, ignorance, and neglect. Of course, she was not a neglectful mother.

That's not what I'm suggesting. I am simply saying that we, and especially Caleb, are neglectful children. Therefore, she is ignorant of us and we are ignorant of her. Our father as well.

Neglect breeds ignorance, which inevitably breeds boredom. I have to admit, it is a somewhat dysfunctional family. Though, to be fair, our situation is not nearly as bad as some families that I hear about through the schoolyard gossip. Parents aren't divorced, there is no abuse. They do love us. We love each other. That is not in dispute. We just don't have that flow that some families do. I suppose that's fine as long as I don't ever go looking for such a flow. Such searches can never end well.

Caleb could be cruel to my parents. He was spoiled, just like me, I suppose. Except he didn't know it. Caleb would test my mom right to the limit. Nothing was ever enough for Caleb. He was a liar, too. I hate liars, always have. There's no use for them because they have no credibility. Once I know someone is a habitual liar, I stay as far away from them as possible. Can't trust someone like that with anything. The more someone lies, the better they get at it. Sometimes, though, it gets so bad that they'll lie for no reason. Just little things. So not only does it affect trust, it also just bludgeons any chances of normal communication in any sort of relationship, whether it be platonic or romantic. However, unfortunately my brother is one of those people. A habitual liar. There's not much anyone can do about it anymore. He's fourteen, and maybe this is just how he is. But I hope not. Nevertheless, he is my brother, so I can't just avoid him like I would anyone else like him. We did have our good moments together when we were younger, after all.

I think he knows I don't like him, though. Sometimes I feel bad about that because he gets bullied and he can become seriously melancholic. I know he goes to a therapist for his depression. He's had depression for a while now. I'm not sure about the specifics.

I'm sure if I really wanted to know, I could ask. No one really wants to discuss it though, so I don't say a word.

To be totally honest, the whole thing strikes me as sort of false. If he can lie about this and that, why couldn't he just make up an excuse for his misbehavior as well? At what point do you just give up and say you're not an amiable person? I know this sounds quite harsh, because it is. I know I'm probably not a good person for thinking these thoughts. That's the difference, though. It's not like I'm telling him these things straight-up. I don't tell anyone about my feelings towards Caleb. Because, unlike him, I'm not a complainer. At some point, he needs to step up and be better. I'm not sure he ever will, which worries me. There's so many examples of his dishonesty. At this point, he lies daily, and I have mostly given up trying to counter him. However, some lies stick out more than others. Some cause more damage than the rest.

One such example was when Caleb lied about getting attacked by another boy at his school. The boy had been bullying him, which is pretty awful. However, Caleb struck back in the worst possible way. He told everyone who would listen that this boy (Roger) had groped his crotch twice. The teachers and eventually the Police got involved. Caleb was 12 at the time. After a brief investigation, it was clear that Caleb was lying. Caleb confessed to my parents that night, and after getting grounded and suspended for two weeks, nothing more was said of it. No one forgot, though.

Other times, it would be more innocent scenarios. For example, sometimes he would stay up to three in the morning on a school night. Other times, he would lie to my parents to hang out with Jakob. He said he was studying. Caleb almost never studied. It was reflected in his grades. My brother had a 49 average overall. There was a real possibility that he wouldn't be passing Grade 8.

Most of the time, though, he just sulked in his room. Caleb would yell at my parents for no good reason, and by this point, they were usually too tired to yell back. So Caleb would just spend hours doing God-knows-what on his iPhone while the rest of us tried to live our lives. It sounds like no big deal, but it can weigh one down after a while.

My brother asked to go for a hike after breakfast, and I obliged. I wasn't really sure what my parents were going to do; perhaps they would just spend their time reading.

A light breeze tickled my skin, goosebumps began to form. There was a bit of a nip in the air. I was glad I had decided to wear a hoodie and jeans. We walked past an attractive brunette about my age and I couldn't help but look over at her. She had a beautiful face, with steel-blue eyes and unblemished skin. I wonder if she is my age. Maybe—-

"Ashton?" Caleb's voice was unusually weak.

"Yes, Caleb?" I asked.

"Do you ever have regrets?" Caleb looked at me with a blank expression.

"Yeah, of course. Why?"

"I'm just wondering. Do you know what's happening tonight?"

"No. Do you?"

"No," Neither of us said anything else. We just walked in silence down that nice hiking trail. The birds were chirping, and the loop took about forty minutes in total. It was nice, but a little boring. If only I had known that would end up somehow being the last conversation I would ever have with my brother.

After we finished the hike, I ran into the girl and asked her to walk with me. I figured I had nothing to lose. After losing my girlfriend, I figured a rebound might be the normal thing to do. I wasn't really interested in dating her or even kissing her, but I was bored and she was pretty. Caleb said he was heading back to the *campsite. I simply nodded and hesitated for a moment as I saw a flicker of sorrow in Caleb's sullen eyes before he turned away from me forever.*

The brunette girl was wearing an expensive-looking white sweater, and she turned out to be from a different city than me. It would have never worked. She was kind of shallow, from the sounds of it. Nevertheless, we had a pleasant conversation. Her name was Rebecca and apparently she was a big fan of reality television and avocado toast. Also, her friends were spreading rumors about her. At least some of them. Rebecca said she was happy that now she knew who to trust. I avoided telling her lots of personal things about me, but I'm sure she figured out plenty anyways. Despite all appearances, I suspected she was intelligent. We exchanged contact information, but I could tell that neither of us wanted to pursue anything further beyond an occasional conversation.

When I returned to the campsite, I was surprised to find that Caleb wasn't there. I played some cards with my mom, but we started to get worried once the sun started to go down. Just when we were about to go looking for him, Caleb showed up all rejuvenated. He said he just needed some alone time. No one said anything to that, not even my mom. We invited him to play cards, but he refused, saying that he was tired and needed to get some sleep. He hobbled his way into the camper and he barely talked for me for the rest of the trip. I remember feeling guilty for ignoring him, but then again...he was just Caleb.

20

Chapter 20

I woke up to find myself cuddling Aelia. She was awake too, and we awkwardly moved away from each other. My head was pounding, and the sun was blinding. It was dawn, and some people were already walking around on the docks, getting ready for their morning fishing. Some seagulls squawked nearby. It was already getting hot out. I felt sweaty and disgusting. The sun was scorching my retinas, so I had to squint. Forcing myself to my feet, a sudden wave of nausea overtook me. I managed to get a few steps away from Aelia before puking up the bread and wine.

"A lightweight, I see," Aelia chuckled, as I lurched forward and spewed another round of vomit all over the ground. I felt a lot better after that second puke, but the headache was still there.

"Whoa.." I moaned. Aelia laughed again. She seemed unaffected by the previous night's escapades.

"Come on, big buddy. Let's get you to the Villa. I'll take care of the shop today. Just be ready for tonight." She threw an arm around me and somehow I made it back to Samuel's house.

The maid, Duccidava, shook her head when we stumbled in.

"Where have you been?" Duccidava asked.

"You sound like my mother," I grumbled without thinking.

"No one knew what happened to you. You should tell someone about your plans before disappearing for the night. The master was waiting at the dinner table for you,"

"I'm sorry,"

"It's very disrespectful. He won't be back until this afternoon. I suggest you wait here until then."

"Of course. I'm kind of messed up anyways,"

"Yes, I can see that," Duccidava sighed. Aelia waved and left me to roam the villa for the rest of the day. No one was around except Duccidava, and she was busy cleaning the house and preparing food. So I just laid in my room where there was a cool breeze and I contemplated the events of the previous day. Was I really ready to become a criminal? I wasn't sure. Besides, Heraclius didn't deserve what we were going to do to him. As far as I knew, the only thing that he was guilty of was potentially taking advantage of Livia for her money. However, that was unproven and there were many nuances to those types of situations. There was a good possibility that he might be doing something but he was doing so unintentionally. He could have malicious intent, but there was no proof. I decided that if I was going to do anything with Aelia, I would demand proof first.

After the awful sleep on the docks, I decided to try to take a nap. Hopefully that would take the edge away. It's not like I had any Tylenol or anything. Duccidava came into my room and gave me some medicinal tea before I drifted off to sleep. It tasted kind of funny but I drank it anyway.

Home. The house where I had played with plastic swords and lego. The house where I cooked in my little easy oven to impress my parents. The house where I spent many evenings watching television with my brother in the basement.

I sat there in my living room and let the steam burn my skin. It was scalding, my skin was red. I was nauseous from the pain, black spots dotting my blurry vision. Why was there so much steam? How could it—-

A sharp pain shot up my leg and into my sternum. It knocked the wind right out of me. I fell off my dad's cloth lazy boy chair and slammed into the hardwood floors. The relative cold of the oak was soothing to my scalded face.

Voices. Someone was speaking. I tried to scream but just like always no sound came out. I lay there writhing on the floor, blinded by pain. I saw my front door and started crawling, but it was no use. The voices were getting louder now. SHUT UP!!!

Duccidava shook me awake. I was drenched in sweat, and I didn't feel any better than when I did when I first took a nap. If anything, I felt worse. Sickly, even. My heart was thumping and my muscles ached. My brain felt squished in my tiny skull and when I went to rub my wet temples, I felt a bulging vein on either side. It seemed like my eyes were bulging. There was nausea.

I groaned and tried to sit up. I wasn't able to. Duccidava said that she had heard me screaming in my sleep and she decided to wake me. She offered some more tea, and I accepted, but I also decided to ask for a bucket as well. Also some water. I decided I needed to be hydrated. This was all just another reason that I couldn't frame Heraclius tonight, I told myself. Yet I had a growing feeling that as soon as Aelia showed up that she would convince me. The woman really had a way with people. I guess that's why she was such a good salesman.

Against my will, Duccidava cut my inner forearm and started bloodletting. I tried convincing her that it was a bad idea, but she wouldn't listen and I was in no position to argue to get up and leave. My head was spinning, and I was pretty sure that the headache had developed into a migraine. I convinced her to draw the curtains and avoid any light getting in. As the day went on (apparently my nap lasted less than an hour,) the room became hotter and hotter. This just worsened my headache, and I almost threw up at least three times. Unfortunately, nothing would come up.

The bloodletting was uncomfortable and did absolutely nothing to help, but Duccidava thought that she was helping and she didn't cut deep. So there was that. It was all just so surreal. I was beginning to worry that this was more than just a bad hangover. Maybe I had eaten something wrong, or caught a bug. It all seemed so extraordinarily unlucky considering that I had been sick not so long ago.

I stared up at the ceiling and realized how fortunate I was that I was free. Sure, it was unlucky to get sick again so soon. But last time I had been a slave in a damp cell all alone. Now here I was in bed with an ad hoc nurse attending to me 24/7 and a beautiful ceiling to stare at.

Why didn't people decorate their ceilings anymore? It really does add so much character to a house. The ceiling in this bedroom was decorated with an elaborate fresco of some sort of mythological battle. A muscular man in heroic nudity wielded a spear and was fighting a three-headed serpent. He was aboard a single row ship, and the waves were rising high all around him in a dramatic storm. It looked like he was going to be killed. I wondered what myth it was from. I really should have listened more to the lessons of Knotts. Maybe I would have learned something. Did he ever discuss mythology? I couldn't remember. I did a mythology project in the seventh grade. That was a lot of fun. I think I researched Poseidon. Kind of basic, I know. But I was young and what can you do?

After drinking about three more cups of herbal tea and six cups of water, I drifted off to sleep again. This time, there were no dreams. Just a nice, deep slumber fueled by pure exhaustion. It felt amazing. By the time I woke up about six hours later, it was already night time and I felt like a new man.

Apparently Samuel, Livia, and Aelia had all been waiting for me downstairs. Aelia had explained the situation to them and they all laughed. EVen Samuel. I still couldn't get over how kind he was being to me. It was much more than I had expected. He was really going above and beyond, and in that moment as he was laughing along with the rest of them I felt a deep surge of real affection towards him. Towards all of them. It was more than I could have ever asked for.

Duccidava cooked a nice big fish for us. It was basted in a lemon butter sauce, and it reminded me of Red Lobster. I had never gone to the Red Lobster more than twice but just eating this fish with this specific type of sauce brought me back. I had last gone there a couple years ago to celebrate the birthday of my friend Jim. I got him a book for his birthday, because he was really into reading at that point in time. I remember he was happy with my gift, but I can't remember what the name of the book was. It was a high fantasy, I knew that. The kind with a map at the beginning and lots of dragons throughout. The kind of dragons that talked. But what was it called? It seemed like a whole other life. I wondered if I would go to a Red Lobster ever again.

"Sorry about my absence from the shop yesterday," Livia

said with her lovable smile. Aelia smiled back politely, but I could tell she was upset. Samuel explained that she had been with him on a personal day. Apparently they had gone fishing for the day. I found that kind of bizarre to think; fathers and daughters would be doing the same thing two millennia later. Nevertheless, I believed him because he hadn't given me a reason not to. I guess Aelia and I were just wrong. She hadn't run off with Heraclius for the day. I asked if this fish was one that they had caught, and their smiles faded. They did not catch anything except a very small fish that they decided to let go. This one that they were eating was from the market.

Samuel said that he was getting close to uncovering the identity of our enslavers, which made me feel strange. Was it excitement that I felt? Or was it dread? I couldn't tell. The rest of the dinner was relatively quiet, aside from Livia mentioning that she was planning on cooking tomorrow, which apparently was very unusual. She was still deciding what meal she was going to cook, but she was craving lamb. We all supported her plans.

After the dinner, Aelia approached me and said that it was time to go. I hesitated and then told her how I really felt. It wasn't right to frame Heraclius. I would need proof that he was leeching off of her, and I couldn't see how she could give me that proof.

"What kind of proof do you need?" Aelia demanded. Despite her short stature, Aelia could be quite intimidating. There was just something about the way she carried herself.

"I'm not sure. It's just that if we're going to ruin his life, then I need to be sure," I explained. Even just talking about this in the middle of the dining room made me uncomfortable. Everyone had already left but someone could be hear from the next room.

"Who said— -" Aelia started.

"Let's go outside," I grabbed her by the shoulder and she shrugged it off. We stepped out onto the streets.

"Who said anything about ruining his life?" Aelia asked.

"You did!"

"This isn't going to ruin his life. It'll embarrass him and it might ruin his relationship with Livia. He might even have to move away! But he's still rich. Nothing's going to change for him,"

"If he's rich then why would he be stealing flour?"

"Because he can and because the hookers said so,"

"The hookers? I still don't understand how you can trust them,"

"They'll pull through as long as we pay, alright?"

"If you say so. But I still need proof,"

"You want proof? I've seen him go to the whore house with Livia's money,"

"What?"

"His daddy only gives him Denarius, but when he asks for Livia's money she gives him sestertii. He never has sestertii. Only Livia,"

"Maybe he just— -"

"There's more. I talked to some of the prostitutes to ask about him, and apparently he brags about how he milks his father and girlfriend for everything they've got. He says he's got it so good, and that they would never go out of business as long as he was alive,"

"The fuck?"

"Yeah, that's what I said,"

"Why would he go to...go there when he has Livia?"

"Don't ask me,"

"Seriously though, she's beautiful,"

"Okay, calm down. Last thing I want to see at this time at night is a little tent in your trousers,"

"Little?"

"Oh cry me a river. So is this enough proof for you?"

"Why didn't you tell me all this before?"

"Because it's disgusting and I don't like talking about it,"

"Wait...how did you even—"

"I saw him go into the whorehouse by complete accident. I was just walking by doing an errand. I mean that's bad enough, fooling around. So I decided to go in and ask about him. And this is why they'll be trustworthy,"

"He gives them good business though,"

"So? Even prostitutes have morals. They know an asshole when they see one. Trust me, they will help if we pay them. They might even do it for free," I couldn't argue with that, so I agreed. We started walking towards the whorehouse. It didn't take long before we had entered a part of the city that I hadn't been in yet. I never let my sight leave Aelia's back. It would be easy to get lost in these dim streets. There was still something viscerally terrifying about the dark. Some sort of primal fear etched into our genetic code. I certainly still had it. Maybe in Canada I didn't need that fear anymore, maybe it had become useless. In this world I'm not sure if that was the case. In this world, monsters might actually be lurking around the corner. Maybe that's the same as in our modern society as well. They just hide better, and I guess people are better at catching them. Regardless, I didn't want to be here longer than necessary.

A group of bums huddled around a street fire were laughing and drinking. Maybe it was the same people that I had heard last night. Doubtful. One guy glared at us but quickly returned his gaze to his friends. The streets became dirtier. Horse manure became more common, and when we made a turn, we had to use the large raised stones that served as sort of a crosswalk so that we didn't soak our sandals in the filth. A baby was crying. A dog was barking. At one point, I heard a blood curdling woman's scream. It sounded like it was nearby. I asked Aelia about it but she said it wasn't our problem.

Even with all of this noise, the streets were deserted aside from that group huddled together around the fire. They must know that it's far too dangerous to be wandering around at night, perhaps knowing something that we didn't. Maybe it was just common sense. I wasn't particularly eager to find out. Eventually though we did reach our destination. There were rowdy noises coming from inside, and there were lanterns hanging from the walls. Colorful pornographic imagery was painted everywhere. It was.. shocking. Every position you can imagine was just painted. Right there. For everyone to see. They definitely hadn't mastered the art of subtlety. Aelia knocked a couple times. An older woman opened the door, and I gasped, looking away. She was completely topless, her wrinkled oversized breasts just hanging out. I felt my face grow warm. Can't unsee that.

"What's the matter, hunny? Never seen titties before?"

"Can you put a top on, Cornelia?" Aelia sighed, patting my back. Cornelia hesitated for a moment, looking at me and then back at Aelia.

"Such prudes," Cornela muttered, and she went to get a top.

"Thank you," Aelia said, and she stepped inside. I followed her. The sounds were even worse. Screams, moans, grunts, thumps, the occasional crash. It stunk like candle wax, incense, and body odor. There were more pornographic drawings inside. Every position you can imagine.

"What's with the..art?" I asked Aelia.

"You're acting like you've never been to one of these places before," Aelia chuckled. She brushed her hair behind her ears and crossed her arms.

"I haven't!" I cried.

"I guess you're sort of young. Well, the drawings are so the customer can pick out how he wants it," Aelia explained somewhat distractedly. She was looking at something on the other side of the room, but I had no idea what it was.

"Oh," I muttered. Aelia let out another light laugh. Cornelia returned wearing an oversized white shirt.

"What can I do for you?" Cornelia asked pleasantly. Her eyes drifted to me. I looked away awkwardly.

"We need two of your girls to testify that they saw Heraclius Amata steal two bags of flour from the guild granary near his house,"

"I see," Cornelia mumbled.

"I trust you'll be discreet," Aelia gave Cornelia a big bag of coins. Cornelia smiled.

"Of course. You can count on us when the time comes,"

"I appreciate it,"

"Do either of you wish to have complimentary services as well?" Cornelia asked as we turned for the door.

"I'm afraid not," Aelia said quickly, and we left. We were walking for about five minutes before Aelia spoke again.

21

Chapter 21

It was well into the evening by the time we reached the granary. Like Aelia had said, there were two guards posted outside the doors. They were laughing and drinking from a leather flask. A mosquito buzzed and bit me on the arm. I slapped it away in surprise. I hadn't seen any mosquitoes yet. There was a big, red, itchy bump. I sighed.

"So now what?" I asked.

"Just slink to the back of the building. I will distract them like planned," Aelia whispered, glancing over my shoulder at the guards. It was very dim, but there were lanterns outside the granary building. The granary was this great big stone structure, with white marble pillars and a dome.

"Wouldn't the back door be locked?"

"There is no back door," Aelia said quickly.

"Then how—"

"You're going to have to go right behind them without making any noise," Aelia looked me in the eye and squeezed my shoulders in a show of solidarity.

"How the hell am I going to do that?" I cried. Aelia shushed me.

"Just do as I say!" She rasped hoarsely.

"Fine," I grumbled. Aelia approached the guards. One of them was much taller than the other one. They were both kind of rough-looking, with cysts on their faces and greasy hair. It was clear even from a distance that their body odor was rank. I went around the back of the building like Aelia said and waited. After a minute or two, I could hear voices. Aelia was flirting with them. The guards were laughing at her, calling her a slut. I was surprised to feel some fury building inside me. This was not the way it was supposed to go.

Nevertheless, they were distracted. It was working. So I started to slowly make my way along the side of the building, keeping my arm against the gray brick wall. My bladder was getting heavy, and I cursed myself for not taking a piss before embarking on this whole thieving endeavor. Look at me, Ashton Beachum! A thief! Sneaking up behind a pair of armed guards so I can take a bag of flour or two. Just to frame the boyfriend of a girl that I like. Absolutely crazy. What's more, I still had no idea how I was going to get the flour out from behind them, even if I managed to sneak my way in. This was all such a bad idea.

By the time I reached the front of the building, the guards were having a full-on argument with Aelia about something. I wasn't listening. I was too focused on the task at hand. It seemed like they were probably distracted enough, so I tip-toed behind them and tried to open the door to the granary. Unfortunately, it was locked. I guess we never thought of that. The sound of me trying to open the door alerted one of the guards, and he spun around with his sword. His face was painted in a scowl.

"Thief!" he cried. I bolted without so much as a second thought. Running as fast as I could. I could hear the footsteps of one of the guards chasing behind me. I had no idea where I was going. All I knew was that I needed to get away. My heart was pounding. I was gasping for air, and I cursed myself for not exercising over these last few months. The footsteps on the street were getting louder. I couldn't think about Aelia, if she was captured or what. What would they do to us if we were caught? The footsteps sounded so close. One foot in front of another. I was running in big strides. Almost skipping. My lungs were burning. I could taste blood on the back of my throat. My feet were aching. Why wouldn't this guy just give up? I tried turning down a narrow alleyway to lose him. He sounded so close. Was he calling out after me? Everything was a blur. He was going to catch me. He was going to catch me and——

I tripped and face-planted onto the brick road. My fall was cushioned by some soft manure. I tried to get to my feet, but the guard that was chasing me kicked me hard in the ribs, knocking me back down. The guard was just as winded as me. If I had just made it a bit farther, I could have outrun him. He spat in my face and cuffed me. The metal was cold and coarse, not like the shiny cuffs that you'd see in the modern world. He brought me to my feet and walked me back to Aelia. She was cuffed as well.

"You two aren't very smart, are you?" The guy guarding Aelia said.

"Guess not," I admitted. My throat was still dry from all the running. I took deep breaths to try to calm myself down. Athletic fatigue was replaced with anxiety and fear. My attempts at deep breathing quickly devolved into hyperventilation.

"Calm down, kid," the guard behind me said. Aelia was staring at her feet, uncharacteristically quiet. She had a black eye. I could tell she was just as ashamed as me.

"What...what happens now?" I asked. They just sighed.

"We'll hand you over to the authorities in the morning. In the meantime, you two will have to stay with us for the rest of the night while we stand guard," the guy behind me explained. So that's what we did. It seemed like forever until sunrise finally came, although it was probably only a few hours. We sat on the ground like little children in time-outs, left to think with the consequences of our actions. It was humiliating, to say the least. Around dawn, Heraclius appeared all chipper. He smiled at the guards and then frowned when he saw us. I wondered what he was doing here so early. Heraclius was many things, but a poor worker he was not.

"What happened?" Heraclius asked, sounding genuinely concerned.

"Caught these two trying to rob the granary last night," One of the guards yawned.

"Is this true?" Heraclius looked at us with shock and disappointment. I felt another wave of shame wash over me. Neither Aelia nor I responded. Heraclius rubbed his eyes.

"You know these two?" The other guard asked. Heraclius let out a short chuckle.

"Yes, I know them. Listen, I'll take it from here," Heraclius said.

"Yeah, whatever. They didn't hurt anyone or anything," One of the guards said. They uncuffed us and Heraclius angrily made us hall his flour to his father's bakery as punishment. He didn't know why we were trying to rob the granary in the first place, which made me even more ashamed. Heraclius told us that he would keep our stunt as a secret, so long as we didn't do anything else like it again. He said something about how he knew that we didn't like him, and that by doing us this favor, perhaps things could be set right. In no position to say otherwise, we promised to be civil with him from then on out.

I couldn't help but wonder what happened to those prostitutes that we had hired to give false accounts of what happened. I didn't dare return there. It was all just so stupidly embarrassing. Aelia said nothing to me on the walk back to Samuel's villa, but when we got there, she squeezed my shoulder. I turned around and really saw her for the first time since we were caught. Her eyes were darkened with exhaustion and shame, probably just like mine.

"I'm sorry," she whispered, coughing a little as she hadn't spoken all night. Neither of us had really slept, although I think I dozed off a couple of times.

"We share equal responsibility," I mumbled and turned away to enter the villa.

"I'm kind of dirty. Maybe we could go to the baths together?" Aelia said quickly. I barely heard her.

"Can we do that?"

"Yes,"

"I am kind of dirty. Actually, that would be nice. That way, I can get all of this grime off." I meant it. Both figuratively and literally, I felt disgusting. I needed to clean myself. I hadn't thought of the possibility that I could go with Aelia, but it sounded like the relaxing break that I needed after such a close brush with disaster.

Aelia told me that she knew a spot nearby that was rarely busy and prized cleanliness more than most of the other bathhouses in the city. She told me that she had been going there for years, and that they knew her well by now. They were likely to get their own private bath, she said. According to her, their masseuses were also superior to even the most exclusive clubs in Antioch.

Supposedly, it was a hidden gem among the Antiochene elite and if they were lucky, they might run into some high-level politicians that even Samuel had little to no access to. Since Samuel was a military man, his experience with civilian politicians and bureaucrats was limited at best. If I was to find Priya, Aelia said, then I would need to do some searching on my own as well. It's not that Samuel didn't have connections, or that he would never find Priya. He might. But if I wanted to hasten the search, which I did, then I might have to take some initiative. I agreed with her assessment of the situation. As stupid as we could be, Aelia seemed to me to be a highly intelligent woman who had made a mistake last night. She had been emotionally distracted.

After all, her best friend was being played like a fiddle by a sleazeball who spent her money on whores and booze. I could understand her blindness to logic. I suffered from a similar, if decidedly less noble, affliction. The affliction of lust. Nevertheless, I realized all hope towards that had been lost. Livia was never going to give up Heraclius, and even if she did, there was hardly a guarantee that she would choose me as a rebound. Horny foolishness on my part, dedicated friendship on Aelia's part. That's what led to the disaster last night, and the shame that has followed like a sentient black cloud ever since.

I suddenly realized that I was more than dirty; my face was literally shit-stained. Somehow I had forgotten about the dried horse manure all over my face, and that's probably why people kept looking at me. Allowing me to see their grief, and the lies they told themselves so they could continue on. I could see that all of this life and vigor in the streets was about as real as the heroic paintings on my bedroom ceiling at Samuel's villa. Nothing more than an artistic impression of what happiness could be. I started thinking about all this because people were staring at my shit-stained face. A fresh wave of shame overtook me, and I realized that my shame was now layered deep, like a tiramisu of self-pity and regret.

I told Aelia about my face and she glanced at me, briefly surprised. Then she just laughed and said it was a good thing we were going to the baths because she hadn't gone unnoticed either. Somehow, I must have gotten used to the stink, and the manure caked onto my skin like black-face. I wonder if this was what Trudeau used for his infamous Aladdin costume that made waves in the media way back when. Or was it way forward when? Technically? I don't know. This whole time travel thing really can cause a mean headache.

We reached the bathhouse. It was a small, unassuming brick building that had received only minor damage in the earthquake. Big, faded Latin lettering was engraved above the wooden door. Aelia knocked and a fat man let us in. He spoke in a heavy Greek accent, or at least it sounded kind of Greek. I guess it was an ancient Greek accent, because something sounded a little off.

The fat man, whose name was Manuel, led us to the hot bath. It was small but steaming hot. I dipped my toe in and it was slightly less warm than the average hot tub. The skinny woman came and gave me a small bowl of cold water and a towel so I could wash my face and feet, so as not to sully the water with my filth. I washed up and sighed in relief. The cold water on my face felt amazing. When I was done, I sat down to start washing my feet as I saw that Aelia was completely naked. She was staring at me, her eyes glassy. I looked away in embarrassment after a second of shock. I grabbed the wet towel and started scrubbing my blackened feet.

"Are you not going in?" I asked her after an awkward silence. I started scrubbing my other foot.

"I want you," Aelia said simply. My eyes locked onto hers and I chuckled instinctively, but she kept a straight face and I could tell that she was very serious. She bit her lip as she entered the pool, her naked body sending ripples across the calm water. I felt an intense warmth growing deep inside me and, in that moment, I ignored everything else and let my body take over. And so it did.

When I returned to the villa later that day, I found I was trembling uncontrollably. For some reason, I couldn't stop grinning either. It was embarrassing. I never imagined that I would possess such a feeble resolve. Yet, in a sense, it made sense. Aside from the shock of the moment, and the ensuing arousal, I supposed that I rather liked Aelia. She was funny, and easy to talk to. Aelia was someone who had my kind of humor. Besides, she found me attractive! It seems shallow to like someone more when they reveal themselves to like you, but it is natural, I suppose.

That night, I had a pleasant dream for once. For the first time in months, I woke up with a smile on my face. Maybe things weren't so bad after all.

22

Chapter 22

In the weeks that followed, an awkwardness began to descend upon the villa and the shop. At the villa, Samuel was increasingly absent and when he was back, he would rarely talk to me. Instead, he would just give a polite nod and a shallow smile. I was concerned he knew something about what Aelia and I did at the granary, but when I asked Heraclius, he assured me that he had told no one. Livia was sweet as ever, but even she appeared somewhat withdrawn. Just like her father, Livia was rarely there for suppers.

So more often than not, it was just me and Duccidava. Which was awkward, because she was a slave and she insisted on standing by my table whenever I ate. This was always uncomfortable for me, but when it was just the two of us, it was even more weird. I would be eating the meal that she cooked for me, and whenever I ran out of water, she would immediately pour more into my glass. It just seemed so wrong. She must be hungry herself! So I asked her on several occasions to sit down and have something to eat, but Duccidava insisted that it would be improper. One time, I tried to help her cook as well. She agreed, but I had no idea what I was doing and I accidentally added way too many eggs into a bread mixture. It ruined the batch and Duccidava was quite upset.

After that, she did not want me helping in the kitchen. I told her I could learn, but she said that I can damn well learn on my own time, which was the strongest language I had ever heard her use. The feeling I got was that Duccidava was used to working alone, and she seemed to be content. Could anyone truly find satisfaction in being enslaved? Her life was better than mine at the fish sauce factory, that's for sure. She seemed to have a fair degree of freedom and she had access to plenty of amenities. Still, though, they labeled her as property. She couldn't sit at the table with me. And at any time, she could legally be beaten, or even killed. It all seemed so brutal to me, and yet there seemed to be slaves everywhere. I even saw some customers who were clearly in dire financial straits hauling around a slave wherever they went. It was awful. I felt like I should do something, yet there was nothing I could do about any of it. I knew that. So I pretended it was normal.

Aelia was distant. When I asked her about what had happened in the bath house, she told me that it was a onetime thing, but that there was nothing wrong with me. She said that she wasn't ready for a relationship, which hurt, but at least she had the courtesy to put me down lightly. I could appreciate that. I guess it was just a physical sort of thing. We had both been humiliated, and we were exhausted as well.

Remarkably, we remained civil with each other. More than civil, actually. The friendship remained, perhaps emerging even stronger than before. Aelia became a great confidant; I told her about everything that I could. From my time as a slave at the fish sauce factory to my friends from the "other world," to my family. Of course, I never told her I was from the future. She would never have believed me. Nevertheless, she knew almost everything about me. I noticed that she usually just listened when I started telling a story. She rarely told a story of her own. It was sort of imbalanced with regard to the dynamics of the relationship. She was my confidant, but I was not hers. I supposed that was fine, but it made me curious about her past. I imagined it probably wasn't good, and I reminded myself that for all my yapping, I still hadn't told her about Caleb. Well, I had told her a little bit, but nothing about what I had done. We all have our secrets, and I had many. It was just nice having someone to talk to, I guess. Someone I could be myself around.

All sorts of interesting characters showed up in the shop over the weeks. There were parthian traders, Germanic refugees, and scholarly Greeks. Flustered fishermen, weary soldiers, and wacky housewives. Shopping slaves and little delivery boys that weren't quite slaves but were so close that the difference was nearly indistinguishable. One time, an actor stopped by and he was rather entertaining. Making jokes and such. Very comical. A dirty sense of humor. Very dirty. I couldn't breathe. Neither could Aelia. Livia was there too, but she didn't seem to get it. She found him to be unnecessarily crass and vulgar. Sometimes we all need a little vulgarity in life, though, don't we? I think so, anyway. It's nice to just blow off some steam. Just to say fuck you to society and laugh at what you want. Say what you want.

Maybe there was a rebellious teenager in me, or maybe this was just who I was. I guess I would find out in five years, but then again, maybe I wouldn't. Places like this, I could just as easily long before then. Besides, I didn't belong here. Who was to say that my mind wouldn't start to degrade the longer

I stayed here? What was that thing Mattheson was talking about? Travel sickness? I was supposed to be a guinea pig. I was supposed to be immune. But if they knew for a fact that I was, then they wouldn't have had to send me. Would they? Mind you, was it something that only set in once you returned? I couldn't remember, although I had no idea why that would be the case. Why couldn't it start here as well? All good questions for Priya.

One day, Aelia and Livia told me that they had found Priya through their own channels. I allowed myself to get excited, but unfortunately, it was a dead end. It turned out to be just an Indian woman who had no idea what was going on. Her name wasn't even Priya, it was Prisheek. I began to get discouraged. Weeks turned into months. I had no concept of the time, so I'm just guessing. But a routine began to develop. I would get up and go to the shop, work for the day, and then go home to the villa and have dinner. Sometimes I would hang out with Livia or Aelia, but never together. I considered making a male friend, but I didn't meet any guys aside from Heraclius and the customers, and I had no idea how to make a friend in such a strange environment.

I suppose Antioch wasn't so strange anymore. After all, it was very possible I had been here for a year now. It wouldn't be surprising if it had been even longer since I was locked up at that fish sauce factory. It was honestly hard to tell, especially since my time at the fish sauce factory made everything feel much longer than it probably was. Yet I could tell it had been a long time because I had grown a beard several times, and I had to keep shaving. They didn't have the handy razors like nowadays, but there were sharp blades that did the trick just fine. I got some razor burns and cuts, but I presume that was normal. It was just shocking for me because when Mattheson took me, I only needed to shave every couple of weeks. I had never had a beard because it grew so slow and beards were out of style, anyway. So I had been here long enough for my last stage of puberty to kick in and enhance my hairy genes. That was a terrifying prospect.

If I had been here for a year, then what had happened to my parents? How were they dealing with this? I was gone, disappeared. Probably presumed to be dead. Did they have a funeral? Jesus, my mom must just be a wreck. Well, at least I can come back from the dead now. Just like in the movies. That would actually be kind of cool in a childish sort of way. Always good to look on the bright side, though. The bright side was that my life hasn't been that bad, actually. Not that bad at all. It was off to a very rough start, but these last months had been some of the best months in my life. I had never met kinder people. Never. It was getting to the point where I asked them why they were still helping me. Samuel just told me that we had a bond and that he would look out for me until I could find Priya. That's the only reason he ever gave.

Everything became a blur. I became complacent, content almost. Sometimes I went to the baths to clean off and relax with Samuel. It was a much larger bathhouse than the one Aelia took us to. The conversations were usually not very substantial. He would ask how Livia was doing, how the store was doing. Things like that. I would ask if there was any progress on Priya or finding the factory where we were imprisoned, and he would always answer that they were still working on it. Mostly we just enjoyed the amenities. We went twice a week. The conversation was usually unsubstantial, that is, until the day that Samuel informed me that he was going to marry Livia off to a wealthy real estate speculator. I had no idea what that was, and so Samuel explained it was how Crassus made his fortune. As if that helped!

"Crassus?"

"Yes, Crassus. Can you believe it?"

"Well, I don't know, I—-"

"Yes, yes. Be quiet, will you? So, do you think Livia will agree?"

"I don't know, she's stubborn and—-"

"You must persuade her,"

"I don't know if I can make any guarantees,"

"That's not acceptable! Look, I've been very generous to you, have I not?"

"Yes..." I didn't like where this was going.

"Let's just say that Priya is going to be a lot harder to find if you don't succeed."

"I don't—-"

"Just get it done," Samuel said simply, and with that, he rose out of the hot pool and put on his towel. He decided to skip the cold pool and massage and immediately went to get changed. I guessed I was walking back alone, which was fine by now. I was actually starting to learn my way around the streets.

When I arrived at the store later that afternoon, Heraclius was already there with Livia and Aelia. He was whispering something into Livia's ear that made her laugh, and Aelia was scowling in the corner, sorting the new shipment of vegetables. I decided to talk to Aelia first. Livia and Heraclius ignored me.

"I see those two are going strong," I commented aloud.

"Yep," Aelia grumbled.

"Those vegetables look a little rough,"

"Yep,"

197

"Well, did Julius say what happened?"

"No, he didn't,"

"These are repulsive vegetables,"

"They're not that bad,"

"We can't sell these,"

"Yes, we can. And we will,"

"I don't know, Aelia. They look rotten,"

"They're not rotten. Just a few bruises."

"I wouldn't eat—"

"Holy shit! Just spit it out! You obviously need to tell me something."

"Samuel is setting up a marriage for Livia,"

"What?"

"He's a real estate prospector,"

"No, no, no. He can't do that. She will leave. I'm serious,"

"Rich like Crassus, he said,"

"Livia's sanity is hanging on a thread. If he does this, it'll push her over the edge,"

"You never did tell me how her aunt died,"

"You don't want to know, alright? She didn't j—t lose her aunt. It was worse than that. Much, much worse,"

"What do you mean?"

"It's not for me to say,"

"It doesn't matter. Samuel is forcing me to convince her. I can't do it alone," I mutter. Aelia cackled so loud that even Heraclius and Livia glanced over at us. That's all it was, though—a glance. They immediately went back to whatever intimate conversation they were having. I could tell they were in love. Or at least deeply attracted to each other.

"You think that she will listen to me?"

"Aren't you her best friend?"

"I was her best friend,"

"What are you doing hanging around here, then?" I blurted out. Aelia slapped me.

"Because it's my business, too, asshole," Aelia grumbled. She was smiling, though. By now, Livia and Heraclius had snapped out of their alternate reality and began to approach us to see what was going on.

"What did you say to Aelia?" Livia chuckled.

"I didn't do anything!" I exclaimed.

"I believe you, man," Heraclius patted my shoulder.

"We were just messing around," Aelia said.

"Of course you were," Livia grinned.

"Let's get back to work," Aelia sighed. There were no customers, but we dispersed anyway.

That night, I knocked on Livia's bedroom door. I had no idea if she was awake or not, since even after all my time here, it was exceedingly difficult to tell the time. There were sundial clocks in public places, but they only worked when it was sunny and they only had 12 hours in the whole day, which was confusing. Whenever I asked someone what time it was, they would say something really weird like "cock stops crowing" time or "lighting of the candles" time. Basically I just had to guess.

"Come in," Livia said. She was in a thin white nightgown, and once again I found myself with some naughty thoughts. My attraction to Livia had never dissipated over the course of the last few months, but I had pushed it aside the best I could. It was clear that she was taken, and there wasn't much I could do about it. A warm breeze blew in from her window, curtains fluttering. She was sitting at her desk, writing something with a quill and ink.

"What are you writing?" I asked, while closing the door behind me.

"Oh, just a love poem," She mumbled.

"A love poem?"

"We all have our pastimes,"

"Poetry, though. Wow," I said. She laughed.

"I was not being serious. I'm actually writing a letter to my father,"

"Has he gone somewhere?"

"No, but I am,"

"Why is that? "

"He plans on marrying me to a 64-year-old man,"

"You know about that?"

"I know about a lot of things,"

"Really? Did you know that Heraclius spends the money that you give him on whores and booze?" I blurted out. I regretted it from the moment I said it. Livia's characteristic smile faded away.

"I don't care what he does to satisfy his needs. He can do whatever he wants with the money I give him. Aelia will have you believe that he leeches off me. Bleeds me dry. It's not true. We share everything, and I know everything about him. I know his darkest secrets, and he knows mine. And yes, he gives me money when I need it. Heraclius is not poor, in case you didn't notice. It's just a matter of having spare change. Trust is the foundation of any good relationship," Livia spoke calmly, rarely breaking eye contact.

"Oh," I said stupidly

"It's true, I know lots of things. I also know that you have a thing for me. It's been going on for a while, hasn't it?" Livia said, while looking me directly in the eyes. My face went beet red.

"I don't, uh, I don't know what you, uh—-" I mumbled. She laughed again. What a beautiful sound that was.

"You're a good man. Someone will love you. I know that as well. Someone will see your goodness and they will be swept off their feet. Personally though, I already love Heraclius. Take care of yourself," Livia said. She walked up to me and kissed me on the cheek. Her lips were warm and soft. I was so embarrassed. Also, what the hell was I supposed to do? She was leaving! What would Samuel do if he found out that I let her go? Should I, like, physically restrain her? Call for help?

"Your—he'll—your father will be furious if you leave," I reflexively rubbed the back of my neck. I had a little pressure right at the base of my skull, which I sometimes got when I was suffering from intense stress.

"I explained everything in this letter. Goodbye, Ashton," Livia beamed. She then quickly went to her closet and took out a big black cloak. She put it over her nightgown and hoisted a big bag over her shoulders. I decided right then and there not to stop her. If it was her decision to leave, then so be it. I went back to my room and slowly drifted off to sleep, the fears and anxieties of tomorrow slowly fading away in the comforting haze of slumber.

23

Chapter 23

"Good morning," I said. Samuel was sitting alone at the breakfast table. He was staring at the letter in his hands, a look of distant sorrow painted upon his weathered face.

"Did you know about this?" Samuel whispered hoarsely.

"No," I surprised myself with how quickly I lied.

"She can be so ungrateful," Samuel growled. I said nothing. Samuel sighed and put the letter down. We ate in silence. I went to the store as usual. Aelia was there already, like always.

"She left," I said simply. Aelia nodded.

"She told me. I helped her last night,"

"You helped her?"

"Of course I did. She's my best friend." Aelia said simply. I supposed they were always friends. True friends never turn their backs on each other when they need it the most. I thought of my own friends. Jim especially. He was my best friend. I'd known him since the first grade. Short of murder or rape, I supposed there wasn't anything Jim could do that could convince me of completely cutting off ties with him. People drift away, but once that bond is made, it's there forever. Brothers. In this case, sisters. I could respect that. I wish I had that bond with my actual brother. I wish Caleb knew that I believed we had that bond. Maybe then...

The next few days were generally solemn and restrained. I originally thought that Samuel would be furious; that he would send out search parties and the whole bit. Instead, aside from that first morning, he seemed to mostly resigned himself to the reality that his daughter had left him. I think Livia underestimated how much she would hurt him by doing this. He no longer showed up to work, which he just wrote off as his well-earned vacation days. Samuel said that the army could do a few days without him, and that after all, he was just a useless old man. Even Duccidava seemed sort of sad. Everyone knew Livia for her positivity, but without it, her effect on our collective morale became ever more evident.

In contrast to the house, the store was as much fun as ever. Aelia was just as upset about Livia leaving as me, but she coped with her specific brand of dark humor. I liked it.

A couple of days after Livia left, I decided we needed to do something big to get the store's financial situation back on track.

"So, I was thinking that we should do some sort of big event to attract more customers," I said.

"What kind of event?"

"I don't know, like a promotional event,"

"Yeah, ok buddy. Promotional event. What the fuck are you talking about?"

"I don't know!"

"Well, you brought it up! Give me something here."

"Maybe we could offer a ten percent discount,"

"Maybe I'll grow a dick,"

"Ok, Jesus, you don't have to be so crude,"

"Why are you bringing the christian God into this?"

"What?"

"You said Jesus. Wasn't he that crazy Jew who claimed to be God two hundred years ago? He's got like a whole cult and everything now. Serious people are converting,"

"I guess, well——"

"No, I've noticed you say that before. It's weird. Are you one of them?"

"Would you hate me if I were?"

"No, I don't discriminate. You know me: I'm just lovey-dovey. Cupid incarnate,"

"Yeah, yeah. Whatever,"

"You didn't answer my question,"

"Does it matter?"

"Kind of,"

"Maybe that's what we could do!" I suggest.

"What? What could we do?"

"We could do a 'christian day'"

"No! No fucking way,"

"Why not?"

"Because they're Christians. They worship a dead God. They are lunatics,"

"They aren't so bad. I heard they're very generous,"

"Oh, you've heard, have you?"

"Yeah..."

"You are a christian!" Aelia cackled.

"No I'm not!"

"Whatever you say, christ-lover,"

"Ah.. screw you!"

"Easy with the foul mouth there, buddy. You're speaking to a lady here,"

"Yeah, a lady. Right," I smiled.

So, we told anyone who would listen that we were having a special...15%! Discount for all Christians who were willing to come to our store. At my insistence, we also included in our message that our store was a welcome place for them to spread "the word of God." In order to implement the discount, I had to confess to Aelia that I couldn't read. She teased me ceaselessly. It was awful. Luckily, she was able to read out the numbers to me and I could do the discount calculations. She was confused by the numbers that I was using.

"What is that gibberish?"

"Numbers,"

"Yeah, right..." She knew that they were real, because they had a pattern to them. But it was impossible for her to recognize where they were from, because they hadn't yet been invented.

The actual event was quite the success. I mean, to be honest, I had some doubts about the whole thing, even though it was my own plan. We made over 30 gold aureus, which was an insane amount of money. That was like thousands of sesterce. I don't even know how much exactly. There were relatively few hiccups, although at one point a fistfight broke out between one of the customers and an adherent of the traditional roman religion.

Luckily, it resolved itself and the pagan roman walked away after landing a few good punches. We gave the beaten customer a free cabbage, which earned praise and even more business from other christian customers. I was shocked to see how many actually showed up. It was incredibly fulfilling, actually. My whole time working at the shop was thoroughly enjoyable, but this event was even better because it was my idea being put into practice. Some good was actually being done. At the end of the day, we had made more than enough to pay off the debt and managed to make 8 aureus of profit. It was amazing.

"Thank you for this," Aelia said that night, as we were counting up the coins.

"We did it together,"

"But thank you," Another peck on the cheek. What was it with pecks on the cheek? This one was more brief, and for the first time I saw Aelia embarrassed. I said nothing, but I tried to hug her before going home. She pushed me away playfully.

"Easy there, bucko. Haven't got to the hugging stage yet," Aelia chuckled. I smiled back and went to sleep. It was a good sleep. A deep sleep. The next morning, I had a little spring in my step. I wasn't exactly attracted to Aelia, but I was honored that she liked me. And I liked talking to her. She was funny. Maybe that was enough. We hadn't spoken about our passionate sex session in the bath house all those months ago, and I thought she made it clear it was just a onetime thing. A peck on the cheek. Maybe it was just a friendly peck, like what Livia did. Maybe she was ready to try a relationship now. I had no idea. It was possible that the debt was really weighing down on her. After all, the shop and therefore Aelia had this debt for quite some time and no one had solved the problem until I came along. Geez, I better watch out for that ego. I might blow it out of proportion. No, it was hard to have an ego when you were just learning to like yourself again. For once, I was doing some good. These were good people. There was a little drama, sure, but I loved my life.

"We found them," Samuel said one morning. He was in full

leather armor.

"Found who?" I said. Maybe he really did send people after Livia and Heraclius.

"We found Ajax and his men. We found the camp," Samuel grinned through gritted teeth, his eyes watery. He had grown a beard, and it made him look old. There were almost no brown hairs in that sea of gray.

"What?" I heard what he said, but I was buffering.

"Do you want to come?" Samuel asked, making direct eye contact. I hesitated; if I did this, then there was no telling how I would react. Something told me they weren't taking prisoners.

"Do you have an ax?" I smiled along with him, taking a deep breath to stop my pounding heart. Screw restraint...I wanted to watch Ajax die.

Luckily, I knew how to ride a horse because of a camping trip a few years earlier. My dad loved horses, even though he was from the city. I hated it at the time; playing a game of basketball or a round of cards would have been much more up my alley. But I praised my reluctant agreement way back then, because otherwise I would have been in an awkward situation. Everyone knows how to ride a horse in this era. I was a little rusty, but after a few tries, I managed to mount the gray horse that Samuel had given me.

We rode outside the city to a field where hundreds of Roman soldiers had assembled. They were in perfect formation, their expressionless faces staring out into the distance. They were holding long spears, and short swords were on their hips. Aside from being all-men, the soldiers seemed to be from every corner of the Empire. It was like a militarized hodge-podge of different cultures. They all seemed equally disciplined. When we approached, they slammed their fists against their chests

207

and extended their arms in what looked like a Hitler salute.

"Hail caesar!" the soldiers exclaimed in a thunderous roar. Wait, wasn't Caesar dead? Also, Samuel was no caesar. I guess it was just like the Heil Hitler thing. Samuel returned their salute.

"At ease, gentlemen. Today, we end the scourge of illegal slavery in this city. For months now, untold numbers of unsuspecting roman citizens have been stolen from their homes and forced into servitude. Good, tax-paying Romans!" Samuel boomed. The soldiers beat their swords on their shield, almost musically.

"Yeah!" one soldier cried out from a distance.

"As some of you know, none other than myself can be listed among their victims!" The soldiers started loudly booing, slamming their swords even harder against their shields.

"My friend here was among the prisoners. He is a good Roman. He tried to help me escape, and killed many guards in his attempt, despite no fighting experience," the soldiers cheered.

"I asked him to join us today," Even louder cheers.

"And when we kill these scum, I can assure you that each and every one of you will get a big piece of their stolen pie. For no reward is enough for heroes such as you!" the loudest cheers of all. Hoots and hollers. They were practically itching to go.

"ONWARD!" Samuel cried. A military band with drums and some strange horn instruments that I didn't recognize began to play a menacing tune. We marched slowly but steadily. The enthusiasm earlier had somewhat dissipated after the grueling thirty minute march to the slave factory.

We reached the factory. The guards had assembled outside the wall. There were probably about 150 of them, standing in a disorganized mass. The slavers were outnumbered more than two to one, but I was still surprised at the number of men Ajax had managed to scrape together. He wasn't going down without a fight. It was also clear, by the looks of things, that he didn't plan on slinking off into the darkness either. He was at the head of his army. Samuel's soldiers seemed surprised by the sheer size of the slaver forces. They expected a pushover. An easy battle. This looked like a confrontation that could cause some serious casualties. Nevertheless, the Romans troops remained in perfect formation, unwavering.

"Ajax! I'm coming for you!" I blurted out. Ajax just smiled, waving his arm. His archers suddenly fired a volley of arrows. The sky was briefly blotted out by a thick cloud of black. How many archers did he have? I couldn't see him. The soldiers scurried into Testudo formation, preventing most of the arrows from hitting any flesh. Luckily, Samuel and I were just out of range, and a bunch of arrows practically landed at our feet. We were lucky, that was all.

Samuel waved his arm and his troops returned fire. The guards had shields, but they were smaller and round. They could not organize themselves into a good testudo formation, and many of them were killed by the volley of arrows. Maybe ten or fifteen of them. Only two of our soldiers were hit, and they were non-fatal wounds.

Our soldiers began marching. Slowly, carefully. Nervously, I asked Samuel whether we should join them. I could kind of ride a horse, but fighting on horseback was a whole different thing. I was pretty sure I would be killed. If we were going to fight, my best bet would probably be to get off the horse.

"No, we stay behind. I'm too old and you're a kid with no training. Don't worry, this is what they do for a living," Samuel explained with glee.

Ajax pummeled our troops with another volley of arrows, but their shields protected them once again. Even the injured soldiers still marched on, keeping in formation. They were like unstoppable steel rectangles. Another volley. No casualties. They kept on marching. I could tell the guards were getting antsy.

Suddenly, Ajax screamed and charged forward with his sword, plowing through the troops. His guards followed him. Intense fighting broke out. Lots of screaming, lots of blood. From the start, I could tell the guards were in trouble. They fought surprisingly fiercely, but they just couldn't seem to break the army's solid formation. No matter what they did, they just kept getting pushed back. Some soldiers were killed, but not very many. Maybe half a dozen. It was hard to tell from far away. But the guards were getting slaughtered. After about five minutes, the early intensity of the battle died down and the guards just kind of melted away, fleeing in all directions. Some of them were caught, but many got away. Ajax tried to flee as well, but one of the soldiers managed to capture him.

"Now we go," Samuel said. I trotted close behind him, and we entered the walls of the camp. I was struck by how much the battlefield stunk. I mean, it was one thing to see dozens of dead bodies strewn across a field, but it was another thing to see them up close. Some of the bodies were not bodies at all; they were live people, gasping for air. Crying for their mothers. Gurgling on their own blood.

Kuhh kuhhhh kuhhhhhh

That awful, wonderful sound again. It stunk like shit, piss, and blood. I guess when people die, they lose all control of their bodily functions. You don't really think of that when you watch an action movie, do you? It also stunk of rotting fish guts. A familiar, jarring smell that one can never erase from their memory once they have experienced it. We entered the gate. The slaves had all left their posts, circling around to watch what exactly was going on. The familiar fishy stench intensified.

Ajax was on his knees, along with the few dozen other prisoners the army had managed to capture. He smiled at me. He actually smiled! Bold son of a bitch. I hopped off my horse, walked up to him, and spat on his face.

"Keep smiling, you filthy piece of shit!" I hissed. The soldiers laughed. Ajax calmly wiped my spit off his smug face.

"I don't regret a thing," Ajax purred.

"What did you say?" I exclaimed.

"Do we, fellas?" Ajax boomed. The guards cheered. They were being defiant, but I knew they were terrified. Ajax included. They just didn't want to admit it. A matter of honor, I suppose. How ironic.

"Kill all of them except him," Samuel ordered one of his junior officers. The officer extended his arm in a salute and obeyed him.

"You heard the man," the officer said. The soldiers slit the throats of the still-cheering guards. Blood sprayed everywhere. Crimson rivers flooded the sandy ground.

Kuhh kuhhhhh kuhhhhhhh

They gurgled and choked. I smiled. I couldn't help it. I was grinning like a fucking cheshire cat. Ajax remained smug as ever...but.... was that a crack in his demeanor? Was that a small glimmer of fear that I saw in his eyes?

"Do you want to do it?" Samuel asked me. Never before had I felt such hate for one man before. I needed him to die. I longed for it. But could I actually kill someone? I had killed people before. That guard during the escape attempt. That was different, though. I had to kill him in order to survive. This would be a cold-blooded murder. Even if he deserved the death penalty, by doing this I would be making myself judge, jury, and executioner. There would be no going back.

"Shouldn't he have a trial?" I ask meekly. Even I knew, as those words left my mouth, that they were intended as only nominal resistance to Ajax's execution. I fully intended to carry it out. I was just going through the motions of feigned reluctance in an ill-fated attempt to satisfy my future conscience.

"He will just buy the judge. He's too dangerous to be kept alive,"

"Of course. I guess... I guess I could do it," I say. Ajax's grin starts to fade. Maybe with the impending realization of his death, the last remnants of his humanity began to kick in. Almost everyone is afraid to die, even a man like Ajax. is human nature. People will do anything to avoid death.

"You don't have to do this," Ajax said. He looked genuinely scared now. He must have thought that we were going to take him for a trial or something, on account of his "status."

"Please, don't," Ajax pleaded, right before I slammed my ax into his neck. He started to scream, but that was over by the second swing. It was like I was leaving my body, and someone else had taken control. Or maybe a dream is a better comparison. A dream where you're doing something so awful, you know it can't be real. You know that you can't be in control, because how could someone as good and normal as you be doing something so terrible? But there I was, chopping and chopping. His warm blood sprayed all over my face like a broken garden hose. His lifeless eyes rolled to the back of his head. Yet I kept chopping. I grabbed his hair to hold him still. My hand was clenched tightly in a fist.

As I chopped, I thought about the beatings. The whippings. How that one guard beat me and spat on me like I was not a human being. How they treated me like property. Like an animal. The hard, 12 hour workdays. The constant stink of the fish guts, rotting away into the glossy black sauce that I would package every day. The heat in the mornings. The loneliness and exhaustion that accompanied every night for what felt like forever.

How I had to spend my sickness wiping the snot off my face with a sleeve. Shivering alone and cold in my damp cell. I was basically on the brink of death. The dry, flavorless oatmeal. And the "treats" they would give us whenever we did good, like we were dogs. I was so desperate I ate them despite my disgust. I remembered how they crucified Paul. He was up there for a full day, slowly dying. That's what Ajax really deserved. To be crucified. A long, painful death like he had inflicted on Paul. If you think about it, what I was doing was merciful. A kindness, really. He should be thanking me.

Suddenly I chopped through the last layer of his skin, and his body slunk to the ground. I was holding Ajax's heads in my hand. You could barely see his pupils. They were rolled right to the back of his head. Blood was still squirting from his headless body, his heart somehow still pumping. I was soaked in it. Absolutely drenched. I could taste it. The salty, iron-rich blood of my victim. It had gotten in my eyes, so I dropped my ax and wiped the sticky blood away. I noticed I was shaking; Everyone was staring at me in silence.

They had to take the head out of my hand. Later that day, we got washed up. I was still clenching my fist, shaking, when I went to sleep that night. Something had broken inside me. It was like there was a doorway to somewhere no one wants to go, and I kicked it down as soon as I could.

What did that say about me?

24

Chapter 24

<u>Before</u>

I looked out my window and saw thick snowflakes falling from the sky. It was thirty-seven degrees below zero, and I had no intention of leaving the relative warmth of my home. It was Christmas Eve and although my mom wanted to drive to church, I didn't think that was going to happen. She was the only christian in the family, and most years we would oblige her out of politeness. However, this year it was just too cold. My dad would agree with me when I suggest that we stay home.

Previous Christmas Eves were far more exciting. After finding out the truth about Santa, I guess the whole thing was just a little less mystical. Yet, it was still fun. My parents still gave me good gifts, or at least they had the previous year. My dad and I had a tradition of decorating the tree. It was a fake tree, because we were a lazy family. Nevertheless, a mess was made. Some of the fake pine needles always ended up scattered all over the place. It was fine, though. We just vacuumed.

I would bake stuff with my mom and Caleb. We had a small kitchen, so usually my dad didn't join. Although there were a couple of years where I remember my mom was working late, so it was my dad and Caleb that I baked with. My favorite thing to bake was snickerdoodle cookies, and we made two big batches today already. The house smelled great, especially upstairs. My dad also insisted on making his signature pineapple upside down cake. He had gotten the recipe from somewhere. I don't know here. Perhaps his parents. My dad was always pulling things out of his pockets. And no, I don't mean literally. He had these great recipes or nuggets of knowledge that he would just spit out at the most random times.

Once in a while, as in the case of the upside down cake recipe, he would turn that knowledge into a tradition. Another example of this would be how he always calls my brother Hugh Hefner because one time when Caleb was sick, he wore his red robe that my grandma had gotten him. His hair was all sweaty because he wasn't showering, and it looked like it was slicked back. With sweat. Disgusting, I know. My dad called him Hugh, and now it was like an inside joke. It made no sense, and yet there it was. Popping up at the dinner table for conversation now and then.

It was late now, and I knew I would have to be getting to sleep soon. EVen though I knew there was no Santa, I was still excited about whatever might lie under the tree in the morning. The pancakes. My parents would make pancakes and bacon on Christmas mornings, usually a rare occurrence. My mom basically made us eat cereal most days, but sometimes she would cook omelets. I hate omelets. I'm not allergic to eggs, but to just eat that much egg without anything is just too much for me. Don't like scrambled eggs either. Over-easy is fine by me, but it must be with bread. Bread and bacon. On Christmas mornings, though, my mom made pancakes. They were good pancakes, too. Seared in butter, topped with thick corn syrup and fresh fruit. Strawberries and blueberries and black berries. I was in BC once, on Vancouver Island and the blackberry bushes groped there like a weed. Sizzling bacon, slightly crispy but not overcooked. Sometimes we would get breakfast sausages as well. Oh! Whipped cream. I forgot about whipped cream. How could I forget about whipped cream?

Caleb had been avoiding everyone lately. It was disconcerting, to be totally honest. Why was he acting up on Christmas Eve? This was supposed to be one of the happiest days of the year, and it was! gifts on the way, good food, good company. What more could anyone want? I guess it's one thing if you're out on the streets and you don't have a family to spend Christmas with. Well, not just people on the streets. There were lots of people without any families. Maybe they had a falling out, maybe they died. Caleb did not fit the category of these people. There was no way he should be sulking on Christmas Eve. He had a loving family that cared about him. Why was he being like this?

He was tired as well. So tired, all the time. It didn't matter how much sleep he got, Caleb would never be energetic. He used to be. There was a time when I enjoyed talking to him. Now, he was disgusting. He didn't shower nearly enough as he should, which meant that his hair was always sticky and greasy. So yes, he stunk. Most of his friends had abandoned him. I had long since given up on what had happened to make him this way. Apparently, it was no single event. It was just an illness. At least according to the doctors. Caleb was doing this to himself. Something had happened. He had done something. My brother was always up to something. There's just some people you can't trust, and Caleb was one of them. He lies all the time, even for no reason. None at all!

At a certain point, one just has to resign themselves to the reality that Caleb was a piece of shit. Take the sentimentality out of it. Look at the situation objectively. People were getting so soft. He *falsely blamed a classmate for rape. He stole seven hundred dollars of my mom's money and then lied about it. He stole two hundred dollars from me and lied about it. Overall, he's just a foul and unpleasant human being. I genuinely dislike him. There's no redeeming qualities that he has beyond the memory of what was. He's a revolting shadow of his former self. At the same time though, he's still my brother. He deserves empathy, if not from anyone else then at least from me and our parents.*

It had been a few months now since he was put on medication by the doctors. They say he has clinical depression and ADHD. I believe it. I try to be understanding. Sometimes though, things just come out. I can't help myself. It's hard for me to hide my disdain for him. I know he must realize what I think of him now. Maybe it will get him to straighten out? I don't know. I'm embarrassed of him as well. My friends come over and he's just up in his room like always. Never showing his face unless it's shoveling his dinner down his gullet. His liver must just be so inflamed. Stretch marks everywhere, he was gaining weight. Not that there's anything wrong with putting on a few pounds. It was healthy to live a happy life, and why give up your happiness if that is food? But food wasn't his happiness, it was his escape.

I know I am an asshole for thinking like this, and sometimes even speaking about my brother in such a way to my friends. I know I'm probably going to hell. But I can't help it! It's just what I think. Maybe that's how he is. He can't help it. That is how he is. There's no dispute. The thing I can't get over is why? Why is he so sad? He has no reason to be. I must be missing something. Something big. If he won't open up, I can't do anything about it. Maybe he was opening up to the therapists. I hoped so.

Thinking like this on Christmas Eve was unacceptable. I needed to relax, and forget about my brother. He would be fine. After all, he was taking medicine. Not all Christmases would be like this in the future. It will get better. An important aspect of having a family was loving them no matter what, even when you don't like them. I supposed that wouldn't be so difficult. All I had to do was wait out the storm and before I knew it, we would be back to our regular old jolly Christmases. Maybe even Caleb and I would be best friends again, like we used to be. At the very least, he would get better. I knew he would.

I crawled into bed and dozed off to sleep. It took me a while as I was an insomniac now, but eventually my brain shut down and I drifted into my usual dreamless slumber. When I woke up, it was six-thirty in the morning. My throat was terribly dry, and I smiled at the fact that I had left a glass of water on my bedside table. I took a couple big gulps of the lukewarm water. It was a habit that my grandma had taught me. My grandma had many ailments, but she had been getting a dry mouth in the morning for decades. I missed my grandma. It had been a good few months since I had last seen her. We had been at an autumn farmers market. I guess that was more than a few months ago. September long weekend? I think so. Anyway, she will be at the house today for Christmas. She always brought two big bags of her own gifts for me and Caleb.

I groaned as I forced myself out of bed. It was surprising to me that Caleb had not yet woken me. Usually when it comes to presents, he was eager. Somehow even that had been affected. 6:30 was still kind of early, to be fair. Everyone was getting older and such. Going back to sleep was well within the realm of possibility, and it was certainly tempting, but I decided against it. I couldn't help myself; the excitement of Christmas morning still hadn't been completely wiped away.

I staggered through the hallway in my pajamas and knocked loudly on my parents door. My dad grumbled a bit, but I was satisfied they were awake. My mom crawled out of bed and went to her en suite to take a shower.

Now, it was time to wake up Caleb. I had never woken him up on Christmas morning before, and it was bizarre. A shift in the family dynamic had taken root, I could feel it. When I knocked on the door, there was no answer. I opened up and was overtaken by the stench. There were clothes strewn across the floor, there was garbage everywhere. Dirty dishes piling up, food rotting. I was surprised it had gotten so bad, and that my parents had allowed it to deteriorate to this condition. I guess on Christmas break they had let up on him. Obviously that was a mistake.

It stunk like something else, as well. Something truly vile. Like vomit or something. I sighed and plugged my nose and I worked my way over to Caleb. He was under the covers, deep asleep. I tried shaking him awake, but he was either comatose or faking it. Chuckling a little bit, I grabbed the half-drunk water glass on his bedside table and poured it all over him. To my surprise, he still didn't move. I furrowed my eyebrows and pulled the cover off his face.

Caleb's lifeless eyes stared right back at me. At first, I couldn't believe it. I just stood there, frozen. His skin was gray, discolored. His eyes were red and dry. His dark brown tongue protruded from his mouth, white vomit everywhere. His stomach and neck were bloated. I looked and saw that his rigor mortis fist was clutching a mostly used bottle of antidepressants. It was an overdose. There was no note.

25

Chapter 25

"Ashton?" Aelia shook me, "Are you ok?"

"I'm fine," I lied. It was cold, so cold here. Someone needed to close the window.

"Samuel told me what you did," Aelia said, a flicker of fear in her eyes. Or was that a look of concern? I couldn't tell anymore. I just wanted to crawl up into a ball and cry.

"Did he?" I said flatly.

"I'm worried about you." She did seem worried about me. That's what the look was.

"That would be a first," I chuckled.

"Shut up," she grinned.

"Look, I did what I had to do," I told her the same lie I had been telling myself.

"Well, I mean, you didn't have to," Silence. I kissed her, but she pulled away.

"That doesn't count," Aelia sighed and stood up, starting to walk towards my bedroom door.

"Please don't leave," I whispered. I didn't want to be alone.

Tears welled up in my eyes. I was scared of falling asleep. Afraid of what I might find once I allowed myself to lurk around the dark corners of my subconscious. What might be living in there...growing...eating.

My hand was still clenched, even after sleeping. Aelia's face softened again, and she sat on my bed. She was sort of short and stubby, but she had an attractiveness to her that's hard to explain. Maybe it was just the way she carried herself. Nothing close to the sheer intensity of what I felt for Livia, but there was something.

"How can I say no to a crying baby?" Aelia groaned dramatically as she sat down on my bed.

"Thank you,"

"Let's talk about something else," Aelia suggested softly.

"Like what?"

"I don't know..."

"Why don't you tell me where you come from?"

"What?"

"You couldn't even tell Livia. Precious Livia,"

"I..."

"I just want to know a little more about you. We talk but don't...talk. You know?"

"Don't get all soft on me," I said.

"No...I mean seriously. Tell me about yourself," Aelia demanded.

"Well, this goes both ways. I don't know anything about you either."

"Because you never asked!" She exclaimed. Was that true? My face went red.

"I'm asking now!" I cried.

"Fine, have it your way. My name is Aelia, in case you missed

222

it."

"Ok buddy, dial it down a little."

"I was born here, and I'll die here too,"

"You sound like those small-town girls from the movies," I said, before realizing my mistake. Aelia furrowed her brow.

"See! What the fuck was that? What is a 'movie?' You say the weirdest shit," Aelia said.

"I guess I'm just crazy,"

"Nah, I've met crazy. You're not crazy. Stupid? Maybe. Bizarre, for sure. Not crazy though,"

"Thanks for that," I said.

"Listen, I know we haven't spoken about what happened that night—"

"The night we had sex?"

"Wow. Subtle as ever. What a poet," Aelia rolled her eyes.

"Were you always so sarcastic?" I asked.

"Sometimes people do things to cope,"

"Fair enough." I was surprised at the maturity of her answer.

"My brother died shortly before I came here," I said shortly.

"I'm so sorry," she sounded sincere. She laid down and wrapped herself around me, laying her head on my chest. At first, I was sort of shaky. I wasn't used to that sort of intimacy. She was deliberately changing the nature of our relationship. I decided to go with it. What the hell? She calmed me, and that was more than enough.

"He killed himself. We had an argument...we had a lot of arguments, actually," I said softly. It was hard to say it out loud. Even this was calming, in a strange sort of way. I never had talked to anyone about this before. Well, I did talk to one person. That was a confession, though. This was different.

"That's not your fault," Aelia whispered. She smelled like

raspberries and honey.

"I just couldn't give him a break, you know? I was awful to him. And then... he killed himself. I saw his empty...his empty eyes. There was nothing there. Nothing at all." I cried and cried. She just held me close. My hand slowly unclenched. It was incredibly sore after being clenched for hours and hours. Aelia slowly pushed my fingers out, so they could relax. Her skin was soft. I just sobbed for what felt like forever, to the point where there were no more tears. I got a headache, but just kept crying. Wailing, even. It was mostly silent, though. Silent, dry sobs. After a while, Aelia spoke.

"My parents died when I was young. My father was killed fighting a war when I was a baby. So it was just me and my mom. When I was five or six, she left me on the streets. To this day, I have no idea what happened to her." Aelia talked so quickly I could barely understand her. I looked over at her; she was almost as emotional as me. I hadn't even noticed.

"I'm sorry," I gasped between sobs, desperately trying to compose myself.

"I was begging on the streets until Livia's aunt took me in." Aelia was staring into the distance. Her breath was becoming shallower.

"The one who just died a few weeks before I got here?" I asked.

"Yes, Cassia. A wonderful woman. Very kind. She raised me as her own. She had so many children, but she took me in any way. Only me. This was my room." Aelia pulled me closer, and I wrapped an arm around her, hugging back.

"So she was like your mom," I whispered, stroking her hair.

"Yes," Aelia swallowed.

"What happened to her?" I asked. Why did I always

find myself asking that question? What happened to them? Everything was so violent, so brutal. Not so long ago, when I asked what happened to them, I was talking about Rudy Giuliani's dramatic fall from grace, or maybe the suspicious sacking of one of my teachers. Not this. Nothing like this. Yet here I was. Maybe it was brutal in the modern world, too. Maybe I just wasn't paying attention.

"When Samuel was captured by the slavers, they raped Livia and Cassia. Livia came over to my place after it happened, with the... the semen still warm between her thighs. Cassia threw herself from a window after Livia left. Livia blamed herself,"

"I don't...I don't..." I muttered. I had no idea what to say.

"Cassia died a couple of days later. The doctors were unable to save her...the skull was just..." Aelia muttered shakily, and I impulsively kissed her on the forehead. She stiffened for a split second, but then smiled lightly. We held each other.

After a while, I pretended I was sleeping. So did she. But I knew she was wide awake. I didn't care. I had no idea what else to say, and I was equally unwilling to sleep. It wasn't really a matter of attraction. It wasn't sexual at all, actually. I think we both needed someone that night. I had old scars, and some new ones too. So did she. So we laid there for hours and hours, and we never let go.

26

Chapter 26

Empty. The field was empty. Not a single building. People were nowhere to be found. No slaves, no guards. But it was the field. It was the same field. I could tell. I don't know how I could tell, but I knew. I knew where I was.

Red. Something was wrong. What was it? I couldn't tell. There was just something...off. Maybe it was the sky? The sky was blue. The grass? The grass was as brown and dirty as ever. No, it was the ocean. It was red. Crimson red. There was more; in the distance, through the heat, I could make out a glimmer of air.

A face. There was a face. In the glimmer of heat. Maybe it was just a trick of the eye. A mirage is all it was. After all, how could there really be a face in the air? Was it God? Coming to judge me? Why did I jump to such conclusions? Only the guilty jump to those kinds of conclusions. What was wrong with me?

Fill, fill, fill, fill, fill the field. Fill it with what? I didn't know. All I knew was that I had to fill the field.

The face was getting angry. Getting angrier. I knew...I knew it, knew what I had done. What had I done? I had done something *wrong.... I knew it.*

MURDERER! KILLER! BUTCHER! DEVIL!

What was that? Something was screaming at me. A desperate howl that scratched at the pit of the throat. I curled up into a ball and closed my eyes. The grass was cold...the dirt was dry and dusty. There was no life in this field. Go away, go away, go away please....... PLEASE NO.

Something hard hit me, and I was flying. FLYING, FLYING, FLYING. No, I was falling. FALLING, FALLING, FALLING. FALLEN. I WAS FALLEN. Like an angel. A perverse, evil, murderous, devilish angel.

"You killed me, just like you killed your little brother," The voice of Ajax said. I opened my eyes. The headless body of Ajax stood before me. The blood was no longer squirting from the wound. His skin was gray and foul.

I didn't kill him!

YES YOU DID YES YOU DID YES YOU DID .... I turned to see my mother holding Caleb's rotting corpse.

Fill the field...what?? Fill the field with what? PLEASE TELL ME WHAT YOU MEAN. FILL THE FIELD WITH WHAT? FILL THE FIELD WITH WHAT? FI——

I woke up to find the entire room shaking. Aelia pushed me off the bed and a chunk of the roof crashed down where I had been sleeping a moment before. The building was collapsing. I cried out, but I could barely hear my own voice among the thunderous quake. It was like the earth was a snow globe and someone was shaking as hard as they possibly could. I tried to get up, but I just fell back down again. I couldn't think. I couldn't see. I couldn't breathe. The dust was getting heavier, clogging up my throat. Something hit me hard. Everything went black.

"Ashton? Ashton!" I woke up to find Aelia shaking me. Her nose was broken...blood was gushing from her dusty face. Her nightgown was blackened in tatters. My head was pounding. I could feel the warm, terrifying river of blood oozing from a wound in my forehead. Thu-thump. Thu-thump. Thu-thump. My mouth tasted like blood and dust.

"Wh-what?" I said weakly. She hugged me tight.

"We need to get out of here!" Aelia exclaimed. I limped out of the rubble to the street. People were screaming in the distance. There were smoke stacks billowing up everywhere. Fire. Catastrophe. Dead bodies littered the streets. Their heads bashed in, or their chests crushed. A woman cradled her lifeless baby, rocking it back and forth. She kept singing a lullaby under her breath.

I looked back on the once-mighty estate that we were living in and found it to be partially collapsed. I suddenly realized that Samuel was probably still in there. Was he? I had no idea.

"Where's Samuel?" I rasped, one arm around Aelia's shoulder.

"I...I don't know," Aelia muttered, furrowing her brow.

We spent the next few hours searching for Samuel, or maybe Samuel's body. We found Duccidava dead within the first ten minutes. She had been impaled by a large wood shard. Just as we were losing hope, we found Samuel. He was barely alive after having his ribcage crushed by a sizeable chunk of rubble. I was no doctor, but I guessed that he had some broken ribs and a collapsed lung. Hopefully, none of his organs were ruptured, and he had no internal bleeding.

It all happened so fast. One second I was sleeping...and now I was here, standing over a rasping Samuel. Since he was wealthy, a doctor came relatively quickly, despite all the chaos. Aelia and I limped behind Samuel and the doctor, as he took them to a relief center. Yes, they had relief centers. I was surprised at the extent of emergency services that were in existence. There were soldiers all over the place, helping people out. There were other people running around with buckets, putting out fires. And there was this relief camp that I had to assume was not the only one within the city. Some of the services were definitely focusing on the more affluent members of society, but not all of them.

I watched in horror as a doctor inserted a tube into Samuel. Surprisingly, he sterilized it with boiling water. I had expected that they didn't know about germs, and they probably didn't, but at least they knew about sterilization.

"The lung has to re-inflate," the doctor said simply, before scurrying away to attend to other patients. We were in, like, a courtyard or something. There were probably a hundred people on stretchers, just like Samuel. And more came in by the minute. I couldn't believe the scale of it. Entire trees had been knocked down, uprooted. Well over two-thirds of the buildings were partially or completely destroyed. Dead bodies were everywhere. Dead people, dead animals, dead babies. I couldn't see how they were going to rebuild the city anytime soon.

"Are you ok?" I asked Aelia finally. Someone came by with blankets. We put them over our shoulders. It was dawn, the sun was just barely up.

"Fuck, no," she chuckled. Her chuckle turned into a coughing fit. At least she wasn't yelling anymore. Maybe her hearing was coming back.

"Did you see Duccidava?"

"Yeah...all that time I lived there and I never even had a full conversation with her," Aelia said tearfully.

"She never expected you to make an effort,"

"I should have anyway," Aelia said. More coughs. A baby cries in the distance.

"Have you seen a contraption like that before?" I ask Aelia, glancing doubtfully at the tube implanted in Samuel's chest.

"No, but I've heard of them," Aelia said, groaning as she sat down on the foot of Samuel's makeshift cot. I looked at Aelia's smashed nose. The blood on her face had started to dry finally.

"You should get your nose looked at,"

"It's fine,"

"Have you looked at yourself?"

"Yep. Hottest girl in Antioch. That's me." Aelia threw her hands up.

"Yeah, maybe if everyone else is dead," I smirked.

"Too soon," Aelia sighed.

"Too soon," I agreed. Eventually, of course, a doctor did come by and fix Aelia's nose. It was hard to watch, but at least it was over quickly. They never bothered to check my head, but I figured I was fine. A lingering fear of a brain bleed was omnipresent. Remember Liam Neeson's wife? She fell down and hit her head on the bunny hill at a ski resort. Some headaches, mild discomfort. Next thing anyone knew, she was dead! Or Bob Saget. Famous comedian, great guy. He was at a hotel and he hit his head on the headboard of his bed. Poor guy brushed it off as nothing and went back to sleep, like most people would. He was found dead the next morning. No drugs, nothing. Usually, when a celebrity dies in a hotel, there's something else going on. Not Bob Saget. Bob Saget just hit his head. So there was some fear there, naturally. Unfortunately, there was really nothing I could do about it. Might as well assume everything was fine. Worrying never did anyone any good. (That's a blatant lie, but it makes me feel better. So what the hell.)

Suddenly, the earth started shaking again. People began to scream. Crumbling building groaned and moaned under the stress. I grabbed onto Aelia and we knelt down, clutching Samuel's cot. Luckily, we were in an enormous courtyard away from the buildings, so we were relatively safe. But I could tell more people were dying in the city. You could see many of the damaged buildings collapsing, disappearing from the cityscape. The screams grew louder. The shakes weren't as bad as the ones that woke me up, but they were still very intense. Before we knew it, the aftershock was over.

Smaller and smaller aftershocks continued throughout the day. Later that afternoon, we found out a tsunami had flooded the port and surrounding area. Many people drowned or were crushed. Luckily, we were far enough inland to avoid the effects of the tsunami. Some soldiers brought us some water and coarse bread. I didn't complain; it was our only meal for the day and I scarfed it down.

In the later afternoon a tween boy, soaking wet, was brought to the camp. He was otherwise unharmed, but seemed completely traumatized. I glanced over to the corner of the courtyard and noticed a leather ball.

"I have an idea," I told Aelia.

"What kind of idea?" She asked. I looked down at Samuel, who was out cold. It was impossible to tell if he was getting better.

"He's not going anywhere," I said.

"And?"

"I'm gonna go play a game with that boy there," I pointed

231

at the tween.

"Why?" Aelia rubbed her forehead in exhaustion.

"Because,"

"That's not an answer,"

"He's traumatized,"

"We all are,"

"I'm going," I said finally. I walked over to the leather ball and found out that it was somehow still inflated. Bouncing it, I realized it was roughly the same as a basketball. I approached the boy. He was only a bit younger than Caleb would have been.

"Hello," I said to the kid. He didn't respond, but he was looking at the ball with interest.

"Do you know how to play basketball?" I knew he didn't, but I wanted to see how he would respond. The kid shook his head. I started dribbling the ball, doing tricks with it. Dribbling the ball between my legs and such. It was a little heavy for a basketball, but bounced well enough. The kid smiled. I gave him the ball, and he started dribbling.

We played for the next hour, and I taught him how to try to steal the ball, and whatnot. There was no net or anything, so we couldn't practice shooting, but it was still fun just with the dribbling and footwork. The kid, whose name was Antonius, caught on pretty quickly. People were looking, unsure of what exactly we were doing. They probably thought I had made it up on the spot. Eventually, even Aelia joined in, and we had a good laugh about it.

That night, we slept outside. It was cold, but we had blankets and so it was basically manageable. Aelia cuddled up to me again, and we kept each other warm. It was comforting. As I was lying there, the memory of the dream came flooding back to me. Ajax's dead body. My mother and Caleb. The face in the distance. The sea of blood. Most confusingly, what did the voice mean by "fill the field." I remembered it so vividly. The voice kept telling me to "fill the field." Fill the field with more victims? My mother, my brother, and now Ajax. I had killed them all. Maybe my mother wasn't dead yet, but she wouldn't last long. Who knows, maybe she killed herself while I was away.

No, she wouldn't be able to do that. She would be under observation. Institutions like the one she was at would have protocols for that. But even if she wasn't actually dead, she was deeply damaged. Because of me. Because of how I treated my own brother. Ajax was just the next natural step forward into cold-blooded murder. I was a murderer. A killer. My subconscious must think that I'll kill again. That I'm going to fill the field with more victims. More worryingly, did it want me to fill the field? Or was it warning me against it? I was overthinking this. There was no supernatural shit. I was in total control. I've seen too many movies. Fortunately, there were no dreams that night. The emotional turmoil could wait another day.

Chapter 27

The next few months were spent helping rebuild the city. I had no construction experience, but basically people just told me what to do and I obliged. Samuel's lung was re-inflated within a day, and it was only a week before he was limping around on his own two feet. A swift recovery. Good! Very good. His death might have sent me over the brink.

An intense relationship began to blossom between Aelia and me. After that night before the earthquake, I just couldn't stop thinking about her. It wasn't lust, not like with Livia. Not that I didn't find her attractive. I did, but it was more than that. I genuinely could be myself with her. I didn't have to perform like I tried doing with Livia. I wasn't doing it for status like with Jennifer. At the end of the day, it was Aelia who I wanted to talk to. She was so funny as well, but in a sarcastic sort of way. Dark humor, rude humor.

My kind of humor. Also, she had this little mole right behind her left ear. It was quite small, but I couldn't help but smile whenever she pulled her hair behind her ears and

I saw it. She found it so funny and teased that I had a fetish or something stupid. I didn't, but it was just these things. I couldn't understand it. It was just absurd. I loved the way her hair smelled like honey, and the way she stroked her fingers across my chest on those lazy mornings. There were more of those now, as things started to get going again. The city was still destroyed, but the soldiers had been helping, and there had been a surprising amount of progress in such a paltry amount of time.

The nightmares continued. Some of them were about Caleb or my mother, some of them were about my time as a slave, some of them were about Ajax. There were dreams that had all three, or none at all. None of them were pleasant. I avoided sleep as much as I could, but my days were filled with endless physical labor in the Mediterranean heat; it was always a losing battle. I started drinking wine with Aelia before bed to soften the dreams.

It didn't work, so I stopped. If anyone could excuse becoming an alcoholic, I suppose I would be a prime candidate. Ultimately, I guess I just didn't think it tasted that good. Wasn't worth it. Besides, I made for an idiotic drunk. That escapade with Aelia involving that old chariot racer was proof of that. Luckily, we did nothing like that again while drinking. It was just too dangerous outside. We did have a lot of fun, though. One night, she managed to get me to dance around in a dress. As if that wasn't enough, she dunked the remaining half bottle of cheap wine all down my head. There wasn't even a reason for it. We were such silly geese. She just couldn't stop laughing.

One day Aelia told me that the baths that we had visited all that time ago had reopened as they had suffered only minor damage. She suggested that we clean off, as we were pretty disgusting by this point. It had been months of only washing my face, armpit, hair, and crotch with a bucket and cloth. I needed a full bath. We set out, waving goodbye to Samuel. After his recovery, he had been busier than ever helping rebuild the city. Just like all of us, I suppose. But he had more responsibility as an officer. There was also talk that most of the Army was getting ready to leave for Parthia in a couple weeks. The enemy was waiting. Samuel would be staying behind, though. He was too old to fight.

Once again I found myself to be entranced by the clamor of the streets. The liveliness of it all. We passed by a stand where a woman offered to tell fortunes with runic sticks. I had no idea what religion or cult she may hail from, but there was a long line filled with people wanting to hear what she had to say. Another woman was standing on a pedestal, preaching the gospel of the Lord. There was a small, but dedicated crowd surrounding her. She praised the miracle of Jesus Christ. Shortly after we passed by, her preaching devolved into an angry argument with a pagan and stone throwing ensued.

Violence. A trio of soldiers nearby looking to buy some dried fruit rushed over to calm everyone down and avoid someone getting seriously hurt. From what I could tell, the soldiers succeeded. They dragged the stoner away, and the woman kept preaching. I was surprised that the preacher was a woman. I suppose gender norms in Christianity were a little more relaxed in the past. Years. That makes sense, I guess. The more people the better. They were in a growth phase, not yet established.

It was hard for me to even grasp the concept of Christianity being a new religion that was frowned upon and disregarded by the masses. It had just been part of the establishment in so many countries for so long by the time I was born, that even the rise of atheism in the modern world could not prepare me for the tense and chaotic religious situation in Antioch.

After the earthquake, large portions of the city were destroyed. What survived suffered serious damage. We stayed in the intact areas, but there was still widespread death and destruction in the early weeks. Now, however, things seemed to have stabilized. The city was lively again. People were singing, dancing, bartering, preaching, drinking, and fucking. It was almost normal, in a surreal sort of way. Even among all of this rejuvenation, there lived a sense of grief and foreboding among the residents. It seemed very much as if everyone was just putting on a show. Not just for those around them, but for themselves as well. A charade to keep themselves sane. It was the only way; adapt or die. It was known among the population that emperor Trajan was within the city at the time of the quake and some of his entourage had died. Word had just gotten out about a week earlier that the consul Marcus Pedo Vergilianus had been killed in the earthquake. I discovered that this was deeply shocking to many of the customers that frequented Livia's shop.

There was a darkness here, hidden among the lively atmosphere. Everyone had lost someone, or at least the majority of people had lost someone. I didn't really care about anyone who died in the quake, but just about everyone I talked to did. The fires were gone now, and most of them had taken place in other parts of the city, anyway. In the wooden suburbs, not amid this marble city center. The cracks in the walls and the stains of blood on the cobblestone were everywhere, the stench and distraught imagery masked by the exotic spices of the food stands and the loud colors of the various murals and mosaics.

We reached the baths and there were some cracks in the

foundation, but it was just as pristine as I remembered. The same fat man greeted us, but I noticed he had lost an eye in the earthquake. His eye was scarred shut. We cleaned off and made love. I decided I loved Aelia. I loved her more than anyone I had ever loved before, aside from my family. I would do anything for her. Anything at all.

Chapter 28

When we returned home later in the day, Samuel was waiting for us. He needed help putting planks up on the roof of the guest house. It was easy work, but Samuel was too old and too injured to be of much use. Aelia and I finished the job pretty quickly. I had become rather efficient with physical labor over the last couple of months. If I ever returned home, I might even be inclined to try to get a summer job along those lines. Those kinds of jobs paid pretty well, I think, but I had always avoided them out of laziness and fear. Fear of bad performance.

The tools would be different, but the temperament required would be the same. And as I discovered, I did have that special temperament for this kind of work. It was helpful, and it provided me with satisfaction in a way that white-collar work never did. I was building something or filing something. There was actually a tangible benefit to my hard labor. Something visible. Something I could admire. Be proud of. It was all useless, anyway. Thinking about summer jobs and money and my past. That is gone now. This was my life. It wasn't a bad life, either. I heard footsteps approaching us from behind. It was a soldier, sweaty and clearly over-dressed in his leather and chainmail armor.

"Sir?" The soldier extended his arm in a salute. Samuel groaned, laboring to sit up.

"Yes?" He coughed.

"Sir, we found the slave you were looking for,"

"Now? Amid all this chaos? Well done,"

"Just doing my job,"

"I'm impressed. What's your name, centurion?"

"I am First Spear Centurion Habil, sir,"

"Well, Centurion, where is she?"

"She's encamped at the hippodrome,"

"Are you sure that it's her? We have had a terribly difficult time,"

"According to the description given...yes,"

"I suppose we will find out when we see for ourselves,"

"Of course. She is a slave of the Legate Hadrian. Arranging a meeting was difficult but he will see you right away," Centurio Habil was looking at me. I was supposed to meet Hadrian. Alone? Jesus.

"Today?" Samuel asked, bewildered.

"Yes," The Centurion confirmed. He allowed a little grin to spread across his stony face. I couldn't believe it. The banality of the whole thing. I had been stuck here for more than a year and now all of a sudden some guy comes up and says that they found my salvation. It was insane.

"You can go, centurion. Well done," Samuel said. The centurion saluted and walked away. My grin was wiped away once I realized just exactly which Hadrian they were talking about. Hadrian, as in the successor to the Emperor Trajan. That guy. Knotts had been talking about him. Apparently he was a good emperor, but I couldn't remember anything else about him other than that Trajan would die in less than two years and Hadrian would replace him.

"He just wants to meet you. Trust me, this is the best you're going to get," Samuel said.

"You can convince him, Ashton," Aelia squeezed my shoulder.

"I don't have any money," I said. Samuel chuckled heartily.

"A man like that couldn't care less about money," Samuel explained. I nodded my head and exhaled.

"He wants him alone?" Aelia asked. Samuel nodded. How hard could it be to convince someone to free their slave? Place like this, there are plenty of slaves. He can afford whoever he wants. Mind you, Priya would be quite the slave, if she was sharing her full abilities. I mean, the woman could pilot a time machine. Not many could boast that achievement.

"I'm ready," I said.

29

Chapter 29

Before

Funerals are one of those events that bring all sorts of far-flung relatives and family friends together in a way that is only comparable to a wedding. I prefer weddings. Up until now, the only funeral I had ever been to was for my Uncle and Grandpa.

Something else that is striking to me about funerals is all the steps that go along with them. I never knew either of the subjects of the funerals I have attended, as my grandpa died when I was young and my Uncle lived far away. In those cases, all the steps seemed quite tedious. Memorial this, luncheon that. I know, I know. I'm a terrible person. It's just that I saw funerals as something that people really dragged out. I knew the reason why it was done that way but sometimes I just wished that it could be done in a few hours. An hour at church, an hour for lunch, and an hour to bury the poor soul. Seemed easy enough.

How wrong I was. My parents could barely hold themselves together. I was devastated when Caleb killed himself, but things were more or less fine for me in the solemn days that immediately followed. Perhaps it was numbness, a state of shock. One day he was there, the next he wasn't. It was like a gaping tear in the fabric of my universe. It was as if the sun had suddenly burned out on a particularly warm day, like God turning off one of his many little light switches. My family was violently plunged into a cold, pitiless abyss. Such a contrast to the warmth that came before.

I complained about him while he was here because I didn't realize what a staple he had become in my life. A staying force of continuity. I always assumed he would grow up with me, grow old with me. Forever a pain in my ass. I didn't cry because I was numb, empty. Almost like my bone marrow had been drained, I felt hollow. Weak. Guilty. Despite this, I wasn't about to break down like my mom, who confined herself to her bedroom and did not leave until the funeral.

My dad was in a similarly rough state of mind, but he pulled himself together and called all the relatives. He took me to the coffin store, which looked exactly like what you'd expect a coffin shop to look like; beige carpets, comfortable chairs, potent air-conditioning, and an occasionally colorful assortment of coffins defined the interior.

The wretched old place was cavernous, but largely empty aside from a couple geriatrics. It took me a few minutes to come to the morbid realization that they were probably shopping for themselves.

A young, energetic young woman emerged from the back to greet us. She couldn't have been older than twenty-five. She struck me as far too transactional, and she had a squeaky voice. A deep, red rage rose up from the pit of my stomach and lodged itself in my chest. I found myself fighting a growing urge to hit her. This was surprising as I am hardly a violent person. But there was just something about her casual demeanor, her high-pitched voice, and the awful Botox that made me want to lunge.

It was shockingly short. There is something visceral in seeing a miniature coffin. My father agreed with me when I suggested that we should get him one that was bright orange. I think Caleb would have found that funny. Bright Orange wasn't his favorite color, you see, but it came with a story. A couple years earlier, Caleb was angry with me for not making his bed. him. So he dumped orange paint all over my bed, as payback for not bending to his will. In return, I dipped his toothbrush in my mom's nail polish remover. He was coughing for like an hour!

After buying the little orange coffin, my father and I had to meet with the funeral director. The funeral home was almost as depressing as the coffin shop, although I liked it better. Instead of giving off an abandoned eighties strip mall vibe, it reminded me of a warm, old-fashioned home from long ago. There was a big fireplace in the reception area and lots of oak furniture. The mounted deer and moose horns all over the walls reminded me of my Uncle Hermann's lake cabin. It was warm and smelled of incense. Or was that smell just some old candles? I have no idea what that smell was, but it was exactly what I expected.

The funeral director was another young woman, probably about the same age as the coffin lady. Except I liked her much more. She looked young, but she presented herself as much more sensitive and mature. This wasn't a transaction, it was a compassionate service provided by a family which had been doing this for generations. The meeting itself only lasted for about an hour, although we covered a lot of stuff during that hour. The funeral home would handle the catering, and they were great with allergies. We would have to use the big room, because of all the people that were going to attend. We talked about a bunch of other things that I paid little attention to.

By the end of the day, my father and I had returned home to a dirty house. My mom usually keeps the house in order but after her withdrawal from the world the burden fell solely on me, since my father was busy planning the funeral. Despite the circumstances, I had no choice but to return to school. Missing high school classes isn't really an option because the classes are so long. They cover so much material in just one class, and though I do okay, I'm hardly an academic student.

Despite my vehement objections, my father must have told the school because on the first day back there was a wonderful announcement. No one looked at me the same. That first lunch back with Jen and the boys was rather silent, at least until some creepy guy came down the street riding a little girl's bike, and we all burst out laughing.

"Nice bike!" Mike calls out to him. We laugh even harder.

It was nice to have a distraction, even if it only lasted for a few seconds. To be totally honest, I was happier with my friends than at home with my Dad. It was all just so suffocating. My mom was MIA right when her family needed her most, and my dad just buried himself in work. Sometimes María would drop by for a visit, always willing to help out in whatever way she could. But she had some mobility issues and could only do so much. As a result, the week leading up to the funeral passed in a blur. My dad was doing who-knows-what while I focused on cleaning up after my parents.

The funeral was on a Saturday. Despite the fact that summer was well behind us, the sun was shining and I don't think there was a cloud in sight. We got to the church around ten in the morning, and no one else was there yet. The funeral wasn't supposed to start until eleven-thirty, and we probably didn't need to come so early.

All the preparations had already been made, and Caleb's little orange coffin had already been placed on the pulpit by the funeral home people. Even just convincing my mom to leave her room was exceedingly difficult. She was a mess and hadn't showered for a week. Dad and I managed to make her clean herself up and put on a black dress, but she was a shell of her former self and she didn't speak a word to me.

As soon as we arrived at the church, my mom just sat down at her seat at the front of the church and gazed off into the distance. It was an open casket, but my mom never so much as glanced at the coffin. She was blankly staring at one of the murals on the wall. It was terrifying.

My dad went to go comfort her, and I was kind of just left standing at the front door of the church, unwilling to go and see Caleb. I had no desire to see my dead brother in a coffin. It would make it too real. At least until now I could always just pretend that he was away on a vacation somewhere, that he would be coming back. After all, just a week earlier I was having conversations with him. Caleb had been gone for longer than a week before. One time, about a year ago, he went on a trip to California for two weeks with his longtime best friend Ralph. I couldn't believe that my parents let him go, it was just unbelievable. I've never got to go on a weekend camping trip with my friends, never mind leave the country! I always knew that he was dead, but I can't accept that he's dead. How can he be dead?

He still has another seventy years to make my life a living hell. What about high school? Making new friends? Or going out with a girl and then having me laugh at him when he gets dumped for being an asshole. What about getting a job? What job would he have had? I don't even know if he had any idea what he was going to do when he grew up. Hell, I don't. What about buying his first car? I don't even have a car but if I did I know he would make sure his car was superior. He would make it his mission to let me know that his car has leather seating, and mine doesn't. Maybe his headlights would be a bit brighter, the engine of better quality. Now that will never happen. Now I will never hear another whiny little word from his mouth again. Now he is dead.

How can that be?

I look and see a priest walk in through the front door. I'm surprised he wasn't here already, but that doesn't really matter. I don't know why I did this, but for some reason I feel a sudden urge to ask for confession. Again, this is very perplexing for me because I'm not exactly the religious type. I'm sure it's probably very unusual to ask for confession right before a funeral, and if it did happen, it would probably be suspicious. The priest would probably be wondering if I killed him or something. I mean, really, who confesses at a funeral?

"Hi," I'm surprised at how loud my voice is.

"Hello, my son, what can I do for you?" replied the priest.

"I know—is it normal for—-I was thinking about doing confession,"

"It's perfectly normal, don't worry about that. And of course, there should be time,"

"Alright then," I say. We walk into the confessional and I kneel. My hands are all sweaty and I can't help but pinch my arm in anxiety. Why is this so nerve-wracking? They say confession is like lifting the weight of the rocks that weigh down your soul. I've only done it twice before so I could get my first communion and then later confirmed as a catholic. My Catholicism was nominal at best, however, and my family only came to church on Easter and Christmas. Nevertheless, I was not an atheist.

The priest, I think his name was father Micheal, started speaking all of a sudden from the other side of the confessional. He said some sort of blessing and then there was an awkward silence. Eventually

I remembered to say "bless me, father, for I have sinned," and do the sign of the cross.

"How long has it been since your last confession?"

"About four years," There was a bit of an awkward silence and then I realized I was supposed to confess.

"I swear sometimes. I have said the Lord's name in vain many times," I pinch my arm some more. Silence.

"Oh.. there was one time I was so angry with my friend Mike that I shoved him and called him a piece of shit. Mike's a great guy, I don't even remember what I was mad at him for. That's out of character for me, it must have been a bad day or something," My voice is unsteady, and I worry if I'm speaking too quickly. It must sound as if I'm rambling. I have a sudden urge to just say what I've said already is all I have come to confess. Why does he remain silent? What does he expect me to say? What the hell am I doing here? I should be out mourning or praying or whatever the fuck you do at the funeral of your little brother.

"I...I was a bad brother," I whisper hoarsely. The lump in my throat gets bigger, and I start to worry if I am going to choke. At this point I'm pinching my hand as hard as I can.

"Any chance I got, I would undermine him. If he ever did anything good and received praise, I was jealous. If he did something somewhat mischievous, I would just get angry with him or report him to my parents. I never engaged with him or his little jokes that he would play on me. Our interests were largely opposites, but we got along when we bonded over a few limited things. Basketball is an example of that. We both loved basketball. Problem was, I always resented him because he was so bad at it. So I would say, 'oh nice job' and kind of slip off, trying to avoid him. Sometimes he would try to hang out with me and my friends. We were never downright hostile towards him, but we tried to get *rid of him as soon as we could. When he...when he was alive I did not like him. I did not like my brother at all. In fact, when I got home from school and I heard him arrive later on, I would just get a headache and wish he came home a bit later," I stop for a second to catch my breath. My throat is completely dry and the lump in my throat is still there, if somewhat lessened. Burning pain radiates through my hand from all the pinching, but it's numbed by the situation.*

"I see," The priest says. Before he can say anything else, I continue.

"You see, I hated my brother. And I know plenty of siblings who said things like that about each other, but few actually believe it. They annoy each other from time to time, but with Caleb my mood darkened whenever I saw him. I think he knew it, as well. My mom would tell me things about how Caleb just looked up to me and whenever he was bitter or cruel, it was just him lashing out. He had a tough life, only a few friends. I think he was bullied a lot. I never batted an eye. You hear of overprotective brothers, but to be honest I had little more than passing sympathy for him. I saw his surface-level anger and refused to look beyond it. Even though I hated him, I loved him as well because I miss him so much. I took him for granted, and now that he is gone I feel like I've lost my left hand or something. I was a bad brother," When I finally finish, there is some more silence before father Micheal finally speaks.

"It is normal to feel guilt after the death of a sibling, or someone close to you. People have complex relationships and that's ok. Our Pope, Francis, teaches us that one should never go to bed without making amends for all the arguments made in a day, because you never know when someone might pass on. Unfortunately, many people do not do this in practice. Familial love, or storge in Greek, is something that runs deeper than day-to-day affections.

A friendship can be destroyed from an argument, or in your case a series of arguments. And that's okay. You will meet many people throughout your life, and few will be there when it is time for you to go. That doesn't lessen the importance of those relationships, but they are fleeting. Family is not," Father Micheal spoke with a soft, comforting voice that I had not noticed before.

"Your brother, while I did not know him, loved you. He was young and while your case may feel unique, I can assure you that it is not. One can love someone and hate them at the same time. If he...if he had lived to a more mature age, I am sure you two would have reconciled. Family, aside from God himself, is the most powerful connection you will ever have," Father Micheal paused, perhaps faltering a bit. By now I was feeling better, although there was still a distant feeling of guilt.

"Let me ask you this, do you grieve your brother?" Father Micheal asked.

"I guess," I mumble foolishly. I pinch myself in embarrassment.

"Yes, of course!" I almost allow my hushed whisper to turn into something much louder.

"Then you loved him. Sometimes one has to lose someone to realize how much they meant to them in the first place." There is another pause.

"yeah...I don't know, I don't know, I don't know..." I start to cry a bit, so I pinch myself again and force myself to stop. That familiar empty ache fills my bones, but Father Michael definitely helped.

"You have undoubtedly still sinned, and so your penance will be to complete the rosary. I also challenge you to be more conscious of your actions around others and how you affect them. Try to be kind when you can. Tolerant whenever possible. Most importantly, you must learn to forgive. Not only those who have wronged you but also you must learn to forgive yourself. In nominee patris et

filii et spiritus sancti. Amen." The priest left his stall and walked back into his office.

I have no idea how long I stayed in that confessional, sitting there, but no one came to find me. I just sat there and leaned my face against the cold oak. So cold. And then my body heat warmed up the oak a bit, and so I shifted. After some unknown amount of time, I realized if someone saw me they would probably think I looked like my mother. Empty and sullen. Except I wasn't empty and sullen, not exactly. With that thought, I left the confessional and walked to my seat. The church wasn't even half-full yet.

30

Chapter 30

Aelia decided to stay behind, to take a look at the shop. I asked her why she didn't do it with me earlier, but she told me that she wanted to see it by herself. She gave me a kiss before I left, and I kissed her back. This one counts, she said.

Samuel could only get one horse because of the earthquake, so we doubled. It was a relatively short ride to the hippodrome. It was basically a large field, with seating on either side. It looked like it was a racing arena. Like for chariots. There were a lot of security and military tents set up in the field. There were plenty of soldiers in the normal uniforms that I recognized from before, but there were also other soldiers in black and purple uniforms.

"Who are those guys?" I asked Samuel.

"That is the Praetorian Guard," Samuel said with contempt.

"You don't like them much?" I asked.

"Ah, they're just so full of themselves. Officious little pricks," Samuel growled. I said nothing. Samuel was in his full military uniform, and some of the soldiers saluted him as we moved our way down the path. The praetorians did not. One of them stopped us before we could enter.

"We are here to see Hadrian," Samuel said.

"Are you now? The Praetorian grumbled. He looked at us up and down.

"I am the Primus Pilus of—-" Samuel started.

"Yeah, yeah. Whatever. ID?" The praetorian scowled. Samuel unrolled a scroll and showed it to him.

"Happy?" Samuel asked. The praetorian sighed and waved us forward. We rode to the center of the hippodrome, to the big tents.

"Get off," Samuel said simply. I obliged. What was the Hadrian going to be like? I remembered vaguely that he would, indeed, be the next emperor of Rome. Rest in peace, professor Knotts. What was I going to say? I guess I could tell him the truth. Or the closest believable version of the truth. I could tell him that I came here with her, that I was a Roman citizen, and she was my only way home. People didn't really require proof of citizenship, but if he did ask, I could explain to him that it was lost in the earthquake. I could do this. It was going to be ok. I was finally going to go home.

A young, bearded man emerged from one of the big tents. He was wearing elaborately decorated black leather armor, with gold embroidery.

"You must be Ashton," the man said, extending his hand. I shook it nervously. He had a firm grip.

"Yes, sir," I said.

"You can call me Hadrian," Hadrian said, with a well-practiced smile I recognized from politicians on TV. I followed into his tent, and Samuel stayed outside. The tent was even more massive inside. There were multiple tables, including one with a large map. Next to his big king-sized bed, there was a wooden desk with an unfinished letter on top. Priya was standing in the corner, her hands clasped over her stomach. She looked sick or something. There were bags under her eyes that looked more like bruises. Her chocolate skin was gray and sickly. Most alarmingly, it looked like chunks of her hair had fallen out. What the hell happened to her? This guy must be abusing her or something.

"Priya!" I exclaimed.

"Hello, Ashton," she sighed. Hadrian gave another broad politician's smile.

"So you two do know each other, then," Hadrian said. His voice was smooth and measured.

"Yes, I know him," Priya said shortly. Hadrian walked up to Priya and put his arm around her. She gave a weak smile.

"Priya has been my most trusted friend and advisor," Hadrian said. I suppose it wouldn't be that hard to believe. It seemed like people used slaves for everything here, so why not political advice? I imagine it wouldn't be beyond her abilities, either.

"I can appreciate that, sir, but I came here with her, and I need her help to—-" I started. Hadrian just laughed.

"Leave us," Hadrian ordered, his smile fading away. Priya nodded and left the tent, closing the door on her way out. Oh, no. What was he going to do?

"Sir, I don't know—-" Hadrian interrupted me again.

"Ah-ah-ah! What did I say?" He waved his finger.

"Sir?" Hadrian slapped me across the face. It stung so much, my face went numb. He didn't hit that hard, although by the looks of him, that was by choice.

"I told you to just call me Hadrian," He whispered hoarsely.

"Ok...Hadrian," I rubbed my face. Hadrian went over to one

of his tables and started pouring two glasses of wine.

"Care for a drink?" He asked. I didn't really know if I had a choice.

"Sure," He offered me a glass, and I took a sip. It was unexpectedly delicious, even though I'm not a wine drinker. Fruity, with a hint of nuttiness. That's what the wine tasters would say. Much better than the booze Aelia and I had been drinking. I just knew it was obscenely expensive. I took another, bigger sip. He sat down, and so I did as well. We just sat there for an entire minute before he spoke.

"Are you familiar with the story of Damon and Pythias?" Hadrian asked, leaning forward.

"No," I answered.

"I'm sure you wouldn't have. You're a Roman, are you not?" Hadrian scratched his curly beard.

"Yes," I lied.

"It's a Greek myth. Some so-called Roman traditionalists object to my admiration of Greek culture. They see the Greeks as little more than learned barbarians. I object to any such classification, don't you?"

"Yes,"

"The Greeks are not barbarians. Greece is the cultural heartland of our empire. We inherited much of what we know from them. Math, rhetoric, architecture, naval technology, and so much more,"

"Yes,"

"Anyways, I'm getting off topic here. Damon and Pythias. They were best friends a long time ago, before Rome. Back when the Greeks and Carthaginians and Egyptians ruled our sea,"

"The Carthaginians?"

255

"Yes, the same ones as Hannibal."

"He crossed the alps, right?" I blurted out. I hoped I was right. It was just something I vaguely remembered. Hannibal crossing the alps. It was a saying.

"Yes! Very good," Hadrian exclaimed, taking a big sip of wine and leaning back in his chair.

"So Damon and Pythias lived way back in the day,"

"Indeed. They lived in the far past, in Syracuse. Damon was condemned to death by the tyrant Dionysius. Damon asked Dionysius to put his affairs in order. Dionysius refuses until Pythias offers to be executed in his stead,"

"What happened?"

"Well, Damon returned at the allotted time, and Dionysius was so impressed with their friendship that he let them both go," Hadrian crooned. What the hell did that story have to do with anything?

"Does that mean you'll release Priya?" I asked. Hadrian smiled wearily.

"Perhaps,"

"What's the meaning of that story?" I decided to ask outright.

"You claim to be good friends with Priya. You claim that you need her to get home."

Hadrian says. Where was he going with this?

"I am," I insist.

"Then...you will be willing to risk even your own life for your friendship,"

"Well..." I mumbled. What was he going to suggest? Was he going to make me?

Fight in the arena or something? Was he going to make me fight a lion with my bare hands?

"I will let her go, if you prove to me that she is as important to you as Damon was to Pythias," Hadrian said.

"How?" I asked, somewhat reluctantly. Hadrian stood and walked closer to me. His

lips curled into a thinner smile that was clearly more authentic than what I had seen so far.

"I have a certain...thirst. Sometimes it must be quenched. Do you understand?" he felt my face with his soft hands. WHAT THE HELL? He wanted to have sex with me. No. No way. No way in hell. I couldn't, could I? I mean, the stakes were pretty high. But my life here wasn't so bad. How sustainable was it, though? How long before the Uber-generous Samuel started to ask questions?

"No," I said. Hadrian scowled and grabbed me. I tried to fight back, but he was massive. He smacked me hard across the face, giving me a nosebleed. I fell down, dazed. He grabbed me by the hair and bent me over the table. In one last burst of energy, I swung and tried to punch him. Instead, he grabbed my hand and twisted my wrist. I screamed in pain. He pinned me against the table again.

"Yes." Hadrian's smooth voice was dripping in lust.

Beige. The color of the tent was beige. Beige was a pleasant color. Unassuming, gentle, kind. It went with everything. I don't care what people say about beige, it's not boring. I like beige.

What kind of fruit was that flavor of wine, anyway? It was fruity, but in what way? Strawberries? No. Raspberries? No. Oh! Raspberries. How I loved raspberries. I remember that one time when I was enslaved, I had a really big craving for...no. Don't think of that. Think of something else.

What was I going to do when I was home? I would hug my

dad and find a way to reconcile with my mom. Hopefully, she was out of the institution. They must be so worried about me. And my friends! Jen and Jim. I wonder if those two got together. They would have complemented each other nicely. A match made in heaven! I bet that—-

Hadrian grunted loudly, and it was done.

"You can go," He said. I couldn't move. I just stayed there, bent over the table. Utterly scarred, humiliated, disgusted. I was shivering.

"What about Priya?" I asked weakly.

"She can go too," Hadrian said. I slowly stood up, acutely aware of the mixture of blood and semen inside me. Carefully, I pulled up my trousers and limped out of the tent, only to throw up on the grass. I vomited and vomited until there was nothing left to come out. I was just gagging. Priya and Samuel ran up to me and asked if I was ok. I wearily looked up at Priya.

"Let's go," I said, before gagging again.

31

Chapter 31

"So you're Priya," Samuel said, breaking the silence. Since the three of us couldn't ride a single horse, we walked the horse back to the house.

"Yes," Priya said sullenly. I hadn't spoken a word to Priya yet.

"What did you do...before?" He asked.

"I was a wife," Priya muttered.

"Where is he now?"

"Oh-he's somewhere," Priya said vaguely. There was no more conversation for the rest of the walk back. Aelia was waiting for us.

"Ashton!" She smiled and hugged me. I hugged back very tightly.

"I missed you," I whispered.

"Geez, you weren't gone that long. What did the rich fool do to ya?" Aelia tickled me. I didn't laugh. Her smile faded away quickly. Priya widened her eyes at the sight of Aelia.

"Priya, this is Aelia," I said. They shook hands.

"Ashton, we need to go," Priya said firmly, looking me directly in the eyes. There was urgency in her voice. She didn't want to stay here another minute. I could definitely understand that sentiment, especially now. "What, now?" I asked. Priya looked at me for a long time before sighing.

"We can stay the night," Priya said.

"There are only two undamaged bedrooms, I'm afraid," Samuel wheezed. It was clear he had no intention of letting her sleep in his room.

"That's ok, I can sleep outside," Priya's voice was weak, and she was staring into the distance. I expected Samuel to offer his room, but he just nodded. Priya's despair wasn't really out of place, either. Samuel had just lost his sister and daughter in relatively rapid succession. Aelia was mourning the loss of a mother figure and now had to deal with my sudden departure, and I had just been raped by a man. Fucking hell.

"Let's go look at the store," I practically shouted at Aelia.

"Now?" She sighed heavily.

"You shouldn't have to see that on your own. That's your life's work," I said. She smiled weakly.

"Ok," Aelia sniffed her nose.

"If you two are going, I'm going to have a conversation with this young gentleman here," Priya said, looking at the aged Samuel.

"Are you finally going to explain the whole story? Ashton's been holding out on us," Samuel chuckled. Priya did not laugh.

"Yes," Priya said. Aelia and I started walking. We said nothing on the way there. A woman was laughing hysterically in an alley. Her eyes were wild, listless. We went up into the loft. Aelia slammed the door shut.

"Where are you going?" Aelia shoved me against the wall.

"I'm going home," I said.

"Where is that? And don't give me another bullshit answer. Tell me the truth," Aelia said. She wouldn't believe me, but who cares? I was leaving. I couldn't leave on a lie. I loved her.

"You wouldn't understand,"

"Then make me understand!"

"I'm from somewhere far away,"

"You've said that before,"

"Because it's true,"

"I could strangle you!"

"I'm from the future. That's why you can't understand," Aelia slapped me and tried to walk away. I had a brief twang of trauma, but then I got over it and impulsively grabbed her by the wrist. I pulled her towards me and we kissed, but then she shook her hand free.

"Don't do that!"

"Don't slap me,"

"I'm sorry, I didn't—-"

"I'm from 2023,"

"What?"

"I'm from 2023," I repeated.

"What is that number supposed to be?"

"The year,"

"The year is 115," Priya exclaimed.

"Yes, it is," I affirmed.

"And you are from...2023?" Aelia asked, exasperated.

"Yes,"

"No, you're not,"

"Yes I am,"

"Ok, then. What am I going to do tomorrow?"

"I don't know!"

"Then how can you be from the future?" Aelia shook her head.

"I just am! I don't know how to explain it to you, but it's the truth!"

"Well, how then? How did you get here?"

"A man built a machine, and I don't know how he did it, but—-"

"Now you're just making words up. What is a machine?"

"It's—-never mind. I can't explain it."

"Was it Saturn?"

"What?"

"Did the God of time send you?"

"I mean, maybe he sent me. I have no idea how it worked, but it did. I guess an ancient roman god is a good an explanation as ever,"

"What other explanation could there be?"

"I don't know, maybe—-"

"Saturn sent you here to realize something. The Gods have something in store for you. They wanted you to discover yourself."

"Discover myself? When did you get to be so religious?"

"How did you not know I was religious?"

"I guess I didn't—-"

"You have way too much wax in your ears,"

"Ok, that was uncalled for."

"No, it wasn't,"

"So you believe me, then?"

"I don't know. I guess it wouldn't be the biggest leap of faith,"

"Really?"

"I mean, you did have to rewrite the business accounts in that strange language of yours. That wasn't Greek or Latin. It sure as hell wasn't Persian, either. You're clearly civilized. You look like us, and yet you write in a completely different language,

"I guess,"

"Obviously it worked, because we had great success at that sale. Maybe it's just a language I somehow don't recognize, or maybe it was gibberish after all,"

"It wasn't gibberish," I said.

"It looked like gibberish," Aelia shot back,

"So if I really think about it...you're lying!" Aelia cried.

"Listen——"

"You're such a piece of shit!" Aelia screamed, tears suddenly streaming down her face.

"Ael——"

"If you're going to go, then just go. I'm going to stay here and help my neighbors. Alright?"

"Aelia, no. We can't leave it like that."

"Are you coming back?"

"I don't...I don't know. Probably not,"

"My mother left me on the streets. Livia ran away with her boyfriend. And now you are leaving me, without even having the decency to tell me where you're going."

"I'm not lying!"

"Get out,"

"Aelia, please. I can't go like this. Don't make me leave like——"

"GET OUT OF MY SIGHT!" Aelia sobbed. I sighed and slowly started to walk back to Samuel's house. I felt terrible. Why couldn't I have just made up some sort of story? There would have been no harm in it. It would have been a white lie. Now, she thought I was lying to her. She thought I was a liar. That I was leaving her. That she meant nothing to me. Aelia and Samuel meant everything to me. They saved me. Livia, too, wherever she was. I needed her to know that.

Unfortunately, I had no idea how I could tell her without it ringing false. Of course, it sounded like I was lying. Of course, she didn't believe me. I knew she wouldn't believe me. Why would she? Maybe I was a piece of shit. Nah, I wasn't a piece of shit. I was a murderer. That was worse. Being a piece of shit was just in the job description. I wished Aelia had known what I was before she got too close. I was toxic. She was a hurting woman, and I hurt her even more. Kicking her while she was down. Intention does not matter. No one cares about intention. Only outcomes matter, and the outcomes of my actions are almost always horrific.

Maybe I deserve everything that was inflicted upon me. Getting trapped here, getting enslaved, getting beaten, getting raped. Now this. Aelia was fucking with me, but maybe she was right. Maybe I was sent here by Saturn, the god of time. Maybe this was my divine punishment.

I reached Samuel's house to find Samuel and Priya in better spirits. Priya hadn't recovered, though. If anything, she looked even more sickly. The day was slowly fading away, the sun was blotted out by the growing storm. The gloomy clouds started sputtering out little raindrops, seemingly unable to produce the full thing.

"Where's Aelia?" Samuel asked, taking a swig from a bottle of wine.

"She's at the store. I think she'll be staying there for the night," I replied.

We spent the rest of the day in relative silence. I went to my room and rested. Not exactly sleeping. Just resting. No one asked what happened in the tent. I imagine they must have heard from outside. There really isn't anything to say. Apparently, after spending the day with Priya, Samuel softened and allowed her to stay in his room.

I didn't sleep at all that night for fear of another nightmare. When the morning finally came, my head was killing me and my eyes were so dry it was blurry to see. Nevertheless, I forced myself up, and we had a nice breakfast of bread and fruit. How Samuel got ahold of such luxuries as fruit amid all the chaos, I don't know. Just one more act of kindness that I could add to the list.

"I don't even know how I can thank you," I told Samuel as Priya was readying the horses that Samuel somehow got for us. When did he arrange? No one knew.

"No need. It's just what you gotta do," Samuel smiled, and extended his hand. I shook it. It was scratchy and calloused.

"But you didn't need to. Why extend so much charity to someone you barely know?" I asked.

"It was just something I had to do," Samuel said simply, exhaling heavily. And with that, I mounted my horse and slowly started the final approach back to the time machine. As we rode away into the distance, I found myself thinking about what I would say to my parents.

Chapter 32

Before

Days lurched into weeks. The funeral was on a weekend, and I took no time off for school. They said I could take all the time I needed, but that was just something they basically had to say.. I don't think many people take offers like that seriously because at the end of the day, what else am I going to do? Sit around at home, watching Netflix and get fat? Wallow in my grief? What good does that do anybody?

No, the best way to get through something such as this was to go back to business as usual. Bury myself in schoolwork, distract myself by having fun with my friends. A combination of both should cure the plethora of memories bursting through the floodgates.

School was undoubtedly more difficult than ever before, and so I decided to start going to coffee shops after school to study. I was never an awful student. I never slacked off in class, or regularly neglected my homework. But I also wasn't the kind of guy who went to coffee shops to study. No one else I knew was doing it.

Effective though it was, the main reason I kept coming back was all the random conversations I would happen to listen in on as I studied. Humanity is the show that just keeps ongoing, isn't it?

For example, one time I was sitting studying some math homework, and I overheard a conversation between an old man and woman. They hadn't seen each other since "the nineties." The man said that he had missed her during his time living abroad, and that it was a shame they hadn't gotten in touch sooner since he had returned three years earlier.

Returned from where?? I have no idea. They continued talking about this and that. I didn't really pay attention to all of it. I was actually studying some of the time. However, I did hear them grumbling about cancel culture.

The frigid December let way to an even icier January. My friends and I spent the time in Jim's basement. He had gotten a new PS5 for Christmas the year before, and we all loved to play on it. The coolest feature on the PS5 was the fact that you could actually feel things with the remote. Of course, it only worked with a couple very specific games, but it was still very cool.

"I can't believe you guys are still XBOX loyalists after this," Jim said one time. "This is cool, but it's a fad. XBOX remains number one for graphics," Mike countered.

"Sorry Mike, but Jim's right on this one. The XBOX is like regurgitated chicken shit compared to this thing," Jen said, and we all laughed.

So we spent hours down there that November. No one really mentioned anything about Caleb after the funeral, and I suppose that's how I wanted it. Time lessened the pain, but I hardly forgot. The biggest problem for me personally was that I was always tired. I was accustomed to being energetic and vigorous, like a teenager should be. It's not like I was getting out of shape either. My exercise schedule was more ambitious than ever.

In the movies, after a tragedy the character will have awful nightmares reliving a certain awful moment again and again. I hear that for some people, this is true. But for me, I didn't dream at all. It was just darkness. Nothing. Go to sleep, wake up. Unfortunately I kept waking up way more than I was supposed to. At ten I would turn off my lights and the world would fade away actually quite quickly. Around one in the morning, I would wake up for no apparent reason. Again at three. Again at five.

Sometimes I would go back to sleep only to start my day at seven, other times I would stay awake after five because it seemed pointless. They say that everyone dreams and that the only question is whether you can remember. I'm glad I don't remember.

Perhaps contributing to my fatigue was my mom's death spiral. The dumb-ass shrink my dad and I made her go to prescribed her some sort of heavy anti-depression meds, which sedated her. I mean, she just wouldn't leave her room. After a few weeks, she had lost her job. Her employers were sympathetic, but as they explained to my dad, her position was far too important to leave vacant for so long. Of course, they would love to consider hiring her back whenever she was ready.

Unfortunately, it seemed like "ready" was a long ways away. There was just nothing in her eyes. It was like she was brain dead, or something. The only way I knew she wasn't was the rare instance where she left her room to come downstairs to collect her supper and the occasional late-night conversation I would hear her having with my dad in the bedroom.

One time, at three in the morning, I heard them discussing something unintelligible, but all I knew was that after a few minutes my mom was dryly sobbing and the conversation was over.

My other friends John and Daniel increasingly started hanging out with another group of guys as the year went on. I guess you learn who your true friends are after something terrible happens. Jen, Jim, and Mike came to the funeral. They were there for me, when I needed it most. John and Daniel just kind of faded away. It's not like I needed them to come to the funeral, that was completely unnecessary. But they had barely talked to me at all since I came back from that damned camping trip. So I treated them the same.

Although it seemed impossible at the time, January eventually did end. February went by a little quicker, and then it was March. Even as Spring approached, the weather did not improve. The winter that year was particularly harsh. There was one weekend in late February around Valentines day when the blizzard was so bad I was unable to walk to school. My dad had to drive me, like when I was a little kid.

"Let's go!" My dad yelled. I was in the middle of eating my awful no name corn flakes, but I knew I needed them if I was going to survive the day.

"Yeah, yeah, in a minute!"

"You're going to be late! I've got places to be too, you know!" he roared. After all the rushing we had to sit there for ten minutes while my dad heated the car. I had to go around and scrape the ice off of the windows, while my dad sat in the car warming up. I think he enjoyed that.

Eventually, we finally got going and my dad turned on the reggae station. "Three little birds" by Bob Marley was playing.

"So..how are you holding up?" This was the first time my dad had asked me that question, and it seemed to come from nowhere.

"I don't know, fine I guess." I wasn't fine.

"You know, you can talk about whatever with me. Whether it's mom, or Caleb, or school," My dad said carefully. I could tell my

269

dad was trying his best.

"There is a social test tomorrow. I'm going to have to study at the coffee shop again,"

"That's fine by me," My dad sighed. The remainder of the drive to school was filled with silence.

Christmas was a somber affair. The school went all out with decorations and a secret Santa thing, which was fun. I got Mike an old go pro from Kijiji for his skateboard, Jen my old Nintendo 3DS, and Jim a nice hoodie. The studying started winding down, as my teachers allowed us to write all our tests when we got back from the holiday break. Some people complained, because they would have to study on the holidays. School was fun, but the rest of Christmas was depressing as hell.

My mom's usual silent trance was replaced with incessant wailing. She refused to come out even for supper, and my dad started sleeping on the couch because she stopped showering.

"Maybe we should get her help," I suggested one especially awful December night.

"It's just grief. She doesn't need to go anywhere," my dad mumbled.

"Dad..."

"She doesn't need help. Now stop talking like that! She is your mother! She just needs time," And that was that.

In comparison to the rest of the Christmas season, the first Christmas Eve following Caleb's death was actually quite a bit of fun. I hung out with Jim, Mike, and Jen during the day. We went on a walk through the river valley, which was nice. The trees were covered with snow. It was that rare and beautiful occurrence where the snow actually stuck to the branches and the sides of the trees. As Jen put it, it was like a "winter wonderland" that day. Anything to forget.

The dinner at home was interesting as well. My Uncle Hermann showed up to the house, but out of all the extended family members who were invited, only he could make it. Our neighbor Marìa also came over for dinner. It was quite the combination.

"So...Ma-rie-ah, how are you doing this fine evening?" Hermann asked once we started eating.

"I'm ok, thank you Hermann," She would reply in her light Peruvian accent.

"Well, ain't that fun? Hear that little boy?" he nudged my shoulder, "Marie here says she's doin' fine! I think that's a damn shame. She should be feeling great, don't you think? Great!" Hermann was yelling at the top of his lungs. Everyone was uncomfortable.

"My name's Marìa, actually," Marìa mumbled.

"What's that, honey? You know, it was a long journey here and my bones are uh-aching," Hermann smiled creepily. The veins on his balding head were bulging.

"Oh-k then! I need a drink. Hermann, Marìa?" My dad stuttered nervously.

"No," muttered uncle Hermann.

"No, but thank you," Marìa responded pleasantly. I got up to go with my dad. I needed to get the hell out of there. As I was heading into the kitchen, I swear I saw Marìa grin a little at my uncle. Trust me, there is nothing more disgusting than the sight which I have just described to you.

The rest of the evening went well enough, aside from my uncle's disgusting remarks and Marìa's increasingly responsive attitude towards them. The pumpkin pie was good, but my dad over whipped the whipping cream. Which is fine, I guess. We played a game of monopoly, my uncle cheated and everyone got mad, and that's how the night ended off. Weird, disgusting, but in a strange sort of way wholesome as well. I enjoyed it. Like I said earlier, interesting is a great word to describe that Christmas Eve.

Throughout all of that, my mom was lying in her bed. She never came out once. Her absence was noticed, but never discussed.

When Christmas morning arrived, I instinctively checked under the tree for presents. There was only one. Despite my age and circumstance, I was disappointed. It's not so much that I wanted something in particular, or that I believed in Santa anymore. It was just that there is something emotional about waking up and finding a bunch of presents under the tree. There is something that much better about unwrapping a gift compared to them just handing you. I suddenly realized that had Caleb still been alive, there would be a bunch of presents under the tree.

The smell of sizzling bacon and pancakes wafted through the air. My dad had already started cooking breakfast. My favorite breakfast, actually. Blueberry pancakes and maple bacon, with fresh fruit on top.

"You're up. Good. breakfast is ready in five," my dad says.

"Sounds good," I replied. I figure I better go brush my teeth for the morning. Some people say it's better to brush your teeth after breakfast, which I guess makes sense. Nevertheless, I like if I were to do that I would just forget and be down to one brush a day. And don't even get me started on people who only brush once a day.

So I brush my teeth and just as I'm about to head downstairs to eat my blueberry pancakes, I hear the most unexpected thing. The voice of my mother.

"Ashton, are you.. are you there?" I hear her weakly call out from behind her bedroom door. This is the first time she's spoken to me since the death of Caleb. I feel tears well up in my eyes as I open the door.

"Yes mom, it's me," My mom is a shell of her former self. Her

eyes are sunken back deep into her skull, with big bruise–like bags under her sockets. The hair which was once carefully cleaned and brushed every day, taking up to half an hour, was now greasy and unkept. Her shirt had two stains; one was brown, and the other was dark yellow. I have no idea what they were from. I couldn't believe the shattered human being in front of me was the same mom that raised me and taught me everything I knew. The same mom who was a warrior at work and at home. I couldn't believe someone could fall so far and still be alive.

"I hate you," my mom whispered.

"What?" I thought I must have misheard her. I feel a huge lump in my throat.

"You did this to him. You never liked him, did you?"

"How can you—–"

"YOU KILLED MY BABY!," My mom screamed that last part as loud as she could, and then just kept repeating it.

"YOU KILLED MY BABY, YOU KILLED MY BABY, YOU KILLED MY BABY, YOU KILLED...." She started slamming her fists against the bed in anger. How could my mom say this to me? How could she believe I was to blame? How could she really think it was my fault? Was it my—–

"Laura! Stop it!" My dad boomed. He looked at me frantically.

"I didn't do anything," I was crying at this point as well.

"Just call 911. I–I think it's time she gets some help." My dad muttered. She kept screaming the same four words right until the ambulance drove her away with my dad.

———————————————————————————————

My mom was committed to a psychiatric hospital. It isn't the same thing as an asylum. Asylums were for the criminally insane. She wasn't a criminal, and she wasn't insane either. Grief strikes people in different ways, and there is nothing more unnatural than a mother losing her child. There isn't even a word for it. There are widows, widowers, and orphans. What is the word for a woman whose son has died before her? There isn't one. Not that I know of, anyway. Probably in another culture or something. Who knows? All I know is that it is unnatural, and it was ok for my mom to be taking things a little hard.

It wasn't forever, and she needed the help. Hopefully after a few weeks of therapy all would be well. At least that's what we thought when we admitted her. I was taken on a balmy afternoon in mid-June, during the exam break. Nearly six months after we forcibly admitted her. It didn't look like she was getting better.

My Dad visited three times a week; I was never welcome.

33

Chapter 33

We reached the time machine after a two-hour ride. It was hard to stay awake, and I found myself occasionally drifting off. Luckily, I always jolted out of it before I leaned too far and fell off the horse. There was a bunch of dirt and sand blown onto the side of it, but the ball-shaped machine otherwise remained untouched.

"Here we are," Priya coughed. We dismounted. Here we were. Finally! I could finally go home. See my friends. My family. Let them know I was okay. I had no idea how long I had been gone for, so maybe they had declared me to be dead. The concept of coming back from the dead always did fascinate me. It was hard to not wonder whether they recorded my funeral. Few people get to see their own funeral. I wonder what people said about me. They probably did, like, a memorial or something at the school. Hopefully not. Hopefully, they were still looking. I'd like to believe people wouldn't give up on me so quickly. Unfortunately, I didn't. I didn't believe that.

"I didn't believe I would ever see this thing again," I sighed.

"Neither did I," Priya agreed.

"We haven't talked," I said.

"No, we haven't. I'm very sorry about what happened to you. This should never have happened. None of it. Samuel told me what happened before you got here, and I also know what Hadrian did to you. He did it to lots of boys, but never me. I had to help him sometimes. Help hold them down. The soldiers wouldn't take part. They said it was a slave's job," Priya said.

"I'm sorry," I muttered. Wow, I was really getting used to saying that.

"Let's get out of here," I said. Priya nodded violently and opened the door to the machine. We climbed in. The two empty seats were glaringly obvious. It all happened so quickly. What had started out as a tour had gone so terribly, unpredictably wrong. What had been excitement turned into dread, depression, and fury? What had been love towards the world became a reluctant hatred. With the push of a few buttons, the machine groaned back to life and the familiar dizziness overtook me once again. This time, I wasn't so scared. I almost wanted something to go wrong. Deep down, I wanted to die. When we arrived safely in the modern world, I was almost disappointed.

34

Chapter 34

I staggered out of the time machine and found Mattheson to be standing there, along with all the lab techs and attendants. They were smiling and clapping. How did they know to gather here? Did they get an alert or something that we were on our way? It had been a year. How did they...I suddenly realized that no time had passed. Everyone was wearing the same clothes as when we left. Matthias Mattheson was in the same white suit. The lab tech all looked the same. Everything was the same. After all, why would we travel back to one year after we left? With a time machine, we could travel back to whenever we wanted. I hadn't been thinking. It was so obvious, but I guess I had other things to worry about.

"Ashton, congratulations! You are the first teenage time traveler! How do you feel?" Mattheson was grinning ear to ear. I tried to speak, but a sudden wave of nausea overtook me and I threw up all over the concrete floor. I retched three or four times before the nausea was gone. I forced myself to look Mattheson in the eyes. His smile was gone.

"Fuck off," I grumbled, wiping the puke off my dry lips with the back of my hand. I walked right past him and made my way to my room. Oddly enough, I remembered exactly where my room was. When I had first been here, probably a year ago now, I didn't know where the room was. Now I did. Explain that! Insanity. Everyone stared, but not a single soul dared to stop me. They could tell something had gone very wrong. Loud murmurs infected the vanilla air. People wanted to know where the other two had gone. I decided I would leave that one to Priya, given she was the adult in the situation. I guess I was an adult, too. Or was I still 17? I was biologically 18, but in this time period I was 17. Bonkers. Absolutely bonkers.

The room looked just the same as I remembered. As if on autopilot, I stripped down and took a hot shower. I hadn't had a shower in over a year. Just baths. Public baths, at that. There's something nice about cleaning yourself in public. You're naked, and so is everyone else. That sounds weird, but after you got used to it, the benefits became more clear. It's a perfect place to do business because everyone is on the same level as everyone else. It's hard to tell who is rich or poor because almost everyone could afford the baths and since everyone was naked, you couldn't judge people based on their clothes.

Nevertheless, I think I still prefer a private shower to the social Roman method. Maybe it's just my psychological preference ingrained in me from a young age, but I liked to be able to just reflect. Even the most busy people needed to shower, and it was in those quiet moments when people could truly look inwards. Perhaps not, though. Perhaps one just likes to sing their favorite song at the top of their lungs, or think about nothing at all. You just couldn't do that in those public baths.

So as I stood there in that sleek modern shower Mattheson

had given me, I couldn't help but stare at the drain as dirty little rivers flowed into the depths of the drainage system. I couldn't wash myself. I just stood there, mesmerized by the steaming water flowing down deep. Away from sight. I watched as those dirty little rivers slowly got clearer. The water stayed hot, almost scalding. It hurt a little bit, but it was just bearable. I stood there for probably twenty minutes before I started crying. I don't know why I cried, but I did. I sobbed and sobbed, but I don't think there were any tears. It's hard to tell in the shower, anyway. But I coughed and my nose was running and I could feel it in my whole body. The relief, the despair, the guilt, the fear, the regret, the anticipation, and most of all...

Most of all, I felt sick. Sick to my stomach. Sick like that, those nights in the fish sauce factory, writhing around in snot and puke. Sick like that man on the toilet when I first arrived in Antioch. I remembered how he collapsed and I did nothing. I felt like cancer had overtaken me. A malignancy. A malignant tumor growing deep inside me, devouring my life force. Growing and growing. Like a weight. Such a heavy weight. Stones holding me down, dragging me down into the depths of the icy abyss. I could see what had become of me, and I was dissatisfied. I felt dissatisfied with the person I had become, disgusted by my very reflection. Maybe I had always been a morally repugnant individual. I don't know when it started. All I knew was that I was what I was. There was something wrong with me, and I knew it. At last, I was aware of the darkness. The malignancy that defined my very existence. I was sick, just like my mother was when she told me she hated me; she looked in the eyes of her only living son with a contemptuous glare reserved for the filth of society.

I was sick, just like Caleb was when he swallowed those pills and choked to death on his own puke. He laid there rotting in his filthy bedroom while I slept, excited for the supposedly joyous Christmas morning to come. I hated him for it, just like I hated him for what he was. I loved him too, but that doesn't matter. He was afflicted by a malignancy, just like me now. A cancer that had found its way into the depths of his skull and had begun to eat away. Caleb let this sickness take root inside him, control him...kill him. I would never let such a thing happen to me. I didn't give a shit about myself anymore. I was going to live like Samuel. Be a good man. I knew it was within me. I knew I could change. When I got home, I was going to be a better son to my parents. Not that I was terrible before, but I was going to do better. Cook more dinners, help out around the house, be more understanding when they have emotional troubles. They were humans just like anyone else, after all.

Be a better friend. No more gossiping about anyone. No more talking behind people's backs. No more hateful thoughts. I needed to be better or I would be left to the wolves. If I wasn't careful, I could be swallowed whole. A change needed to be made. So, here in this shower I made the change. I vowed to myself that I would be dirty no longer. I would cleanse myself, redeem myself. This was going to happen regardless of whatever it may cost me. Regardless of what I might be leaving behind.

Even as I made these promises, I knew they were probably just lies that I was telling myself to feel better. Thoughts don't matter. And that's all these were...thoughts. I started sobbing again, but the water suddenly became icy cold. I stepped out of the stream of water and considered drying off, but I hadn't actually washed myself yet.

So, I quickly lathered my skin with the luxury body wash and ran my body under the frigid water. Shivering, I dried off and got dressed. Happy to see the tv, I turned on an episode of Seinfeld. Someone knocked on the door after a while, and it happened to be a lab coat. She led me to a room where some other lab coats insisted I undergo tests. I didn't see Mattheson anywhere, but I had a strong feeling that they would not send me home until I complied.

Naturally, I did what they wanted. They poked and prodded, sucking out some blood from all different places on my body. The forearm, the hip, even the neck. The neck needle really hurt, and I asked them why they couldn't just get the blood from my arms. They were not very talkative. I went through scans, and X-rays, and who knows what else. Oh, they did a neurological scan on me as well. How fantastic! The whole thing took at least five hours, and by the time they were finally done, I was sore and exhausted. I almost wanted another shower, but as I found out, that was impossible.

Mattheson was waiting for me outside the lab. I asked if I needed to sign an NDA or something. Mattheson laughed and said not to worry about that; I was under 18 and therefore couldn't sign anything. I got the impression that they had other ways of making sure I stayed quiet.

It didn't matter anyway, because I was keen on putting this all behind me. I just wanted to get home and be with my friends and parents. I had never missed home more than I did right now. It was one thing, far away in Antioch. But now that I was here, I just needed to get on a plane. Mattheson's eyes sparkled as he ushered me to the plane. It all happened so fast. Priya was nowhere to be seen, and as I walked across the tarmac to the jet, I half-expected her to be there to wave me goodbye. I still felt bad about leaving her to answer all the questions regarding the missing crew members. I suddenly realized that I had to see her before I left, so just as I was getting on the steps of the jet, I sprinted back to the building/elevator where Mattheson was standing. I demanded to see Priya, but he informed me that wasn't possible. I asked why and he said that she had fallen violently ill with traveling sickness. Again, I demanded to see her.

"I'm afraid you have to get home now," Mattheson sighed, patting me on the shoulder. I tried to push past him, but he was surprisingly strong and managed to hold me in place. There were two armed guards glared at me, hands on their holstered pistols.

"I have to apologize to her," I muttered desperately. Mattheson gave a warm smile.

"Your cure will be your apology for whatever it is that you did."

"I'm sorry?"

"It seems like your blood is immune, just as we expected. The technicians in the lab are already formulating a cure. At the very least, an effective treatment," Mattheson explained. With that, he convinced me that I could go home. I got on the plane and didn't look back.

35

Chapter 35

The plane landed at a small regional airport outside the city. It had been a long flight, but I had managed to stay awake the entire time. I just watched movies and ate the fresh fruit they offered. They offered some candy too, but it was just far too sweet. Unlike on the plane ride to Turkey, Margarethe was not the flight attendant. It was some stern-looking man named George. I only knew he was George because I heard him talking to the pilot and that's what the pilot called him.

George avoided any sort of conversation beyond what was necessary, and he never smiled. The whole plane ride he was just stone-faced. I could see him from my chair, and he could see me. Maybe that was the idea. But he wasn't watching a movie, and he didn't sleep. No book either. He just kind of sat there and stared off into space. Something else...he didn't blink. At least not as far as I could tell. It was uncomfortable to watch, so I did my best to ignore him and instead relax and focus on what was to come.

There was a big black Cadillac Escalade waiting for me when

I got off the plane. The driver had an earpiece; I felt like a world leader or something. He drove me home, and I stared out the window the whole time. It was shocking to see all the modern buildings and such. It was nighttime and I could see the glowing cityscape as we approached.

My hands were shaking and my chest was aching. I was going to see my parents for the first time in a year, but for them it would be like I had only been gone for like five days. They probably thought I had run off or was staying with a friend. At the time I was taken, my mom hated me and I didn't see how that would have changed during the time I was gone. I was going to walk into the same shitty situation I had been taken from, except now I carried all this extra emotional baggage from my time in Antioch. I glanced at the driver with his earpiece and slick suit, and realized that I would never be free of this. Mattheson could get to me whenever he wanted. I had no idea what more he could want from me, but from now on, the reality that I could be taken at any time would always be in the back of my mind.

The car pulled up outside my house. I took a deep breath and stepped outside. It was brisk, and the air was still. Silent. It surprised me, but then again, it was one in the morning. As if reading my mind, a motorcycle engine roared in the far distance. The driver left, and I stood there outside my house for the longest time. My breath quivered with unease.

Finally, I decided to walk up to my front door and knock. At first, there was no reply. But then my dad answered the door, and he stood there, shocked. I tried to say something, but nothing came to mind. Suddenly, he hugged me and then called for my mom to come down. She looked just as rough as I remembered her, but when she saw me, she broke out into tears of joy and joined the hug.

They asked me where I had been, and I realized I didn't know what to say to that. Mattheson never gave me a lie to tell them, but I couldn't tell them the truth either. It was just too unbelievable. Regardless, they were clearly worried about me. I had been gone for a week and they had reported me missing. The police had been unable to find me anywhere. They knew I had been taken because the house was completely destroyed when they came home. So I told them as close to the truth as possible; I had been kidnapped, and I didn't know why. I couldn't believe how happy they were that I was safe.

Over the next couple of days, I had to undergo questioning by the police, and I told them nothing about Mattheson. Just as I promised. Instead, I said that I heard someone break into the house and I hit a guy with a lamp before someone else drugged me. I said that I had been held in a basement and that they did nothing to me that I knew of and made no demands. I told them that they had let me shower and fed me regularly, but I never saw their faces. I told them that I had escaped. They believed me, and they searched the city some more for the kidnappers. It was a couple months before they finally declared the case to be unsolved.

My mom kept going to the psychiatrist, and he really seemed to be helping. She got some antidepressants and although she still wasn't her usual self, things were getting better. It was beginning to look like she might be able to return to work soon.

Sometimes, late at night, I would reminisce about my time in Antioch. I would think of Aelia, Samuel, and Duccidava. My peaceful life there. Sometimes Hadrian would pop into mind, or Paul screaming up on that cross. However, every day with my friends and family was a day where I would think of these people less. My past life was fading away into the back of my memory, never completely gone, but always there. I started to write poems, and there was one I was particularly proud of:

"The Field" by Ashton Beauchum:
When the dirt and dust blow an ugly gust
When the farmer starves and the children leave
When all they slaughter can't help them grieve
When the sky cries and still Our river dries
When the mustard field becomes a brittle shield
Will we finally see?

36

Author's Note

If you've made it this far, and you didn't skip ahead, then congratulations. You made it. I know my writing is pretty dark. Oh well. That's just what the English teachers taught us. It's possible to write positive material, but it's also that much more difficult. It's just as much easier to write about pain and suffering. So basically that's why I did what I did. It's my first book, and I started it when I was 16. Give me a break.

I realize that some may see this as a vanity project. You know, just so I can say that "I wrote a book." I can assure you, however, that was not the intent. The original intention of this book was to practice my writing skills. I did well in English 20 and I guess I had enough undue confidence to undertake this endeavor. Perhaps it was arrogant of me. Oh well. If it started as a writing exercise, that is not what it has become. After a year's worth of work (If I'm being honest, it took only about a month but I didn't write consistently, so the work was in short bursts.) But after a year's worth of work, I'll say for convenience, somewhere along the way I decided that I wanted people to read what I had made.

Writing is one of those things that is absolutely magical in the sense that you are creating something that wasn't there before. Now, maybe it shouldn't be around, but now it is and no one can do anything about it. Just like music or art, although I wouldn't go so far to compare this to any art that is worth mentioning.

The idea for the story actually came from my Tourettes. Yes, I have Tourettes. You may have a vague understanding of the term as someone who walks down the street jerking their head and yelling "fucking fuck, fuckaroo my doo!" compulsively. I am not like that at all. Most people have no idea that I have Tourettes, since I hold in my tics all day. When I get home, I kneel in the bathroom and let them out for up to an hour and a half. It is physically and mentally draining, and it drags out any homework I have to do. But it is also a fountain of creativity.

The doctors don't seem to understand when I say that I see a movie when I tic all at once like that. I see all sorts of things. In a strange sort of way, I almost look forward to ticking because it is like an escape. This just happened to be one of the movies. Obviously, I didn't have all the little details when I started. The main plot, however, was already well-thought out before I began. So that made the entire writing process both easier and more frustrating, because I knew exactly what to write, but I didn't know what to fill the quieter bits with. That's where the actual writing came in, I guess.

To those who know me, I am not Ashton. Although I borrowed some details from my own life in an attempt to convincingly fill the modern world of Ashton Beachum, he is in no way me. Also, I apologize for all the swearing. Typed words don't count.

Also, in case you were wondering, this is somewhat historically accurate. There really was an earthquake in 115AD. Ancient roman society was colorful and full of different religions and ethnicities. Slavery was pervasive, and not necessarily considered being wrong by any significant sector of the population. Trajan was emperor in 115, and he was invading Parthia. There were indeed ancient Garum fish sauce factories. They were run by slaves, just as described in the book. The process might have been slightly different, but I wasn't focused on accuracy so much as authenticity. Women could run businesses, and while roman society was regressive towards women by modern standards, women held many rights that were unmatched until liberalization in the 20th century. The details about the Roman baths were carefully researched, and so were countless other details.

Anyways, thanks for reading.

37

Acknowledgments

I would first like to thank my grade 8 English teacher, Mrs. Robson. When I first entered her class nearly five years ago now, I was terrified. She had distinguished herself as a strict teacher but quickly began to show her softer side. Of course, no one could speak in her class while she was speaking. Even whispers were swiftly condemned. Yet her program of making us write every single night helped to develop my skills into what they are today. Without the foundations that Mrs. Robson laid down, I probably would never had the skill to attempt something like this. Nor would I want to.

To all my elementary teachers who helped build the platform on which I could build from in Mrs. Robson's class—thank you.

To my grade 10 English teacher, Ms. E.

To my grade 11 English teacher, Mrs. Petrovic. Without your class and the exceedingly high grades you gave on my essays, I would have never had the confidence to embark on such an endeavor.

To Mrs. Pospisil, who not only was great English teacher

but who also helped me edit this book. I could not have done it without you.

To the illustrators, Althea and Maya. Thank you so much. I realize I can be difficult to work with, but you guys did great jobs. The covers really complete the whole thing, and I couldn't ask for better art work.

To my parents, and especially my mom who have been so supportive of all this. Those Starbucks drinks that you bought me while I was writing will not go forgotten. Thank you.

To my friends and all my classmates. I have barely heard any sort of skepticism or anything. Just pure confidence. That support was what made me continue on, so thank you.

To my sister, Caitlin.

If I forgot you, I am so sorry. I am pretty sure that I'll be in the dementia ward before I turn fifty, so rest assured it's not you. It's me. That's why I'm doing all this writing so early in my life. Get it all down. Out of the way, eh?

Thank you everyone! This may have been my idea and hard work, but I could not have done it without help. Rarely anything worthwhile is a one man job.

Made in the USA
Las Vegas, NV
27 July 2024

93002355R00164